Praise f

2002 HURSTON/WRIGHT AWARD FINALIST FOR DEBUT FICTION
2001 WASHINGTON POST BOOK WORLD RAVE

"This is a novel that should be read by everyone who wants insight into modern Africa and the women who mother and daughter it."
—NIKKI GIOVANNI

"Writing in a stark but delicate style that seems to mimic the terrain, Haulsey unsparingly depicts the miseries of East African tribal life: routine domestic violence, alcoholism and disease, as well as the complications of polygamy and ritual circumcision. . . . This unflinching tale marks Haulsey as a promising young writer."
—*Publishers Weekly*

"Haulsey deftly plays tangled personal and cultural differences against one another [in her] smoothly written, engrossing novel."
—*Washington Post Book World*

"*The Red Moon* is an impressive first novel [that is] moving, shocking, and unforgettable."
—*Essence*

"Haulsey very effectively handles the colliding themes of tradition and modernity in the lives of a Kenyan family. . . . [She] does an excellent job of mapping the intricacies of a shifting world and a people striving to manipulate what they know and what is to come."
—*Mosaic*

Also by Kuwana Haulsey

Angel of Harlem

THE *Red Moon*

THE Red Moon

A NOVEL

Kuwana Haulsey

ONE WORLD

BALLANTINE BOOKS

NEW YORK

A One World Book
Published by The Random House Publishing Group

Love is not love

Which alters when it alteration finds,

Or bends with the remover to remove:

O, no! it is an ever-fixèd mark,

That looks on tempests and is never shaken

Ever and always for you, Yvonne

ACKNOWLEDGMENTS

. . . .

I HAVE BEEN BLESSED by God repeatedly and abundantly. First, He gave me a clear vision that I could grab hold of and immerse myself in and call my own. Then He offered me His guiding presence and support, which helped me see it through. And finally He surrounded me with the free-flowing love of my family, friends, and even certain strangers, who looked at me and said *yes* although there was absolutely nothing telling them to do so.

Mommie, I love you. Without you, none of the things I do would be possible. Daddy, Grammy, and Papa, I am slowly becoming the person that you always knew I could be. Sadie Haulsey and Lucy Ann Stevens, you have been the embodiment of true wisdom and kindness to me throughout my life. The safety that you provided yesterday is what enables me to risk everything today. Yvonne, James, Jenny, Janell, and Kelly, I thank God that we've got each other. Little Kelly, Mandy, Naiya, and Christian, you inspire me. To the rest of my family: your support guides me in everything that I do. I hope I make you proud.

Micheal, this book would never have been written without you. For so many reasons.

Beresford, thank you for believing in the future.

Everyone who blesses us with his or her presence in this life is a teacher in some form or another. Thank you, George Davis, for helping me realize that and many other truths that I knew but had somehow forgotten along the way.

To my agent, Eileen Cope, thank you for believing in this book from the very beginning and never wavering. To my editor, Melody Guy, thank you for making this process so much easier than I thought it would be.

And to all of my friends who took me in, treated me as family, believed in my vision, and aided me in every possible way—I love you. May other people know the joy and blessings that you've brought into my life. Special thanks to: Geofferey Lengunguyo, Sammy and the Wamboi family, Augustin Lolowas, Julias Lekolua, Francis Masika, John Das, Towanda Sylcott and family, Parvawattie Tilak-Raghunandan and family, Mary Oyaya, Idia Achionbare, Patrick Parris, Robert Wamalwa, Mr. Karanja, Christine Wambui Karanja, Teresia Lengees, Sophia Lepuchirit, Elena Eaton (Tiger and Chief too!), John McLaughlin, Purvi Raicha, Carolyn Tshiaka-tumba, Tiffany Lockett, Maya Ellis, and David Mulligan. God bless you all!

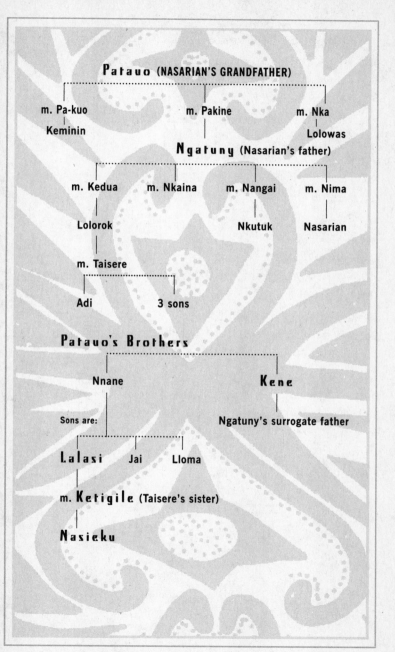

Patauo (NASARIAN'S GRANDFATHER)

m. Pa-kuo   m. Pakine   m. Nka

Keminin   Lolowas

Ngatuny (Nasarian's father)

m. Kedua   m. Nkaina   m. Nangai   m. Nima

Lolorok   Nkutuk   Nasarian

m. Taisere

Adi   3 sons

Patauo's Brothers

Nnane   **Kene**

Sons are: Ngatuny's surrogate father

Lalasi   Jai   Lloma

m. **Ketigile** (Taisere's sister)

Nasieku

BEFORE *Harlem, New York—1998*

. . . .

LOOKING AT HER MAKES ME REMEMBER. I can almost
feel the heat rising, riding the backs of broken cobblestones, gray
and scraped smooth by a ceaseless parade of tired, black, sandaled
feet.

But that was far away and long ago. Here, this woman peers
almost timidly around the curving, splintered wood of the brownstone door, blinking furiously now as the wind and rain whip her
face. I stare, and a sudden longing whistles through my mind,
dancing around me on each restless gust of cold, wet wind that
slams into my chest as I walk down 132nd Street in Harlem.
Harlem. So far from my home. So far from the endless Kenyan
plains that I still dream about each night.

The rain pelts my face, and I shiver as it shimmies down my
neck and creeps underneath the thick, scratchy collar of my coat. I
cannot stop staring into this woman's face, this African mother
draped from brow to ankle in gold and wind-crushed linen. As she
descends the stairs, the rain seems to disappear around her. Now
that she has committed herself, she does not blink or falter. If any-

thing, the rain has become a tightly woven fruit basket bearing down on the crown of her head, under which her pride demands that she stand erect. The only concession she gives is to pull her head wrap up out of the folds of her long, dark cloak and clutch it tightly underneath her chin. The scarf is a replica of the same gilded hijab my mother wore as a child, long before she became my mother. I know this because it is the outfit that she chooses when she comes to me at night in my dreams.

This woman looks nothing like my mother, yet somehow my heart tells me that they are almost exactly the same. She tucks her curling braids underneath the edges of the wrap, attempting to cover the wildness embroidered in her hair. I don't understand why; modesty is no kin to women like her. She cannot help but walk like a mountain's peak through the raunchy streets of Harlem, wearing her continent on the high bridge of her nose, with the valleys curving round like clattering rings into her nostrils. Her exposed heels are lined with the deep furrows of an elephant's trunk. She wears sandals in the November cold, in the hard, trash-swilling rain because the thirsty leather straps remind her of deserts and home (at least that's why I do so).

I see silence around her. She peels it back, like the papery skin off a wine grape, cuts her wide mouth open into a smile that cramps my stomach, and says hello to someone who is way across the street and thus outside the juicy reach of her quiet. Following her gaze, I see a man and a young boy huddled underneath the green striped awning of The Brothers bodega. The man holds the child's hand, and with his free hand he waves. If I squint hard enough, I can almost trick myself into believing that he is waving at me.

I sigh softly and touch my swelling stomach. For a moment,

he looks like my Ubuntu, but I know that Ubuntu is dead and that I killed him.

As soon as I think it, I see it. Again, I'm back there in my mind, trapped in that alley in the old part of Nairobi, the part where the flies whirl in thick, confused black clouds over upturned carts. They dance blissfully on tiny black bananas and oranges split open, sticky and stinking from the heat. I can see a wrinkled little man apart from the crowd. He sits with his head wrapped in his blistered hands on the broken edge of one of the wooden wheels of his cart. He is mumbling out loud, "Oh, what can I do now?" And I look away because I feel so much like him. My mind wanders freely here, here where the heat and the smell are the worst. Here where I'm watching Ubuntu die.

But that thought snaps me back. I cannot stand to look at the man anymore, so I concentrate on the child. The little boy holds a tattered, green umbrella with the spokes sticking out in the back. Looking closer, I realize that I recognize him. I have seen this child sitting on the stoop in front of this very same brownstone almost every day on my way to and from the library. And he has always looked exactly the same. Mute. Passive. Obedient. But I don't believe that he really is all of these things. Not inside, anyway.

I wonder how this woman and this boy can have anything in common at all, much less share the same roof or the same bloodline. Then I think about Nima and how different we were from each other. And that's when I realize that the boy's presence on that stoop, whether in rain, sunshine, or trapped under a cone of lamplight, makes me tremble because, in his faded eyes, I see myself. I see my home and my mother. I find myself remembering my mother and how she died and how her death was the catalyst that began my life. When I think like that, I feel myself to be the worst sort of parasite, fat and slippery with blood that is already cooling as the twilight descends on the life of another. But I try not to think that way very often.

Most often I see my mother singing. She is wading through a field of tall grass that is so rich and green it almost appears to be blue. It shines in the sunlight, like her skin and the tight, black curls of her hair. She is singing softly to Jesus in Kiswahili like the missionaries do as she strides through the field carrying a straw basket with the long handle fixed across her forehead, trailing down past her ears and onto her back. Her lesso is rich, woven with hues of gold and scarlet, the cloth tied tight over her shoulder. The folds of this cloth strike against her body, flowing into the wind like the probing fingertips of dawn as it reaches into the soul of the day and draws out, with tender care, life and birth and beginnings. Atop her head rides a calabash fashioned from the black-and-white skin of a cow, which is filled to the brim with warm blood-milk.

She fed me with blood, hers and others'. Maybe this is why I equate her existence with the existence of all life. The comfort of the earth, the curve of her hips, the stinging night wind that carries her voice—all of these things birthed me. They break like wild tides against my breast. They need freedom. My memories need to feed themselves. Only then can I be free.

Nima calls me. I must reply.

THE *Red Moon*

CHAPTER *One*

. . . .

SAMBURU, KENYA

THE MOON WAS RED on the night my mother died.

Fat, fairly bursting, as I remember, it rode so low in the sky that it grazed the backs of the leopards who hissed and spat and cursed it for interrupting the hunt. It caressed the thorny tips of the acacia trees, bending them, seeming to crush them with light.

Close to six years have passed since that night, and when I think on it, the moon is always the brightest image. I remember quite clearly my breath catching in a painful bubble in my chest as I stumbled out of the compound just after dark and looked toward the sky. For the rest, I must dig back far and dig hard, past the heavy sounds of weeping and swells of humiliated rage. The memories and images hide, season after season, deep inside the soul of my marrow.

But the moon is what I was speaking of. I had never before noticed it so red. It seemed to me to be crying blood. Perhaps this is how and when my fixation with my mother's blood began—on the night she died. To me, then, the red moon is death.

That night, I sat outside the manyatta as my father's other wives prayed in my mother's hut. I remember the manyatta as it was before my mother's passing as a world of singing women hidden away from all the rest of the world behind a fence. The thick, circular fence had been constructed from thorny branches of the acacia trees that dot the hills and groves of the highlands and that reached much higher than my short head. We kept our animals close in bomas opposite the low-roofed, bark-colored huts. Sometimes, late in the night, we even brought some of our sheep babies and our goats next to us in the huts, at arm's reach. That way, no lions could creep up on them as we slept, slipping through the fence and disappearing into the brush with their jaws full before any of us had even opened one eye. Outside that fence lay a vacuum of dead space, sulking and creeping like the leopards, immense and terrifying.

That night, I watched as the clouds began rolling in slowly from the south. Soon I could not tell where the earth ended and the horizon began. It all merged together, confusing me, lying to me. But for once, I convinced myself not to be afraid of the leopard's darkness. I sat down, closed my aching eyes, and invited the dark inside.

The hours passed, and when I opened my eyes, I found that the wind had pushed the clouds behind me out over the valley's edge. Once again, I saw the stars. They glittered violently against a rich indigo sky, bathing the plains and bushes, the distant forest and smoky mountains, in a pearly, cascading shower of secrets and light. When I breathed, the night sky breathed with me, soothing me, molding the white warmth of starlight like a clay cast against my skin. I settled into the night shadows with thorns pressing angrily at my back and waited.

My mother's co-wives and I had known since the passing of my Father that my mother, Nima, was also marked to die. Still, I prayed and watched and hoped that she would spare herself for my sake.

We all knew it wouldn't be long, and I wondered whether the prayers of the three other women's hearts were actually for Nima or if they were frightened of what her death would mean for them. She was the last wife and, therefore, according to tradition, deserving of little or nothing. And yet she, the outcast, had been the wife of my Father's heart and an unprecedented prize. They, the respected ones, had gotten the remnants. There was no sense of propriety or traditional justice in my Father's heart regarding this matter. There was only a love that, at times, even I couldn't understand. I knew only that my parents' devotion made me conspicuous, a target for the other women's children, my older sisters and brother, who were outraged in a way that their mothers could never express. And so no matter how I tried or coaxed or begged, their hearts refused to open to me. After a long while, even their mothers relented (Nangai and Nkaina, at least) and began loving Nima as well as they loved and treasured their own hearts. But my sisters and brother nursed a hate so old that they couldn't even remember it firsthand.

To the hut of my Father's first wife, Kedua, they would run, and she would stoke the withering flame in their minds. She would invoke the image of her dead sons, of all the dead children, until they were so real that even I, as I hid listening in the smoky shadows of her entranceway, could feel them breathing and gurgling in my ear. Kedua always mangled the story to make their deaths all the fault of my mother. Even after I was old enough and I learned the truth, the sound of those tiny ghosts rising from the past and flying up out of Kedua's mouth terrified me so that I always ran and hid under my mother's sleeping hutch. I covered myself in Father's brown-and-black bull skins (thinking that no ghost would consider looking for a little girl tucked away under the skin of a bull) and prayed to my dead brothers and sisters not to kill me. For in Kedua's stories, that was always the right and justified end.

By the time Nangai and Nkaina began bringing my younger brother and sisters into the world, I was already in school. So while these young ones never hated me, we were never particularly close, as I was often gone for months at a time. As hard as I try, I cannot remember a time when I did not feel alone. When I was not different. It was Nima who protected me, Nima who gave me worth. Nima who stopped my fear. And I hid behind her skirt or wrapped myself up tight in her lesso like an infant, so I could always feel her warmth. Her voice singing softly in the pale half-light just before dawn was the balm that soothed my spirit, even when we were far apart. But now Nima lay dying.

"*Ngai inchunye ana nkerai naji Nima ichero marou lino lomelok lemeylo likatingaui.*" *God give this daughter called Nima the healing power that only you can give to people.*

Over and over they chanted the same inane request, until it began to sound like the bleating of a dying goat inside my head and I wanted to cry out loud but I couldn't. Perhaps that is not even what they said, only what I remember. Anything is possible. I make no claims to accuracy. I can only report my heart, which is flawed. But I do know that I passed nearly the entire night sitting outside that thick thorn fence, which had been built by the hands of my father's sons so long ago and which separated me from the huts and the animals and the people that were my world.

Sitting alone, shivering in the dark dust, I refused to dwell on these things. Instead, I stripped the thoughts from my mind as completely as possible and concentrated on things that I could see or feel and understand, like the night sky and the cold. Especially the cold. I wrapped my ragged brown lesso around my shoulders as tightly as I could. But it was cheap and thin, with holes the size of silver shillings forming all along the edges, and no match for the night air. The wind leapt and danced, numbing my bare feet and covering me in dirt and nettles. It bit into my thighs, climbing higher, growing stronger in the dark, and carrying with it the sharp odor of sickness that wafted out of the smoke hole in my mother's tiny hut. The smell, mingling with the stale scent of goat meat and cloves, merged again with thin trails of smoke and hollow voices, drifting up then spreading out, catching the cold night by its throat.

If only I could speak.

The chanting got quieter, and I could tell that my mothers were tired of waiting. This death was long in coming. I hated them then, stupidly and without consequence, because I was too much of a coward to do anything about it. I didn't understand them or myself. I only knew that they planned to give my mother over to Lowaru Nyiro. He knew and was waiting close by and laughing at me.

Soon after the moon reached its apex, I saw him. He ran, crouched low to the ground, with hungry, powerful strides, his sleek, rippling body weaving in and out of the moon shadows across the plain. He stopped dangerously close (as though he was taunting me), lingering between two stubby cactuses directly ahead. With his head cocked to one side and his jaw slack, it seemed as if he was tasting the air.

"Not this night, Lowaru Nyiro," I whispered and let the wind carry my thought rather than my voice on its back. "Not this night. We have yet time."

The beast, sensing my thought, sent back his own.

No, I have time, he told the wind as he rolled out his long tongue and yawned and stretched insolently.

No hurry. I'll wait. Plenty of time . . .

Then, suddenly, he bolted, disappearing into the blackness of the brush. But I could still feel his gleeful eyes as he stalked, hiding behind the night. And somehow I knew that his thoughts were of feeding.

THE STARS AND THE MOON SHIFTED.

The prayers, too, shifted, dropping and waning in the early-morning hours, but never ceasing. We women were generally forbidden from taking part in the formal daily prayers, so my mothers took full advantage of this opportunity, which allowed them to stretch open their throats and feed their minds to God.

"Come," said Kedua.

She appeared beside me all at once, like a bad spirit. I looked up at her, startled and ashamed. I had no idea how long this haggard woman had been standing there watching me as I slept. It shouldn't have mattered, but her eyes made me feel like she had just caught me in the midst of doing something obscene.

I tried to scramble quickly to my feet, but the hard ground and the cold air had numbed my behind and my legs. I stumbled against the fence and the thorns jabbed me, scraping my shoulder. Swaying and a bit unsteady, I finally righted myself and followed Kedua into the manyatta. My mother's hut was the one farthest from the entrance. We first passed Kedua's hut, immediately to the right of the opening. She had the largest and most honorable position for her dwelling because she was the first wife. Nangai's hut and then Nkaina's followed before we reached my mother's. The remaining camels, goats, and cattle were all shut up for the night in their separate bomas just opposite the huts. Next to them, tucked away in a small pit, the embers of our family's prayer fire cast a frail and pitiful glow onto the hooves of the two black heifers standing closest to it. Each dawn, we lit the fire and gave thanks to Ngai for keeping the animals safe through the night. And every evening, we lit the fire again, always and forever grateful for their safe return from the plains.

My Father's fat, plentiful herds (most of which lived on the plains under the guidance of three or four trusted morans because there were too many animals to fit in the manyatta) bought us respect and good standing throughout the district. Therefore they required Ngai's constant attention and care so as to ensure our family's place of privilege among our people. I had never once heard anyone raise their voice over that fire for my mother's sake. When they did pray for her, they prayed inside, in secret, far from God's sight. When Kedua turned her head toward my mother's hut, I leaned over the prayer fire as far as I could and I spit in it. The tiny hiss that escaped from the embers comforted my heart and made it warm as I crossed the quiet courtyard.

Kedua strode quickly ahead, and I had to run to catch up to her. As we approached the entrance of my mother's hut, I vaguely made out a flickering light from the tired, smoldering fire inside. It scared me, this little, sleepy fire with its little dancing goblins of light. Or, rather, what scared me was what I knew the fire would be illuminating. The closer I got, the slower I walked, until I stood there in front of her doorway, rigid and breathless, needing so badly to turn and run. But there was nowhere for me to go. Every direction led back to this door. Every route converged on a thick thorn fence with one entrance and no exit.

Kedua, tired of waiting, gave my head a quick, rough shove, causing me to smack my chin on the top of the doorway. My teeth clamped down squarely on the edge of my tongue. A sharp, sour-tasting pain shot across my jaw and through my ears as my mouth filled with blood. I spun around and stared back at this awful woman, my other mother. Her long, ropy arm instantly shot up and poised just behind her back. Holding her breath, she waited hopefully for me to say something so she would have an excuse to beat me. The corners of her mouth twitched as she lowered her head, peering at me from underneath fleshy eyelids, like an angry, charging bull.

To Kedua, I was a disease. She always complained that she couldn't understand why Ngai had allowed me to enjoy life and grow into maturity when all but one of her children had died. She blamed my mother for her children's deaths (though it was not my mother's fault) because she could not comprehend what life without blame could be. Perhaps, she liked to say when she thought Mother and I were not around, it was truly Ngai's will and desire that her children should die in their mother's arms; but if the world had any justice in it, I would have died right along with them. Never mind that I hadn't been born when the tragedy occurred that brought my mother to these plains. Nangai and Nkaina always looked away and got very nervous when Kedua talked that way. It was blasphemous. Children were a blessing and a reward to a household no matter where they came from. All good women felt that way. But Kedua never believed that.

I stood there bleeding and staring back almost defiantly into her small, malignant eyes for a long moment. She met my look without guilt or shame, waiting for me to move. There was nothing that I could do. I turned, spit, and then, bending slightly, stepped through the narrow entrance.

My mothers barely looked up from their prayers. Nima lay in her little sleeping hutch just opposite the fire, wrapped in a thin, brown synthetic blanket. Her eyes were yellowed and her cracked skin gray. I sat down next to her on a stiff, colorless animal skin that reeked of the sour smell of her sickness and, gently, I took her hand. A fat, shiny roach, startled by the movement, scuttled across her wrist and tried to hide in the dry crease between her thumb and her first finger. I jumped back in disgust and slapped it off, sending it flying into the fire.

I didn't mean to hit her, but I did and she winced. Immediately I wished myself to be that roach in the fire. How could I hurt her? She was already so cold and uncomfortable. The skins were no better than rocks against her back. I had seen pictures in foreign magazines of sultry-looking women resting carelessly atop beds covered with feather pillows and satin duvets. I knew we couldn't have such things here. But still, my eyes welled up with tears and I trembled, shame bursting like a hot, bitter spring from the well of my stomach at the thought that my mother had to die like this, degraded, laid up on a hard, corroded cow pelt, covered in roaches and ash from the fire.

"Yieyio," I began, but then found that no more words would come. That this beautiful woman who was forever brimming with laughter and mischief could be brought so low mystified me. I curled up next to her, nuzzling my nose into her neck and wanting desperately either to get inside of her and wrap myself within the safety of her womb or to hurry up and have her dead. I would gladly have one or reluctantly take the other, but her suffering was unbearable.

"Nkima," she said, and it was the first word that she had spoken in nearly two days. It startled us both, and even my praying mothers looked up momentarily. "My little Nkima. But wait. You are not my Nkima."

I reckoned that she was out of her head again, that she would probably start seeing my Father standing in the doorway and talking to her, but I didn't care. At least for the moment, she had seen me! It was me this time and not him. And I needed her to keep on seeing me. Just this once. Just for now.

"Yes, yieyio, yes. It's me. Please," I begged, "please look close. You'll see I look just like you."

"I see that you look like me, but you are not Nkima," she said. "Not anymore. Nkima is a pet name for a small child, eh? You are a woman now. No matter what the others will tell you. You should never be called Nkima again. Your given name was Nasarian, and that is who you shall be."

"I am whatever you tell me to be," I whispered, "only stay with me awhile. Let me bring you something, eh? What do you want?"

She didn't answer. But she opened herself to me, which she hadn't done since the day after my father was laid out. On that day, my cousins Lloma and Lalasi had come to tell us that Lalasi had outbid his four brothers and would be taking possession of my mother without delay.

No one had asked her. The men had conveniently averted their gazes from her ashen face and the broken slope of her shoulders. They couldn't (or they refused to) confront the ugliness congealed in her eyes, too thick to cry out. And they had no real reason to do so. We were a traditional family, staunch in our beliefs and uncorrupted by the ways of outsiders. Traditionally, it was Lalasi's God-given right to take possession of any of his dead cousin's wives if he wanted to and could afford to feed an extra mouth or two.

Lloma and Lalasi did not let the dust from my mother's hut settle on their feet. They made their pronouncement and were up and gone.

Nima let them get across the courtyard and as far as the entranceway to the manyatta. Then she called to them from her doorway.

You don't want me, my mother said. *I am dying.*

Now everyone was watching. Lalasi walked back to her slowly, his white shuka fluttering in the hot breeze. He studied her for a moment, and then he laughed in her face.

You look healthy enough to me, he said. *Since when did you decide to die?*

Since today, she replied.

From that moment on, her mind was closed to me. She remained closed for the next three months. Even as she began to waste away and cough blood, she would not let me in. Witch doctors with rainbow-painted faces came and charged exorbitant fees to rattle pebble-filled gourds or slice open goat intestines and chant. She got worse. We even resorted to sending for a medical doctor from Maralal-town, who also charged exorbitant fees and did even less than the witch doctors. At least the witch doctors had put on a colorful show. None of these so-called experts could even guess at the problem, much less make it better.

Only I knew what was wrong.

My mother was dying from pride.

She refused to be passed from hand to hand like an unclean woman. The men call these uncircumcised women, women like me, loose shoes because we are fit to be worn by all. My mother wasn't like that. But no one offered her any choices. They told her what was proper and fitting. After all, she had no sons to care for her. Just me—a pampered, uncircumcised woman-child who cared more for books and poetry and decidedly foreign ideologies than for the real-life business of children and livestock. I was useless to her. No protection at all.

So she took the only choice she thought she had left. She gave up her spirit.

And it was this that she tried to save me from until the moment of her passing, when she opened herself to me again and, all at once, it was just like it was when I was a child. In those days, she could call to me with only her mind and no matter where I was, I would come running. We stayed snuggled together for a while, each couched in a lonely silence and bound by a silken web of guilt because neither of us had been able to make things any different.

Nima was tired. She had nothing left. She caressed my face with her smiling eyes to reassure me. Then she opened her mouth to speak, but died instead.

D AWN FOUND ME ALONE on the plains. The crisp morning air carried the sweet scent of fresh manure. Before me, rough scrubs and bushes and thorn trees stretched to the horizon, where I could dimly make out the beginnings of a forest. Herds of elephants, buffaloes, and giraffes lumbered along, wavering in the brilliant golden glare of the new sun like a mirage. They were headed back to the peace of that dense forest after a long night of foraging amongst us. It did not take long for the herds to vanish, leaving only hovering clouds of red dust to mark the pathways they had taken. When even the clouds were gone, I closed my eyes and tried to remember every detail of their retreat. I would soon be with them.

But first, I had to be with Nima.

I walked back to the manyatta to wash, dress, and shave my

head for the ceremony. As I stepped through the fence, Kedua grabbed hold of me and pushed me down in the dirt. She stalked into her hut and returned almost instantaneously with shears and a razor. Without a word, she grabbed a huge lock of my hair and cut it off at the scalp. She did this over and over, haphazardly flinging the locks into my lap and my face until there was nothing left. Then she picked up the razor and swiftly dispatched of every last bit of stubble on my head. She didn't even slow down when she cut me just above my hairline and sent blood dribbling down into my eyes. I sopped it up with pieces of my hair and wondered how I would ever survive my new mother now that my real mother's spirit had fled this place. Kedua cradled my future tight within her arms now, and she knew it and relished it.

As a young, unmarried woman with no prospective husbands in sight, I had to be under someone's rule. Kedua had been the first wife, the decision maker on the women's issues, so she and her son, Lolorok, would be making my decisions for me now. For all I knew she could be planning to keep me away from school. She could quite possibly have already picked my husband for me. Then all that would remain would be my circumcision. Having to live with all these things, the things that most girls giggle and dream of, would destroy me inside, in places that I had only recently admitted to myself even existed. Kedua, I believe, sensed this. And it filled her heart with light.

I looked neither to the right nor the left as I thought these things. I cast my eyes straight into my lap for fear that if Kedua saw my eyes, she would catch a glimpse of the fear of her that I held in my heart and be even more encouraged.

Her every action toward me was filled with spite. I could sense the joy she felt as she stripped me of my hair, which had always been an issue with her. She hated my hair because it was not thick and woolly as, by rights, it should have been. It was soft, full of waves and tiny ringlets, and, as such, a constant reminder that I was a Somali half-breed and that my mother and I should have been outcasts. I did look different, almost exactly like my mother. We had the same straight, slim nose and wide black eyes, which slanted, my Father had always said, like a halved kola nut filled with a sacred knowledge that only he could divine. He'd said this often because it always made my mother laugh. My lips were full and dark like Nima's, almost the same shade as my face. Our complexions were the only true difference between us and the only way in which I favored my Father. I had Father's dark brown skin, while Nima glowed copper. But when Kedua looked at me, all she saw was Nima. And to make the situation even more unbearable, I had the audacity not only to look different but to act different, and that caused Kedua such anger that oftentimes she could barely look at me.

When she was done, she pushed me away and, without a word, walked back into her hut. I got up, trying to pinch the edges of the cut on my head together to stop the bleeding, and went into my mother's hut to dress her body for the ceremony. Nangai and Nkaina helped me wrap Nima in a thin white sheet. They seemed so pitifully lost and forlorn without their friend. Searching her face with their eyes and their fingertips, they patted her arms and kissed her temples in the last moments before we covered her and carried her outside. We placed Nima's body in the center of the manyatta and sat down to wait.

The family arrived slowly. It was still early, and word was just getting around. But already my Father's son Lolorok and his wives, my uncles and neighbors were easily visible in the distance, carrying long staffs and decorated spears to mark their approach. Nangai had sent her son Nkutuk as a runner to tell the relatives in the neighboring manyattas to come. I'd seen him leave at dawn, running off toward the east. He still wasn't back, but then, there were many more people to tell.

The last of the stragglers arrived by midafternoon as the sun's blazing heat reached its pinnacle, searing through our skins like the lash of a white-hot whip. And so it began. Lolorok, Kedua's son, slaughtered their favored heifer for the ceremony. Being my mother's only child, I knelt before her body alone, holding her head, sweating and crying under the burning gaze of the sun. I was lost and felt somehow violated as my family watched me watch my mother's hard, gray face. Most of their eyes held a thinly veiled curiosity that mingled and flirted only slightly with genuine sorrow. So I stopped searching the rows of cool black eyes that somehow ignited a cold blue fire of shame deep inside me, a flame that made me feel as small and lifeless as my mother. Instead, I turned my concentration fully upon Nima. How beautiful her gray skin, hard and smooth like dying marble or wilted stones washed clean and level in the green sea. I whispered to her, trying to draw out the time, letting the sun shine down on her face. Remembering how she loved the glittering pinpricks of light that fell haphazardly onto the lakes and streams where we would walk to get the day's supply of water. And I whispered in her ear her most favorite poem, one of the ones that I'd memorized in school and brought home to her, reciting it first in English and then translating it as best I could into our language, Maa, which she would understand. I spoke it now, one last time, the last time in my life. Leaning over her, sharing our final secret, I said:

> *Now launch the small ship, now as the body dies*
> *and life departs, launch out, the fragile soul*
> *in the fragile ship of courage, the ark of faith*

with its store of food and little cooking pans
and change of clothes,
upon the flood's black waste
upon the waters of the end
upon the sea of death, where still we sail
darkly, for we cannot steer, and have no port.

Have you built your ship of death, O have you?
O build your ship of death, for you will need it.

You've done well, my heart, she would say to me every time she asked me to recite that poem by Lawrence and I did. *You know, I am not a smart woman, I am not like you or your father. So much of what you bring home to me from that school, ah, it is not for me to understand. But this, the words of this Lawrence fellow, I understand. Yes, my heart, this is what I understand.*

And she would mull these words over, sometimes for days, turning them round and round in her mind like a fat, juicy fowl on a spit above an open flame. They made her long to see the sea, but she never did.

Lolorok filled a little clay bowl with fat from the heifer he had just slaughtered and placed it in front of me. I took a small bit of the warm, slippery fat and smeared it tenderly over Nima's mouth. Traditionally, this gesture was considered a sign of respect, but I hated it. It made her look like she was rabid and frothing. Like she'd died angry and hard. But it had to be done. And with this final good-bye said, the morans carried her body out of the gate and laid it out at the foot of the great thorn tree about a hundred paces beyond the back of the manyatta. They stretched her out on her right side facing Mount Kulal so that she could watch Ngai thundering around in his home at the mountain's summit. Once, when I was about nine years old, I'd asked my mother, If Ngai really lived at the summit of Mount Kulal, then why was it that when the Mzungus came with their guides and their backpacks and their Range Rovers to climb the mountain, they never found him?

"Because they are Mzungus, my heart. That is why," she had said without ever looking up from her boiling rice. Her calm annoyed me so terribly that it made my head hurt. So when she turned her head, searching for her salt pouch, I scraped a fistful of tiny pebbles and sand up off the dirt floor and tossed them into the boiling water. The fact that I would have to eat the rice later on didn't occur to me until after.

"But how can we be certain that he is there," I'd sulked, "if no one has ever seen him, not even the Mzungus?"

"He tells us. In here," she said, striking her breast.

"He's never told me anything," I pouted.

She laughed. "You never asked."

As I watched them place her body on the ground, for the first time I asked. I prayed to Ngai, to Jesus, and to His Holy Spirit, which I had heard and studied so much about and yet had never seen. I prayed to anyone who might perchance be listening, even, tentatively, to her old God, her Allah, with whom I had no acquaintance but who I figured might be somewhat sympathetic. I didn't care who heard me, as long as someone did.

Guide my mother to the place of her ancestors, her people, I begged silently. *Finally, her people will greet her and welcome her to them and she will bear the burden of being an outcast no more. No more weight strapped to her naked shoulders, laden down with cares like a tired mule. Give her peace.*

The morans placed her on a bed of leaves and sprinkled more leaves over her body. Then they left.

AFTER TWO DAYS, the body still remained untouched.

No one spoke inside the manyatta. We barely even looked at one another. Perhaps this was Nima's condemnation, a sign of her evil intent to those who had treated her badly during life. Kedua was so petrified that she barely left her hut, even to fetch water. I'd be lying if I said that I didn't enjoy watching her face grow ashen, then waxy each time she peeked out of her doorway, saw Nima's body still lying there in the distance, and dashed back inside.

Me, I watched the sky for signs of favor or rage from her spirit, willing to accept either as my due. I knew that, though I'd never meant to, I had always countered her love and devotion with misfortune. She'd had every right to hate me. Thoughts like these suffocated me. I couldn't eat. I couldn't sleep, because as soon as I closed my eyes, I would hear the sound of my mother's sobbing seeping through the walls.

Late in the evening of the second day, Lolorok was sent for again. He slit the throat of a scrawny black kid and then laid the goat's body next to my mother's.

That night, finally, the hyenas came.

I heard them, or *thought* I heard them, ripping at cloth and flesh, laughing, growling and slashing at their brothers in their unwillingness to share the feast. And I lay prostrate in my mother's sleeping hutch, the faint sounds of the night magnified in my mind until they reached a gleefully cruel crescendo.

"Lowaru Nyiro," I said to the darkness, to the ravenous appetites outside, "you have won this night. It is finished."

I thought of Nima and wished her and her ancestors peace.

"Sleep alone, yieyio," I told her. "Sleep alone."

CHAPTER Two

. . . .

THE NEXT MORNING, we moved. Once a person is turned over to the earth, their family never stays on that spot. It becomes a sacred place, reserved for the wanderings of the dead. So we collected our things and moved on.

The packing was done quickly because we didn't have much. I had the most—a frayed gray satchel full of school clothes and books, in addition to my mother's cooking utensils, kindling, beads, and lessos. By midmorning, we began our trek to Lolorok's manyatta. Since he was Father's eldest son, we became his responsibility, and he dutifully assumed the role of our guide and protector.

We should have joined his family almost immediately after Father's death. If not for the imminent death of my mother, my other mothers and I would have been parceled off to him or perhaps other relatives directly after Father's burial. But Nangai and Nkaina pleaded with Lolorok, sitting at his feet as they reached up to stroke his hair and his ego, begging to be allowed to remain with my mother, whom they loved devotedly. They dared not move her because they feared that, as weak as she was, even a very short journey would kill her. Lolorok scoffed at them. When they wouldn't give up, he screamed that they were unfit to be mothers if they could even suggest that a scraggly handful of women and children should be allowed to live on their own for even one day.

Nangai reminded Lolorok that her son Nkutuk was a moran; though he was only fifteen, he could look after us. That swayed him somewhat. We were allowed to stay, but only with the provisions that Kedua agree to stay also to supervise and that some older male from our family would come by each day to check on us. We agreed.

From that time onward, I viewed my family much differently. My Father, Ngatuny, had dictated the order of our lives, conditioning us to live almost exactly as our ancestors had for centuries. He'd lived among the Mzungus, those foreign devils, he'd said, and their ways were poison. He would not have us infected. With the exception, perhaps, of the Maasai tribe, we Samburu were the only Kenyans who hadn't been fooled into accepting and living with these foreign beliefs. Ours was a tribe, a family, that would never change, I always thought.

But as I grew, I began to see that there were forces snaking their ways around us, a vortex of concepts and ideas and subtle mental shiftings that not even my Father could control. Father had been trying to hold back the forces of the wind, and those forces finally broke him.

Our families, our clans were, in fact, changing and modernizing. For many, it happened against their will and their better judgment. For some, it happened even without their knowledge. But, as is almost always the case, the prejudices of the old could not complete with the industry of the young. The mzees who were not quick enough to outrun the capricious, swelling tides of change got pulled into the undertow. Like my Father.

I remember once walking into Kisima-town with him while we were visiting relatives who lived close by. There was a group of about five morans lounging around on the dusty wooden porch in front of the general store drinking Coca-Colas. Three of them wore Seiko watches displayed prominently on top of the red blankets slung over their shoulders, and another one, a pair of Birkenstock sandals. They moved away when they noticed me approaching, but they did so grudgingly. It didn't matter, because after they settled in a spot around the corner, I could still see them drinking their colas. Father was outraged. A young woman was never supposed to see a moran eat or drink. I looked up at him fearfully, watching him gnash his teeth, the veins in his neck and temples jumping and popping. My stomach churned painfully as I wondered what he was going to do to them.

But in the end, he just walked away.

I also began to see a pattern of things happening within the family that would not, could not, have been allowed in years past. Looking back on it, I believe that Father's decision to allow me to attend school was the beginning of it. Lolorok's decision to allow us to stay in our home had been the culmination.

But now Nima was dead, and the three remaining wives packed up the five remaining children, myself included, and, together with our herds, we began the trek to Lolorok's. It was a very short journey, actually. No more than nine or ten kilometers due southeast to Porro. The flat terrain, brown and cracked from lack of rain, stretched endlessly ahead of us. Weeds and tiny thorn-bushes scratched at our heels and snagged our skirts. Songs fell flat against the hard, white sky, only to be trampled under the patter of the galloping hooves of a herd of antelopes. We made way as their babies leapt playfully through our train, unmindful of the resounding heat, on their way to a nearby salt lick.

Lolorok had sent his three young sons to look after our herds. They walked ahead of us, hopping like rabbits as each tried to smash his brother's toes with the long, heavy walking sticks they carried. The animals, meanwhile, ambled off in search of shade.

Kedua led the women, trying not to look as overburdened as she must have felt. She stumbled from time to time, but she never slowed enough to risk being helped. Nangai and Nkaina walked in the middle of the train, still singing to the younger children to keep their spirits up. I brought up the rear, walking slowly, falling farther and farther behind. I made a point of admiring the landscape the few times we passed unusually rich fields or frolicking herds of zebras, both of which, luckily, became more plentiful as we approached Porro. That way, if any of the other women looked back at me, they would think only that I was being lazy or absent-minded. But I did not want to reach our destination. I simply couldn't bring myself to face down my brother Lolorok.

Lolorok was the eldest of Father's seven sons and one of only two that survived childhood. He is ten years older than me, was almost a warrior by the time I was fully weaned, and yet, when we were children, he tormented me worse than any of my age-mates. His crooked, ugly mouth held the forked tongue of a snake. He was always full of vicious tales of how my mother, the slave, had been dragged to Samburu all the way from Somalia after Father had slain all of her kinsmen. Father walked home from this battle across the bottom of the Great Suguta Valley, looking every bit a triumphant warrior, leading a thousand morans and ten thousand head of cattle, oxen, sheep, and camels, while my mother, his concubine, swung from the end of his camel's ass like a stubborn turd.

Lolorok said that, like all Somalis, Mother had never bothered to bathe, and her hair was full of gnats and maggots. He loved to tell me how her breast milk had sour curds in it (though he refused to say how he knew that) and that she had walked around the manyatta shitting her skirts until his mother finally told her that civilized people didn't do such things. Every day, I would run to my mother in tears. She crushed me against her chest and caressed my cheeks and pleaded with me to tell her what was wrong. But I never told her anything. I couldn't bring myself to foul her ears or hurt her feelings with Lolorok's cheap talk because I knew that even if I told her, she would still never tell Father. It would just give her one more thing to hang her head for in front of Kedua, since Lolorok was obviously only repeating the jokes that he and his mother shared in private. Eventually, I trained myself not to hear him anymore. When he told me that my mother was a whore cursed by Ngai, I told him that his animals were looking very healthy and he should be quite proud of himself.

Each time I answered his slight with a kindness, he became enraged. After a while, he took to beating me when there was nobody else around. Mother cried and begged me to tell her how it was that my eye had become blackened or I had lost one of my baby teeth, but I refused. I didn't want her to find out and tell Father because it would get back to Kedua. And there was no telling what Kedua would do to Nima if she thought that Nima was the cause of her son losing esteem in his father's eyes.

It went on like that from the time I was five until I was seven years old. Every few weeks or so, I would show up for the evening meal with a new bruise or a cut or a funny little limp. If Mother ever guessed who was hurting me, she never let on. But when I turned seven, I was sent off to the missionary school in Kisima. All of the other children laughed at me and said that my Father had decided to send me away because I was a bad little half-breed. But I knew the truth. Mother was trying to save me.

I didn't know what a formal education was when I went off to school. I had absolutely no idea what I was going to be expected to do. The other children whispered to me that the missionary teachers ate little black girls for supper with biscuits and milk and then hid their bones in the churchyard. I was terrified. I didn't know which could possibly be more deadly, Lolorok or the cannibalistic nuns. I decided to take my chances with the nuns.

Perhaps I owe my brother a debt of gratitude after all.

WE ARRIVED AT LOLOROK'S manyatta to find his whole family waiting for us. His sons took our animals and put them in his bomas as his women took our packs and led us to our new places. My mothers each had a spot where they were to build their new huts. Kedua, as usual, got the most revered place—a shaded niche immediately to the left of the manyatta's entrance. Nangai's dwelling would be next, followed by Nkaina's. The children would sleep in small rooms that they would build behind their mothers' huts. But I had no mother, no shade in which to build my room. So Lolorok's first wife, Taisere, pointed me in the direction of her daughter's room.

"You will sleep there with Adi," she told me, "until other arrangements are made. Adi! Come! Welcome Nkima to you."

"Nasarian."

"Eh?"

"You called me Nkima and that is not me. You are mistaken,

Taisere. I am Nasarian. That is the name that my mother gave me and bid me to use," I said as quietly as possible with my eyes cast humbly at her feet.

She stared at me for a moment, perhaps trying to figure out if I had a dull mind or if I was joking. But I knew exactly what I had just done. I had just corrected a first wife on her land, where nothing but her charity would mete out the ease or discomfort of my days. I waited out the silence that followed, praying to Ngai that she would not take offense and set her heart against me.

I looked up cautiously and caught her eyes, which were huge and thoughtful like my mother's, not at all hard like Kedua's, as I might have expected them to be. For a brief moment, she even looked like my mother. Her skin was the same shade of sweet honey-eyed brown and as firm as the flesh of a ripe piece of fruit. Her body was slim and small, dressed in a bright red skirt and matching lesso. Nima had been tiny, like a doll, and she'd loved bright colors too. But honestly, there was little else in this woman that was like my mother.

While Nima's strength had always lain deep in her eyes and in the gentle stroke of her fingertips, Taisere walked with brazen confidence. I could immediately tell that she had been doted on as a child because she carried an air of ease, grace, and assurance that was rarely seen in our women. She looked almost as comfortable as any man, as though she thought that her opinions counted. It gave her eyes a secret smile that, in the few times I'd met her, I had always noticed and envied.

Her head was shaved, and she wore yellow, red, blue, and white beads wrapped around it, circling her forehead like a headdress. A heavy silver medallion in the shape of a triangle hung down between her eyes. She wore necklaces made from thick strands of vibrantly colored beads fashioned into perfect circles that started off close to her neck and got wider and wider until they spilled over her delicate shoulders. She was beautiful, even startling. And to top it all, she had the loveliest ears! I could tell that her earlobes had been perforated when she was very young because it takes years and years for them to be stretched, and yet, though she could not have been much older than me, her earlobes had already reached down to her shoulders. Taisere showed them off very simply with four small gold hoops that hung from each lobe, jingling softly against her collarbones.

Without thinking, my hand went self-consciously to one of my own ears. After I was sent away to school, my mother had stopped the stretching of my ears. I had only tiny little holes, something you could barely stick a straw through. I looked at Taisere and thought of myself in my drab, dingy school frock with my little ears, and I suddenly felt very ugly.

Taisere touched my hand lightly and pulled it down from my face.

"There is no need to hide when you are with family," she said. "Believe me, there will be time enough to hide when you are among strangers. Now go to Adi."

But she pulled me close for a moment first, squeezed my hand and kissed my neck. Even after she let go of me, I stood there looking at her and feeling so grateful for her generosity that I wanted to cry.

"I said go, woman. Move!"

She slapped my bum, laughing, and shooed me off toward Adi's room.

"And, sister Nasarian," she called as I struggled to pick up my packs, "the only way to stay out of harm's way around here is to move quick. Do you understand? Move quick. My husband does not tolerate laziness, eh?"

I nodded. She didn't have to tell me that. I doubt that anyone could have known that better than I. Lolorok was not forgiving, even when he had not been wronged.

"Eh. And thank you, sister Taisere," I called back. "You are generous and kind. I will not forget it."

Then she looked over her shoulder and smiled at me. Her smile seemed so free and innocent that I fell in love with her at once. To my childish, fevered brain, she held all the secrets of belonging that I dared not seek out for myself. As she walked away, I struggled to choke down every morsel of her appearance. Her walk was like the ripple of a stream, with its soft undulations secretly carrying the might of Ngai at its depths. Her shoulders sloped gently, like the green hills that shaded her home and her fields. Her hips swung like a pendulum in an intoxicating rhythm. I watched her tiny body blend in with all the other people and the animals and I wondered what type of black magic Lolorok had to use to bind this woman to his side. What laisi had given him the power to subdue this female who flashed sunlight through her smile like fire and who looked so much like Nima.

But that was none of my business.

However, I couldn't help but think about Taisere for the rest of the day. I stayed as close to her as I could when we started building the new huts. Lolorok and the boys left us to do our work, and this gave us the chance to talk and laugh freely amongst ourselves. Taisere and Nkaina kept trying to draw me into the conversation and the singing, but I stayed quiet so I could better hear their voices and laughter.

My three mothers and I, Lolorok's three wives, and their girl children worked quickly and well together. We used sticks and branches from dead thorn trees for the framework of the huts and covered them over with layer after layer of cow dung. The entrances were chest high and the roofs were not much taller. None of the huts had windows. A small hole dug into the center of each roof that would let out the smoke from the shallow pit where the fires would be built.

We finished Kedua's and Nangai's huts by early afternoon the next day. The dung was left to dry out and harden as we began working on Nkaina's dwelling. By then, it was the hottest time of the day, the cow patties were melting in the sun, and I was covered in mess up to my elbows. But I was close to Taisere. And Nangai and Nkaina were finally happy and laughing. Until then, it hadn't occurred to me that they had stopped laughing some time ago. In my selfishness and grief, I hadn't bothered to consider that they had had their own grief to deal with. It shamed me deeply to think that Nangai and Nkaina had been so gentle with me and I had repaid them with evil thoughts and cruelty.

This can be a beginning for us, I thought. *Even if they do not realize it. I will know it.*

So I redoubled my efforts, smoothing, patting, and scraping as though they could sense my love in my dedication to my task.

But I never got to finish it. Lolorok sent for me.

One of his little sons came running through the gate, grabbed me by my skirt, and began pulling me out of the manyatta.

"Father wants to see you, Nasarian. Hurry up. Be quick!"

Everyone grew silent and stared at me. I turned back and tried to catch Taisere's eye. She looked back at me, but from a distance I could not make out her expression. She masked her thoughts with a placid face, smooth like a stone at the bottom of a reflecting pool. She had known that this was coming, whatever it was, and she hadn't warned me. I had felt an instant bond with this woman, the likes of which I had never experienced. I knew that she couldn't have felt it too, but I thought that she had at least felt something for me. I had been deceived. Or more correctly, I had deceived myself.

Lolorok's boy led me to a clearing at the edge of an acacia grove in front of a forest and, as promised, there he was. My brother.

He sat with his back against a gnarled thorn tree using an old iron-handled knife of Father's to carve a new ntotoi board from a block of podo wood. Having delivered me, the little boy bowed quickly to his father and ran as fast as he could toward the other end of the clearing, leaving me all alone with Lolorok. During the long pause that followed, I looked neither left nor right but straight on, over the top of his head.

"Nasarian," he said finally without bothering to look up at me, "I will be brief because it is late, I am tired, and you stink."

"Of course, Lolorok."

"Your cousin Lalasi is coming for you in three days. You will be in his care from now on. As you may or may not remember, Lalasi wanted your mother, Nima, for a new wife when Father died. But then she died too," he said, chuckling as if Nima had played some sort of prank on them all, which, in a manner of speaking, I suppose she had.

"So your uncles and I discussed it," he continued, "and we decided that it would therefore be fitting that you go to live with him and his family. He lives in Maralal-town with his wife, who, by the way, is Taisere's older sister, and their young daughter, whose name I don't recall at the moment. Ask Taisere. She knows. At any rate, you won't find the arrangement disagreeable. He's allowing you to finish out the last two years of your education and take those bloody A-level exams that seem to be so important to you."

He stopped speaking for a moment and began toying with the blade of the knife, tracing circles in the dust. The line of his jaw bulged as he ground his teeth, and instinctively I backed away. Father had refused to send him to school and Lolorok had never forgiven me for it.

"Perhaps," he said softly, "you will be able to get a government job like Lalasi since you have repeatedly declined to be circumcised and so appear to have no desire for marriage. You, Nasarian, are not at all like your three older sisters. Prosperous women they are, living far away in their own homes with many, many children. I can't help but wonder what went wrong with you? But I suppose that is what happens with half-castes. Of course, you could marry after you go away, but then you would have to marry one who is outside of your people and without any blessing," he sneered at me. He was enjoying the moment and trying his level best to prolong it with every cheap, irrelevant jibe he could think up. It was almost hard for me to believe. It was just like we were small again.

"Only then you could never come home again. Still, I hear that there are many tribes that will take in a stray, uncircumcised woman. But that is not the point.

"When you go with Lalasi, all that you need do is help with his household and watch over the little girl when you are home from school. Now, that is more than generous. In fact, too generous. Schooling is not cheap. Added to that, you are merely a cousin and not a wife, so you are of no real value to him. And yet, he provides for you willingly.

"At your age," Lolorok grimaced and dropped his voice to a low, disgusted whisper, "you should be providing for your own household with at least two children at the breast. That is, if you were a real woman. But, ach!"—he spit at my feet—"you're still a small girl, not even circumcised and already nineteen years. On my life I will never understand why my Father indulged you the way he did." (Finally we got to the heart of the issue!) "How he could favor you over all his other children. There's no sense to it. You did nothing. We did everything. And now look at you. Some would say that you are a disgrace. However, I am a man with a very progressive mind. I am open to other ways . . .

"You, Nasarian," he said, looking directly into my face for the first time, "are very lucky. Not many girls have men looking after them like you do. Never forget that. Now run home."

"Thank you, Lolorok."

I walked away in the direction of his manyatta, but as soon as I was out of sight I doubled back around toward the forest. I would go with Lalasi in three days if I had to, but I would first prepare myself to take that journey. I had to be alone in the forest. And if it was just a few hours of freedom, that was fine. I knew what the consequences would be when I returned, and I was not afraid. I needed to be away from people. The hills and plains and forests were my peace. The trees were my drums, and the high, dense leaves danced my dance, the one that my own legs could not master, the one that defied reason and boundaries and bitter fear. The one that issued from the wind's song of power and life. For these things I would gladly suffer. My life was dead. These things were all I had left.

CHAPTER *Three*

. . . .

I AM LOTIMI. My family is part of the lmasula clan, and within that clan there always have been and always will be lotimi, people such as myself who are known elephant charmers. It is said that we have shared ancestral blood with the beasts since the time when our people walked the world from end to end and found it, without exception, a lush, dimpled paradise, stroked and washed in the sweet, heavy green of Ngai's tears. All men and all beasts shared the same tongue, could read each other's thoughts, and respected their kills. But, much like the Bible story of the Tower of Babel, avarice and bloodlust prevailed, and we were all dispersed to our dry, separate hells. Still, we lotimi have an infinitesimal kernel of that power flowing through us like thick, gray storm clouds, ever rising, being tangled in the high winds of Heaven and rushed out of our fingertips toward the sea. I am a descendant of a privileged lineage, many times blessed.

I counted on this that day as I entered the forest.

After leaving Lolorok, I doubled back onto a tiny, rocky path where the sun had bleached the earth a powdery shade of orange.

I kicked up dust with every step, and it covered me completely, even becoming trapped in the creases of my neck and my eyelids and my armpits. It covered over the layers of splattered shit on my arms and legs, which had dried into a cracked body mask the color of burnt wood.

I walked quickly, resisting the urge to crouch for fear that Lolorok was following me. As I approached a small, crooked opening in the wall of trees, I suddenly heard a terrified mewling off to my right. The sound was as sharp and soft as the cry of a newborn and immediately followed by a slight thud. The tiny fallen body rustled the stalks of the dead weeds and thornbushes that had long ago choked the life out of this soil, even as the echo of the shriek still floated in the wind just above my head. I dropped to my knees unsure of what I had seen, curled up into a ball, and listened. All I could hear was the sound of angry squawking and the *beat beat beat* of wings against body and air. Vulture, hawk, or eagle, I didn't know, but none would welcome me in the midst of a kill. I pressed my nose almost to the ground, with scraggly, sharp blades of sun-bleached grass whipping me in the neck. And I was immediately rewarded with the low-lying, coppery smell of blood. I crawled toward the smell, inching along, afraid to move but needing to know. And, just as I thought, about five meters ahead lay a newborn lion cub. The downy yellow fur (it couldn't have been more than a few days old, a week at most) was matted with gore and shredded where a hawk had ripped half of its head from its neck.

I crouched in the brush, breathing in dust, with the sun blazing down like falling fire onto my back and being only momentarily eclipsed by the circling expanse of thick, black wings as the bird cast death shadows over its prey and over me. I didn't know what to do. The hawk itself was not so much my worry. If I didn't bother it or its food, I was in no danger. However, a half-crazed lioness roaming the area searching desperately for her baby—well, that was something else again.

Should I crawl home and face Lolorok or continue on and take my chances? It would be foolish to continue, I knew, but perhaps, in realizing that, I discovered for the first time what the demon was that drove me. It was the vision of myself, crouching there, kneading the dust and saliva in my mouth into a gooey paste and trying to scrape it off my tongue with my teeth. The vision of me crying, ripping slim trails of water through the blanket of dirt that had obliterated my face and threatened to suffocate and blind me. It was all the other visions of myself that crowded down on top of me, leaping across my mind like skittering bugs across the surface of a pond: always the same, always crouching, kneeling, bowing, bent, resolute.

The dust had gathered in a smoky film over the whites of my eyes, and the swirling particles wriggled like hungry little maggots up past my eyelids. I couldn't take it anymore. I stood slowly, quivering and blind, and stumbled toward the forest.

But I had unwittingly passed some invisible boundary. I had gotten too close to the cub, and the hawk, thinking that I meant to steal its kill, fell on me almost instantaneously, beating me about the head with its fetid wings, shrieking and squawking, tearing at me with bloody talons.

I screamed and doubled over, stumbling toward the trees, shielding my face and neck as best I could, running and falling, panting like a wounded animal. The seething bird made another angry swoop, and I felt its talons swipe the air directly in front of me. Without thinking, I dropped and slid on my knees straight into a dense wall of deep green shadows. At once, the forest trees engulfed me on all sides, seeming to open up then close around me, like a dark, dank womb. I lay there, curled up against the trunk of a gnarled, broken cedar tree, choking and dribbling up dirty phlegm.

It took a while, perhaps three-quarters of an hour or more, but eventually I moved. My chest burned as if it had been pierced with hot metal and my legs trembled painfully, so at first I crawled. But when my knees, scraped raw, began to swell, I stood and willed myself to walk by pretending that my mother was waiting for me just beyond each turn and bend in the footpath. I followed behind her smiling, imaginary shade, always and forever too late, reaching for her like a small child, alone in the dark, grasping at starlight.

One devilish little velvet monkey flew out at me from a high tree limb. The second before he would have hit me, he reached out and snatched up a thick fig vine from the tree in front of me, sailing gracefully past my left ear. He landed in the crook of a skinny branch just behind my head and scampered fast-fast up that tree. As soon as he was nice and safe behind the stoutest limb, he puffed out his chest and bared his teeth. Then he proceeded to curse and deride me in his shrill little voice for being an interloper, I suppose, and a clumsy one at that. He hopped up and down, waving his tiny fists, shrieking and shouting until I became afraid that he would fall out of the tree. At last he grabbed a handful of unripened figs from the branch and threw them at my head. He missed with all but one, which popped directly off the center of my forehead as I ducked to avoid three others. Then, quick as sunlight through a hole, he scampered off, screeching and spitting at me, daring me to follow. In my mind, I turned his screech into Mother's laugh and hobbled fast-fast along after it. The game was tremendous fun, but not one that I could long sustain in my condition. So after a few minutes I let my little friend go, sadly, waving him off when he stopped to wait for me. Finally, with the deep, exaggerated sigh of a master clown, he disappeared into a thicket of ferns.

Anyway, I had to be serious. I needed to find shelter and enough drinking water to last for the next couple of days. So I limped along, surveying the forest, which was remarkably peaceful and quiet in the late afternoon. The most prominent sound was that of the scarlet-winged turacos darting and flitting through the forest canopy. They trailed silver strands of music, weaving the strands into the leaves, the branches, the spotted butterflies, and the air like the pulsating web of a golden spider. I stepped carefully over the skinny carcass of a fallen umbrella tree, watching out for the snakes that liked to hide in decaying trunks, and sat down on the other side.

No sooner had I sat down than I heard the faint rumbling of a fast-approaching herd of elephants. They came into view through the dense battlement of sycamores moments before they reached me, two old, gray mothers leading what appeared to be three generations of their children. Despite their skinny, half-dead appearance, I knew that the old hags were the backbone and the strength of the herd. As they came closer, I realized that I recognized the two mothers. They were Xana and Cosa, said to be the oldest elephants in Samburu and known by their identically scarred trunks. It is told by the old men, some of whom claim to still remember it, that the sisters each had a long, deep hollow gouged from the top right side of their trunks at the same moment in a skirmish with some men from the lorokushu clan. What started it was this.

One day, about two generations ago, a woman named Kalo, who lived in a manyatta on the outskirts of Kisima, was walking home from town carrying her marketing in a basket dangling from her chest and her baby wrapped up tight in a scarf on her back. The trip was long and hard and Kalo must have been quite weary, for she happened upon Xana, Cosa, and a bad-tempered young bull who we'll call Ejo (since I've forgotten the name the old men gave him) and she didn't even know it.

Now, elephants may be stern and unsympathetic at times, but they are not dishonorable like, for instance, the buffalo. So as honor and tradition dictate (and in spite of Ejo's stamping and huffing), Xana and Cosa gave Kalo fair warning before they struck. The three ran at her, thundering and raging like tiny gods, arcing their trunks and throwing back their ears. But Kalo didn't run. In fact, as the story goes, she supposedly didn't see them. Xana and Cosa were understandably perplexed. So they went back a hundred elephant paces and charged again. This time, they were terrifyingly loud and fearsome. But, *ei!*, poor Kalo, she was either deaf or stupid, because she did not run.

The sisters gave her one more chance, as by elephant law they were bound to do, but still Kalo refused to flee. Well, at this point, Xana and Cosa didn't care, because they had fulfilled their obligation for fair warning, and as far as they were concerned, they were free to kill her. With Ejo leading the way, they thundered down on her one last time. Kalo finally raised her head, startled and terrified at the menacing approach of the beasts, and began crying out to Ngai to save her. Perhaps Ngai had lost his patience with her as well, for he did nothing. Now the woman and the beasts were face to face. They closed on her and she dropped to her knees, pleading and screaming for help.

Then Xana noticed something that she hadn't seen before. She pushed Ejo out of the way and, rubbing Cosa roughly with her trunk, directed her sister's gaze to the naked baby cowering on its mother's back. They couldn't very well kill an innocent baby. Xana turned and backed away. Ejo flapped his ears at her in open disgust and stomped about, dredging up plumes of dust. *Why shouldn't both of them be killed here on the spot?* he was asking. Humans murdered their babies all the time. Cosa and Xana looked from him back to each other. It seemed to be a reasonable question. Why not? But it was only a thought to be entertained for a moment. Deep down, the hags knew that, though they would never be able to control or even understand the behavior of humans, to turn around and emulate it for spite was something they simply could not do.

So they did the only thing that seemed right: Cosa gently slipped her trunk around the baby's hips, snaked it down one of her legs, and lifted her up off her mother's back. As she held the child upside down, high up in the air, Ejo reared back and, with a shrill, trumpeting cry, came down with all his might onto the crown of Kalo's head. The woman's body jerked and twitched madly and Ejo, just to be sure, fell on her again and again. It is said that when they were done, there was nothing left of Kalo except blood-soaked rags from her lesso and a smattering of scattered beads.

But now the trio had this small, screaming baby to consider. Since they weren't prepared to raise a human infant, they decided to take her back where she belonged. So they walked to the doorway of the nearest manyatta, set the child down, and left. As soon as the child was out of sight, the hags turned their attention to other, more important issues. They hadn't yet decided which direction would be most beneficial to take the herd in order to find food and water. The dry season was fast approaching and they didn't want to be caught unaware. Ejo was young and strong, so they had been using him as a scout, but he had turned out to be too much trouble. He was too rowdy, always ready to pounce on things. Tired and disgruntled, the sisters led Ejo back toward the herd.

The walk was long, and the sun, draining until it began to sink lower and lower, losing its force, dying, once more, for the night. They were so tired that they could concentrate on nothing more than returning to their forest. So this time, they were the ones who did not hear the loud, angry feet of their enemies approaching until it was too late. One of the women in the manyatta where the baby had been left alerted Kalo's brother and husband. When they found Kalo's remains, they led a small band of morans to hunt out the murdering matriarchs. The men ran forward, spewing out vengeful curses and chanting for blood.

The brother was a small, sinewy man who had one leg slightly shorter than the other and therefore ran with the loping gait of a baboon. He reached only to the shoulders of most other men, but he also had the most heart. Screaming in rage with his spear raised defiantly in the air, he was the first one to reach the sisters and the first to be cut down. He had been running toward Xana with his spear aimed for her heart when Ejo blindsided him, knocked him back, and pierced his groin with a thick, curved tusk. With one quick snap of his head, Ejo's tusk burst out through the man's back covered in blood and crushed bits of his spine. He flicked the skewered body off his tusk and lowered his head to charge again.

The other men, who were not quite as brave but also not quite as stupid as the brother, backed off and fanned out, hoping to, at the right moment, close back in and catch the elephants in a net of pointed spears. Thinking Ejo to be the most dangerous, the men surrounded him first. In the confusion of Ejo's death, the sisters managed to slip away almost unnoticed. Almost.

To make a long, bloody battle short, the men were forced to re-treat, but not before the husband had struck Cosa with his sword hard enough to rip a deep crescent moon into the folds of her trunk. At the same moment, one of the other men struck Xana, and she also began to bleed.

I know that the story is true, mostly true anyway, because the baby that they left in the doorway still lives in Kisima, although she is getting older now, and is already a grandmother five or six times over. But everyone knows her and is well acquainted with the story of her misfortune. As for the sisters, they have attained the status of legends, made of myth and gray forest mist, lumbering along, mostly trapped within the shifting, solitary confines of children's imaginings.

Now here I was, facing down my grandmothers and wondering what they would do. They stopped perhaps twenty meters away from me, hidden by a line of Doum trees, and the dozen or so others that they led immediately stood still and attentive. One of the sisters stepped out of the shadows and walked toward me, crushing the small bushes and saplings in her way. I stood, let my hands drop to my sides, and cast my eyes humbly at the floor. Somehow I knew the one that approached was Xana, the elder of the two. As she walked, the ground shook slightly beneath me, and I closed my eyes all the way in order to better feel Grandmother's steady advance. I did not look up at her, but I felt her hot, wet breath in my face and her heavy gaze traveling the bruises on my body. She reached out with her withered, mutilated old trunk to caress my head and shoulders. The touch was as dry as desert sand, but surprisingly gentle. Cosa walked around behind me and, bending low, nudged me softly with her forehead, urging me to join them.

So I went with them, walking in the middle of their train, being guided to my feet by the younger members of the herd when I stumbled (which was often). I don't know how long we walked because the sun was not often visible through the canopy of the treetops, but I do know that it was a long time because I felt the forest floor grow cooler, as it does in preparation for the ending of another day. My knees cried and ached and cramped and spasmed until I was dizzy and nauseous from pain. The sisters would slow almost imperceptibly from time to time, and I knew that it was a small concession for my sake, so I tried doubly hard to keep up. When we got to the water's edge, I was so exhausted that I didn't even realize it at first. I had been walking in a daze for probably the last half of the journey. But as the herd stopped and began milling around, I finally saw where we were. Xana and Cosa had led us to a tiny oasis in the middle of a clearing. The body of water could scarcely even be called a pond. What had most likely happened was that the heavy rains that had fallen throughout the district the week before had collected in small basins all across the area. The water was not enough for them to bathe in, so they lined up along the bank, dipping their long, dusty trunks deep into the cloudy water to drink.

I, however, could bathe, and I did. The water was frigid and full of stinging insects, but I sat at the far end of the pool soaking, scraping off the caked layers of shit and blood, because I knew that if I didn't I would almost definitely become diseased or infected. When I had finished with my bath, washed what was left of my clothes, and laid them out to dry, I rejoined the herd. Cosa stood off by herself, beside a ring of flame trees, waiting underneath a tangled mural of bell-shaped crimson tulips. I followed, coming softly up alongside her and reaching as high up as I could to rest my fingertips on the side of her knotted, wrinkly old head.

She flapped her ears in the dimming light, motioning me over to a high pile of plants and leaves that lay neatly at the base of a hollowed-out tree stump. The stump had either been cracked open by some animal or had simply splintered over time, but half of it was gone, leaving a tight semicircle of wood that was just big enough for me to squeeze myself into. I quickly gathered some stones, twigs, and leaves and, with Cosa watching carefully over me, started a small fire in front of my stump. Then I snuggled deep down into the leaves that she laid out for me and found that she had lined my bed with ripe figs, berries, and sweet, pink flowers, dripping with a thick, fragrant nectar that I had never tasted before. It was balmy and rich like sugarcane, yet underneath the goodness, there was another heady, more bitter flavor. I picked the papery wings off the black ants that had come and started their feast without me, absently crushing them and flicking them into the fire as I sucked at the syrupy nectar. It numbed me and took my pain away.

I stayed awake late thanking Ngai for blessing me with the sisters' many kindnesses. The night opened up around me, stretched, and sent its many creatures flying out of its mouth to finally fill the shining silences of the dawn and day. There was shimmering, slithering, prowling, hissing life all around me, and I fell into it completely, determined to get some piece of understanding.

I lay there, as naked as I came from my mother's womb, replenishing my blackness with the unassailable blackness of the night and feeding my freedom with open air.

And my mind leapt about and shook and danced like the leaves on a toppled tree in a storm. That night I happened upon the beginning that I had set out to find. My mind turned over and over to many different places, but eventually, invariably, inevitably, it had to turn back to the past.

CHAPTER *Four*

. . . .

MY FATHER

THEY CALLED MY FATHER NGATUNY and he was but ten
years old when he saw his mother murdered for her cattle.

SAMBURU — 1950

THE THIEVES HAD come without warning.

Ngatuny lay snuggled up tight in the tall grass, away from his
mother, brothers, sisters, and the grazing herd. The others had
long ago given up hopes of finding him, shaking their heads and
clucking their tongues at that lazy little beast. If it were left to him,
his mother said, the cattle would starve and so would they, because
when it was time to work, Ngatuny simply vanished like a sulking
ghost, not to be seen again until the work was done.

In anyone else, this would have been a fatal flaw. As it was,
Ngatuny received his fair share of spankings from his father, plus

a hefty serving of miscellaneous slaps and pinches from his father's wives for constantly neglecting his chores. But somehow the scrawny little boy had only to lift his eyes, which were huge, turned up at the edges, and always looked wet, as if he lived, from moment to moment, on the edge of tears. At that glance, all was forgiven. He charmed them mercilessly with his wild stories and his dramatic pronouncements and so, despite his shortcomings, he was the most well-loved and pampered of all of the children. The only ones he couldn't charm were his two older brothers. They felt that it was their sacred duty to counteract all of the hugs and loving and attention that Ngatuny got with their own special brand of teasing and torture. So, of course, they were nearly always the subjects of his daydreams, because his mind was the only place where Ngatuny ever got to exact any revenge.

On that particular day, his eyes were closed as he lay on his stomach, baking contentedly in shimmering gold waves of sunlight, while he conjured up a dream that was a well-worn favorite. It had many variations but it was always the same at its heart and he carried it around in his mind, where it perched like a faithful, shadowy familiar, waiting for the moment to make itself of use.

In this dream he was a man already, wise and powerful, and he owned hundreds, actually thousands of animals. In fact, he owned so many animals that no one had ever been able to count them all. His herds always appeared as a vast brown, tan, black, and white ocean that rolled slowly and passively across endless plains. No matter how many morans he had looking after his herds, they could never keep track of all of the animals. But he could always tell when even one heifer had been lost by careless hands. He sensed it. The punishment meted out in these cases was swift, severe, and awesome. He knew that he was very harsh, perhaps too harsh with those who worked for him. Even the whis-

pered sound of his name was enough to strike fear into the bellies
of people in manyattas in all directions. His older brothers were
especially fearful and, come to think of it, he had to hurry the day-
dream along or else he wouldn't have time to get to the part where
his brothers came begging and pleading and groveling before him.
He loved it when he got to turn them roughly away.

"Sorry, Keminin, no cattle for you. *No!* Not even one head! You
should be ashamed of yourself to ask, ashamed"—he loved this
part because he always had just the right amount of contempt in
his voice—"to come pleading to your *younger* brother for help.
Ha!" He threw them a chilling sideways grin. "In fact, you should
be supporting me. Ha!"

But he grew somber when he considered the depths to which
his brothers had sunk. However, their degeneration was inevitable, considering the miserable way that they had treated certain people around them in their past. The thought vindicated
him, and he felt better almost instantly. Once again, he drew his
haughty, condemning manner up around his head like a warm
blanket. His eyes narrowed to slits and, one by one, their knees
began to tremble because they could see him reading their
thoughts. He loved the ripe, bitter smell of their fear.

"And, Lolowas, you beaten-down cur, what would even pos-
sess you to ask? Ah, rejection is as natural as breathing to some."
Lolowas could only shiver in horror, his round, scabby knees
clanking together loud as the hollow beat of a drum. On and on
Ngatuny went until his brothers practically swooned at his feet.

"Flee," he said coldly. "Flee for your lives, you ungracious
maggots!" And he knew how forgiving he was for allowing them to
keep their worthless lives as their own. He was too good.

"Now," he continued (and no matter where he was, he always
laughed out loud at this part—he couldn't help it), "you must go

out into the bush and tramp around like ignorant savages for the rest of your lives."

There was a collective gasp from the crowd that had gathered around to watch. Where this crowd came from, he never figured out. They just appeared. But it really didn't matter because he liked the brothers to be humiliated in front of as many people as possible. Realism never particularly troubled his little mind.

"Never show your monkey faces around here again." He paused dramatically. "Or you will face death by my own hand."

A woman fainted; another screamed—presumably the wives of the outcasts. The crowd turned on the brothers, who scurried like beetles from sight. But Keminin and Lolowas couldn't lose the angry mob that ran behind them, pelting them with flying rocks and sticks. Ngatuny sighed in the midst of his triumph, realizing that everything had its price.

This is how he would while away his long days, as a fearsome warrior, a king among men, a wise elder in a youth's body. But for all his majesty and wisdom, he was simply lonely. Sometimes he wished that his brothers didn't need such harsh discipline as stoning and banishment. Sometimes he wished that they would just play with him. But his brothers were morans. They had no time for childish games. So he and his stories wandered sluggishly after the grazing cattle or lay, like today, covered in the high grass, feeding each other on wishes and nursing old slights and injuries. Creases and furrows lined his little face as he thought with regret that nobody really knew him. That is to say, nobody knew him as he was in his dreams, as he would be after he had been circumcised and was allowed to enter into a man's world of cattle, wars, and wives.

But living with the loneliness *now*, the heartache *now*: it was crushing. He sighed from way deep down in his soul, and his eyelashes grew moist as he contemplated the awful price of being (one day) revered. Ngai must have pity on his poor, poor soul. A soul in agony! Oh, it was just too much for one person to bear. He stretched his arms above his head and groaned in happy, melodramatic misery over his aloneness, thinking himself the most wretched person in the whole world.

He never even heard the Pokots.

CHAPTER *Five*

. . . .

THE WANDERING RAIDERS stumbled onto Ngatuny's family quite by accident.

They had climbed up out of the depths of the Great Suguta Valley the night before, stalking the scent of the land and its people as it traveled gracefully on top of the midnight wind.

The men were as black as the bull skins they wore. As they walked, hidden behind man-sized Panda plants and the winged acacia trees that wore their thorns in the thick of the night like bright and regal feathers, they resembled dancing shadows. Hot, sweet, and sticky thoughts of unshed blood flowed freely through their minds, but their faces held steady and expressionless. Even the looks exchanged between the men were as barren as the plains they crossed, conceding nothing. The desperation in their hearts shone only in the glint of their spears, which occasionally caught the moonlight.

They had people waiting at home—fathers, mothers, and sisters—with distended bellies and deep, running sores spreading across their arms and legs that couldn't be explained. The animals in the village were almost all dead or dying, and no one could figure out what they had done or not done to be punished so viciously. The famine that resulted from this pestilence had taken at least two lives every day since the last new moon. The village wasn't that big. These young men, these warriors, needed to steal and perhaps kill to survive. So they walked, each step a testament to the understanding that if they failed, Death would soon be tickling their own heels, caressing their cheeks and licking their trembling lips with her scaly tongue.

But the warriors had misjudged the first manyatta they'd sought to attack. They hadn't seen the shivering little girl wandering in the dark outside of the fence. She whispered as she walked, fearful of disturbing the vast, sleeping darkness with her tiny voice. She was searching for her naughty baby goat that had run off because she'd scolded him and slapped his pudgy little snout after he'd dipped it into her bowl of cabbage. It was her first goat of her very own, the first thing that she'd ever been responsible for taking care of, so she'd had no idea that they could be so sensitive. Yieyio had pushed her out of the doorway (*and don't come back without him!*) and there she was, eyes wide, wrapped up tight in a thin, dark shawl and stumbling through the bush. When she saw the Pokot warriors walking toward her, she almost screamed out loud, thinking that they were ghosts or devils, but then, as they approached, she realized that she recognized the shaved heads and the feathers dangling from their ears.

In that instant of understanding, as the warriors' purpose became clear to her, her belly suddenly got warm and loose and she soiled herself. She fell back against a tree trunk, whimpering, whispering to her mother and sisters to get out. She wanted to warn them, but the Pokots had now passed her and were standing in between her and her family, so there was no way to turn around and run back. She needed help, and there was only one place close enough that she could think of where she might get it. She ran off to get her brothers and the other morans who she knew were spending the night in the communal warriors' hut.

It couldn't have taken more than a few minutes to reach the hut, which was tucked away by itself at the edge of the maize field, but it didn't matter. Each time her foot touched the ground the sound vibrated through her body, mocking her, singing out in her mind *too late, too late, too late.*

She burst through the entrance of the solitary little hut, wheezing and trembling and collapsed on the ground. The small circle of morans had been sitting around a dying fire in the middle of the floor, eating porridge and boasting about the size of their families' herds. They stopped and stared at the child, scarcely breathing as they waited for her to come to her senses and tell them what had happened. They knew that nothing short of death would bring a young girl into this place, the warriors' house, from which women were strictly forbidden. Jai, one of her three brothers that were among the group, gently touched her back and called her name.

The girl flipped over onto her side, gasping and wheezing, as she fought for the breath to speak.

"Brothers," she finally managed. "My brothers, come . . . come home . . . Pokots . . . "

"How many?" Jai demanded, at once reaching for both his sword and his spear.

"I d-d-don't know. Per . . . perhaps eight or ten. But the dark hides them. There could be more. I could not tell."

The warriors flew out of the hut, one running off in the opposite direction to warn others and bring more young men. If the child had been right, then their group was just about evenly matched. But if there were more of them than she had seen, then the morans would need more brothers to back them up.

By the time they got to the manyatta, the raiding Pokots had already rounded up more than half of the animals and killed two men. The morans, raising their spears and machetes before them, ran in without thinking, ready to defend their clansmen.

Two old women and two young ones with their babies were cowering and crying to Ngai from a small space between the goat boma and the fence. The grandmothers had covered their faces and the faces of the littlest children with dark blue and black lessos, as though the cloth would make them invisible. Jai's father and another man lay dead, strewn in a burning heap in the center of the manyatta. They had been finishing the evening prayer of thanksgiving over the pit fire next to the camel boma when the raiders had invaded. Having no weapons readily at hand, the men had taken up the largest of the smoldering sticks from the pit to defend themselves. That was all the excuse that the Pokots had needed to cut them down.

The morans ran in to find the deep red flames hugging the faces and necks of the dead men. The fire moved steadily, languidly, seeking out the intimate places in the lower regions of their bodies even as the blood, which had collected in the pit, bubbled and spit. Jai stopped.

father?

The Pokots began screaming and rushing toward them. Jai felt his brothers push past him, and the motion gave him back his legs. They charged and clashed, both sides perfectly matched in strength, skill, and hatred. Jai came up behind a tall, wiry Pokot and grabbed hold of his arms as the man was raising one of them to strike a moran with his knife. The invader pushed back against him, and for an instant Jai could feel the other's heartbeat crushing into his own chest, becoming his. He tasted the sour smell of his enemy's sweat at the back of his own throat just before he stumbled over his father's legs and went sprawling into the fire pit. He immediately smelled the heavy scent of fat and red ocher as it melted off his hair and his long plaits began to burn. The last thing he heard was his own heart beating, but in his mind the sound came all the way from behind the young Pokot's breast. When the Pokot flipped over, dove at him with his knife, and plunged it deep into his chest, the last thought Jai had was, *Why doesn't he die?*

Each man redoubled his efforts after that first kill between warriors. One side needed to keep the momentum flowing, the other to avenge. The first moran to hear the call of their brothers in the distance was Jai's younger brother Lalasi.

"They come," Lalasi yelled. "They come now!"

At that point the Pokots heard the rumble and the shouting in the distance as well. They each knew that, with an untold number of morans racing toward them, they had no other choice than to retreat immediately or die.

"Brothers, we go," screamed Mfante, the leader, as he kicked Jai's smoldering body to the side and grabbed a burning branch from the fire underneath.

He tossed the branch at the dry thorn fence, which immediately ignited and began racing around the circumference of the manyatta. Mfante seized the confused moment and bolted for the gateway. The other Pokots followed as the morans ran into the huts for water, two or three others dragging the women and their babies out of the manyatta.

Under a cover of ash and smoke, the invaders disappeared into the brush. They spent the remainder of the night racing through the maize fields and across hillsides, trying to navigate their way back to the valley's edge. There they would await the next nightfall and make their descent back across the valley floor. All the while, the nearby screams and shouts of their enemies, a hungry pack of tireless hunters, burned their ears like the bloody fire from the pit.

The rising sun found them in a small dugout where they crouched, praying that Ngai would show them favor by leading their pursuers far away from them. The men had decided to climb down into the Suguta's mouth and hide within the rocky crevices of the valley's steep walls. That way, when night came and it was cool enough to cross the valley floor, they could escape with no delay.

They sat in the dugout waiting for the proper time to cross the wide field that lay in front of the valley's edge. As they waited, the sun rose higher and higher and the oppressive heat of the day settled in to keep them company. The rocks that they sat on got hot enough to burn as the morning progressed, so the warriors found themselves squatting in the dust and cursing their foul luck. By now, all the manyattas in the area would have been alerted to their presence. There could be no surprise attacks, and the party was far too small to wage open war. A call of alarm would immediately be raised, and a hundred morans would descend on them and slaughter them like small children crushing ants between their fingers. The Samburu wouldn't even find any fun in a fight like that. But to go home with nothing! They could not. Perhaps they would fare better with the Somalis at Garissa. But with that prospect lay the knowledge that they would have to endure a long and exhausting trip. Disgusted and dejected, the Pokots cursed the morans and their own black luck.

But then they saw the herds of Ngatuny's family lumbering toward them in the distance. This particular family must not have been warned about the commotion the night before, for only one woman, two very young morans and some girls walked alongside the animals. Mfante could not take it as anything but a heavenly blessing. He raised his head toward the clouds and sent up a silent prayer of thanks to Ngai as the warriors set up their ambush.

NGATUNY'S MOTHER, PAKINE, had conferred earlier that morning with her husband's other wives, and together they'd made the decision that she would take the herd out into the fields since their husband, Patauo, had not returned from his brother Nnane's house the night before. They all agreed that some urgent business must have kept him there, because Patauo was not one to delay any more than necessary when he knew that he had things to attend to at home.

Patauo was a tall, well-built man with very black, very commanding eyes. He had a heavy set of whiskers and hair that was already graying on top at the relatively early age of thirty-seven. It gave him a powerful air that set him apart from most of his age-mates. Patauo was determined that his persona would match his outer appearance, so he always walked with solemn authority, his head high and his eyes focused straight ahead. He never drank more than was prescribed for any particular event, and he always thought carefully about his answers before he gave them. Consequently, people sought his opinions on matters ranging from weather to cattle to women and marriage.

His wives Pa-kuo, Pakine, and Nka were generally considered to be the three most beautiful women in the region, and they always walked with pride. Their husband was hardworking, prosperous, and the perfect picture of propriety and stability. So, the night before, when he did not appear at the designated hour in the evening, the women became very worried. Pakine kept his thick cabbage stew and ugali quite hot for him all the night through in her smoky hut, for it was her night to entertain her husband, but Patauo never arrived to eat it.

By dawn the women were tired and irritable, all of them having slept fitfully, but not daring to voice their concerns, not even to one another. They rose from their cramped mud huts stretching and yawning, with dark, baggy circles around their eyes. Each woman wore a deep brown skirt, but they draped themselves in their most festive red and orange lessos to ward off the chill and the dampness of the dawn as well as their dour moods. They stood around the goat boma fingering the thorns in the fence and the rough, dry wood, staring down sullenly at each other's legs and idling, none of them sure what to do. Each wife had the same thought—that they should send Ngatuny running to his uncle's manyatta to inquire for Patauo's whereabouts. But the place was much, much too far. And, besides, it would be unseemly for any wife to question her husband's whereabouts because it would say indirectly that she questioned his judgment as well. To do such a thing in the privacy of their own manyatta, much less in front of others, was unthinkable for the wives of Patauo.

He had mentioned that on his return he would send word to his two oldest sons, who looked after the cattle, that he wanted them to move the animals to the southwest. His sons lived on the plains with the animals, constantly searching out new and fertile grounds. They had not been home since the rise of the last full moon, but they were known to be close by.

If they stay close to the valley wall and walk toward the west, just past the watering hole where the zebras gather at dusk, he had said, *they will come across the best lands, where the herds will be able to rest properly.*

The women knew that when Patauo said something, he meant it and he meant it immediately.

"Well," said Pa-kuo finally as she sat on an upturned pot, rolling up her long earlobes and placing them behind the tops of her ears, "he has probably been detained by that rascal brother of his. What can a woman do? You know how men are."

Of course, Patauo had never been that way, but the women said nothing.

"If we let the animals get too far away," she continued, "we will be hard-pressed to get them back to where our husband wishes for them to be."

"Shall we go tell Keminin and Lolowas ourselves?" asked Pakine. "I will go if that is what you wish, Pa-kuo. That is, if you will bring back enough firewood for me too this morning."

Pa-kuo, being the first wife, had the final say, and she consented. And so Pakine strapped her tiny baby girl to her back in a soft tan cloth and left with Ngatuny and two of Pa-kuo's young daughters for company.

As she waved good-bye to her co-wives, she smiled, and the new sun lit up the apples of her cheeks and the precious dip where her slim, graceful neck met with her collarbone, making her look exceptionally pretty. It was this innocent picture that the wives would long remember.

"Ei!" she called over her shoulder, laughing. "Won't our husband be so proud of his clever, clever wives!"

THE POKOTS SLUMPED over in the tall, brown grass, hanging low like morning fog across the valley floor, waiting and praying.

Mfante thought that he could even smell the pungent, woodsy odor of the cattle wafting toward them and hear a symphony of guttural lowing. His heart sped up and the palms of his hands got moist. He liked it. The few times that he had been forced to go on raids, he had always tried to look solemn and resigned in front of the others but, in all honesty and truth, he enjoyed fighting for the kill. He loved the power of being so close to Death and yet never embracing her.

"Now is almost the time," cautioned Mfante, never taking his eyes away from the approaching herd. "Stay low to the ground and wait until I move. When this is all over, there shall be much feasting and thanksgiving. Just remember, be swift and careful. None must escape. If they are allowed to get away, they will run for their warriors. The morans are swarming all across this place, and their anger has already been aroused. We are a tiny circle and desperate. We are not prepared to fight that fight."

"But surely there is some other way," ventured one young warrior. "To murder women—"

"It is not murder!" hissed Mfante, turning slightly so that he could stare this young warrior in the eye. "It is just and sanctioned by Ngai for the sake of our people. Do you question Ngai? Do you question me? What is it that you are saying to me, brother?"

"Nothing. I die willingly for my people," the young warrior mumbled.

Mfante turned back around to watch for his prey. The other warriors also turned back to watching, waiting tensely for the animals to get just close enough.

"It's just that the women are like the animals—stupid and innocent creatures. This fight is not theirs."

Mfante turned full around and stared at the young man. Mdeme was his name. Had he always been this troublesome? Mfante couldn't remember. The leader's steady gaze made the young man warm and fluttery in his stomach. Mfante was a man of quick action who despised being questioned. Mdeme knew that if he did not do his part to ensure victory on this venture, he very well might never make it to the other side of the valley. These thoughts made him cast his eyes toward the ground and stutter.

"And . . . and the moran, the one in the back waving the carved herding stick, even from this distance you can see that he is but a child. His circumcision must have only just passed. I am sure of it," Mdeme continued quietly, unsure of why he was pushing so hard, except that this kill felt wrong. "I am no coward, Mfante, if that is what you are thinking. In fact, that is my problem. I have always been taught that it takes a coward to kill those who cannot defend themselves. I would rather have stayed and fought last night, even to my death. At least I would have died with honor."

Mfante crouched silently, hugging his knees to his chest and rocking back and forth on the balls of his feet. He had to handle this delicately.

"You have honor and a fighting heart. That must be respected. But how much respect do you think it will get you if we return home and tell our people that they must die? And not only that they must die but that they must go to their deaths, to meet their ancestors shamed and unmourned, because Mdeme could not dirty his hands?" asked Mfante.

The other looked off into sky.

"We have no choice. And look, they are almost upon us. If it eases you, I will take care of the women myself. You know that if they escape and tell, the warriors will catch us before we even get down the valley wall. We will be lost. Come! What will you do? Are you with or against?"

No one watched Mdeme. They all looked straight ahead. But each man listened intently to the sound of his breath.

"With," he said finally. "I am with."

"Ei. That is how it needs to be, young one," said Mfante as he moved carefully away from the group. "Don't think, just act. You only need to remember two things. First: when we get home, we will be heroes and saviors. Your rewards will be great. And second: don't look them in the eyes."

"NGATUNY! NGATUNY, you rascal, where have you got to?"

Pakine shaded her eyes with her hand as she scanned the expanse of trees, scrub, and weeds to her left and to her right.

"Keminin, where is that incorrigible brother of yours?" she asked as she fell into step beside him, wiping the sweat off her forehead and blotting the moist area between her breasts.

"Hiding, of course," Keminin answered. "Hiding and sleeping. What else could he possibly be doing while there is work to be done?"

Pakine looked at the boy and laughed. Keminin cut a very striking figure, in her opinion, with his bright red shuka tied around his waist and his red blanket tossed over his shoulder. Though he had just made sixteen, he already walked with the grace and ease of his father. He seemed comfortable with himself. He had somehow managed to completely bypass that awkward, ungainly time most young men go through that makes them so hard to cope with. His time as a warrior had done much to ease his transition into manhood.

Pakine watched Keminin flick his long hair over his shoulder, and she thought back to the time when she and Pa-kuo had first helped him do his hair. It was after he had passed through the ritual of circumcision and gone from being a boy to being a moran. They had sat together for hours talking and laughing as the women had braided his hair and then applied the thick mixture of red ocher and cow fat to each tiny individual plait, until at the end his head glowed. The red of his hair mixed with the deep black of his skin suited him, she decided as she watched him walk. It made some boys look pasty and orange-skinned at first. Or perhaps one just got used to looking at them that way. The longer his hair got, the more attractive and mature looking he became.

Keminin wore traditional beads of yellow and black in three slim bands across the top of his head, with a short yellow tassel standing up out of the center. He wore two long strands of red, black, and orange beads crisscrossed over his chest and more around his neck and wrists. His club swung from the waist of his shuka on the right side, and he walked clutching his spear on the other side. Pakine watched him with pleasure. Though he was Pakuo's firstborn, Pakine couldn't have been any more proud of him.

Nka's boy Lolowas, on the other hand, was a pocketful of worries. He was exactly ten months younger than his brother and they had been circumcised at the same time, but somehow Lolowas didn't mature in the same way as Keminin. However, his heart was good and pure, and for that she was grateful.

"Yieyio, I believe that I have spied him over there in the tall grass," Keminin said.

"Where, eh?" Pakine asked. "Oh, yes, over there. I'm sure that I see him now. And you were right. He is hiding. Ngatuny! Ngatuny, you bring your little self to me just now!"

She started over toward the bushes, trying to look sufficiently annoyed.

"Just remember who spoiled him in the first place," Keminin called behind her.

"Shut it, you! I can still beat you quite soundly if I have to. Just remember that, eh? Ngatuny, you nasty thing! Come here before I knock you! I am through . . . Oh . . . Ngai . . . Ngai ai ntejeu ang. . . . Run!" she screamed. "Run! Help us! Keminin! Keminin! Lolowas! Girls, go! Go now! Run!"

Pakine turned and tried to run herself, but the baby on her back bounced and screamed and almost flew out of the wrap. She swung the baby around and grabbed her by the neck, piercing the tender newborn flesh with her fingernails. The child screeched in pain and confusion, but Pakine took no notice. Her terrified heart swelled inside of her chest. The child sensed her mother's panic and began to scream in a shrill, horrified voice, and her face went a sour shade of purple.

The two girls had been up ahead of the herd, so they couldn't see the Pokots from where they were standing. All they saw was Pakine lurching toward them and waving at them frantically with one hand while she clutched her baby to her breasts with the other. Then Pakine stopped. The girls watched as her face went blank and ashen and her whole body sagged. She dropped to her knees, sobbing. She was trying to speak to them, and they couldn't hear her. But they read her lips instead, and the last thing that she said to them was *God protect you* . . .

It was then that they both felt Mfante's breath moving like a silent, stinging wind up the backs of their necks. The girls never turned around. There was no need. They saw their deaths in the eyes of Pakine.

Pakine watched them fall almost in the same instant. From behind them rose Mfante, walking toward her slowly, a machete dangling slackly at his side, savoring the heat, the dust, the smell of the animals and the flesh. And he breathed his blessings in deeply.

NGATUNY HAD HEARD his mother's cries from the secret place where he had been hiding. At first he thought that he had fallen asleep again. But he wasn't sleeping. The ground beneath him was hard and hot, and the weeds that he had been lying on still whipped him in the face. He was awake. That meant that his mother and the others were in trouble. His body trembled, and suddenly he couldn't fill his lungs with enough air. Ngatuny was a brave boy. He had never been really afraid of anything in his life. But now here he was, unable to move, unable to breathe, unable to think. All his mind could process was the sound of his mother screaming.

The thought that something was hurting her made him get up and move. One leg . . . the other leg . . . slowly, slowly, slowly. When he felt sure that his knees would hold him, Ngatuny began to run. He saw the herd up ahead of him. They were terrified of something, bucking, milling around haphazardly, many on the verge of stampeding. He heard a tearing sound and then a muffled voice. Ngatuny stopped and peered out from behind the tall grass and saw his brothers lying prostrate on the ground, a mingling stream of blood spreading out underneath them, coming toward him, following him, pointing him out to his enemies.

He stared straight ahead at his brothers, at their wide-open eyes, gaping mouths, and useless knives still wrapped in clenched fists, and at first he felt nothing.

Oh, they seem to be dead, he thought stupidly. *Yes, they're dead. And I'm alive. I'm alive.*

For years and years after that day, Ngatuny would curse himself for a coward for not running into the mouth of the fight and dying with honor and dignity like his brothers. But he was ten years old and terrified. He saw the Pokots and, in his mind, they loomed over him and his brothers and life and death like wrathful demigods, encased in black and surging forward to strip his soul from his bones and suck them clean.

Then he heard her again.

He looked across the field to his left and he saw the machete go up.

"No!" she shrieked and flung her body over her screaming infant.

"Please, for the sake of Ngai, don't do this. Take the animals. Only you can't murder a child," she begged, hugging the ground and inching backward, trying to buy a moment's more life for her daughter. "Look, look—you see, I'll put her far from me. When they come to collect our bodies someone will find her and take her home to her father. There, there where that tree is. That is where she will be. Over there. But you cannot murder a newly born baby. She is even a girl. She could never avenge her family or harm you in any way, eh? There is no reason for you not to spare at least her life. Please. *Please.*"

Mfante couldn't understand her words anyway. He hefted the machete up and flung it down straight through the blades of the woman's shoulders. Pakine screamed and tried to wriggle away, but she was impaled and so was the baby underneath her. It had stopped screaming, but Pakine didn't seem to notice. She had lost control of her senses. She tried to get up and walk away.

"My son is hiding," Ngatuny heard her say as she struggled to get to her knees. "Where could that rascal Ngatuny be? When I catch him . . . "

Mfante wrenched the machete out and brought it down again, and a stream of blood poured out of her mouth and she started to choke.

"When I catch him . . . "

The machete came down once again, and Pakine lay still.

And Ngatuny ran.

CHAPTER *Six*

. . . .

THE BOY BOUNDED DOWN on them suddenly, in a frenzy.

"Apaayia! Apaayia!" he screamed at them.

The small group of morans had been sitting in a circle in a clearing. They were eating porridge and passing around a calabash of blood-milk as they tried to shake off the remnants of the long, disastrous night. The hunting party had grown from ten to nearly one hundred throughout the night as word of the raid spread to the nearby manyattas. They had searched and searched the night by torchlight but still found no traces of the invaders. Someone suggested that they break up into smaller groups in order to cover more ground. But the Pokots were crafty, and they knew their enemy's land well. They hadn't been caught. So anger festered within the campsite, popping and crackling inside of each man, seeping, rolling, and twisting from one to the other like a flaming river that had no end, because hate had no end.

When the men caught sight of Ngatuny, they prayed that he was running with news. Nabo, the oldest member of the group, jumped up and raced to the boy just in time to catch him as his little body stumbled and fell.

"Make room! Give way! Gather the blankets. Yes, put them there," Nabo directed the others as he picked the child up and carried him to the center of the campsite.

He dropped to his knees, set the boy down on a pile of blankets, and then grabbed him by the back of the neck. Ngatuny's skin was cold, despite the fact that he had been running through the bush, and he wasn't breathing properly. Nabo took the calabash, parted the child's lips gently, and slowly poured the last of the blood-milk down into his throat. Ngatuny retched and gagged and brought it all back up, spraying Nabo's clothing and his blankets.

The morans leaned over the boy, their bodies tensed and anxious, waiting for a word or even a hint.

"Lai yelai," Nabo whispered. "Boy, are you there?"

He took the child gently underneath the chin and lifted his head, praying that this young messenger would meet his gaze. But Ngatuny lay senseless, babbling and cooing underneath his breath, not seeing the men who stood around him with their fists clenched in frustration.

"Lai yelai," Nabo said again. Still the child would not answer.

Then, without warning, he gave the boy an astoundingly hard slap, and Ngatuny fell to the side in a crumpled heap and lay there motionless for a long minute. Nabo watched closely. The child was so still that he was afraid that he had mistakenly taken away the last bit of spirit that he had left.

Then Ngatuny moved.

"Boy," Nabo urged, leaning in so close that he could smell the stench of hot, sour milk on Ngatuny's breath. "Boy, speak! What have you seen? Who has harmed you? Could it be the cattle raiders? Damn it! Listen to me, boy! Have you seen the Pokots?"

Nabo slid his legs underneath the boy's back and cradled him in the crook of his arm. The soft touch, the hot skin of Nabo's arms lying across his ribs consoled him. From down in the deepest, coolest well of Ngatuny's soul, he reached up for the familiar comfort of a gentle touch.

But even though his mind was not aware of what was going on around him, he still sensed that something was wrong. The arms were too strong, and the scent was unfamiliar.

It was not his mother.

Mother.

Did he say it out loud? Could she hear him? Was she dead? Was he dead too?

Ngatuny opened his eyes. He couldn't exactly tell who these people standing around him were, but he could make out some colors. He could see from the flaming red hair and the shukas that he was with his own kind. Morans. Like his brothers Keminin and Lolowas.

Were they his brothers? No. No. His brothers were dead. His sisters were dead, and his mother was dead.

"You will find my mother's body," Ngatuny finally said so softly that none but Nabo could hear him, "at the juncture where the fields of wheat are still green and they run together with that white farmer's maize field. There is a stretch of tall weeds next to the path. There. They are there. And just beyond, at the edge of the valley, you will find my father's cattle. They are right now crossing to the other side."

THAT NIGHT, Ngatuny prepared for his parents' funeral. For his brothers and sisters, there would be no ceremonies. They were young, unmarried, and had no children. So according to tradition, their bodies had been gathered together, taken away, and left to rot in the bush. Only the morans who had been circumcised with his brothers were allowed to mourn openly. They took turns shaving each other's long red hair, which had been growing since they first became warriors and which was their most intense source of pride. They shed the brothers' memories with each shining lock.

Ngatuny had been carried home by the morans after they had caught up with the Pokots, battled them, and murdered each of them with slow precision. Mfante had been the last to surrender his spirit, and not before he'd cursed each moran and vowed that he and all of his ancestors would hunt the nights ceaselessly until they found and slaughtered every last moran that had been responsible for this outrage against God.

Nabo and the others gathered the cattle and Ngatuny and walked the distance to his father's manyatta. Although the women and the warriors had been murdered, Nabo felt that the father would be able to take some consolation in the fact that the entire herd had been returned unharmed, as well as at least one of his sons. But when they arrived at the manyatta, they found the women lying face down in the dirt, screaming and crying out to Ngai for mercy.

"Woman, what is this?" Nabo asked, stepping slowly through the entranceway.

"They have murdered our husband and his brother," Pa-kuo sobbed, ripping at her clothes and her hair and pounding her small fists against the sides of her head. "Last night this happened. Cattle raiders came to his brother's manyatta as they were praying the evening prayer over the sacred fire and killed them both. *Oh, Ngai....* What shall become of us? What can we do? We can't live. There is nothing we can do."

Her body rocked and heaved until Nabo became afraid that she would injure herself. He was saved from having to make any decisions about helping her by the shout of another man's voice.

"Brother," called out the man who stepped into the light from inside Pa-kuo's hut. "Brother, I see you bring my nephew home to this cursed house. We have lost so much . . . so much in no time. My two elder brothers are dead. Did you know? And I am the one who has come here to tell these women and children that all that they had is lost. I am Kene. Brother, what are you called?"

"Nabo."

"Brother Nabo, do you know what it is like to be the harbinger of death and misery for those you love?"

"Before you ask that question," Nabo replied with his head bowed very low, "please, father, hear out what I must say."

CHAPTER *Seven*

. . . .　. . . . .　. . . . .　. . . . .　. . . . . .　. . .

NGATUNY HAD NO MOTHER. Ngatuny had no father.

"I'll be inherited now, you know," he told Nabo.

Simple words that held all of the misery and longing and fruit-less dreams of a lost child.

"I'll be inherited now, you know."

These small words haunted Nabo, though he wasn't sure why. But he couldn't get the boy off his mind. He rolled the image of the child's searching eyes around in his mouth like stale tobacco, and he found that it held a savage and sour taste. This child's guardian spirit was obviously either asleep or impotent, because it certainly hadn't been about its job of protecting him. Since Ngatuny was far too young to have done anything to offend it or Ngai, Nabo reasoned that it had to be Ngatuny's wayward nkai that was at fault. It had been the same with Nabo when he was a child and his parents had died. Only no one had stepped forward to help him, especially his nkai, whom he had stopped praying to long ago. On those few occasions where he had needed intercession between him and Ngai, he had gone without.

In the end, he'd stopped trying to understand his feeling and decided to approach Kene with a proposition. Let Ngatuny come into service with him. Nabo worked for a rich, crazy Mzungu whom they called Mzee Wilheim. Nabo and a group of five others had been hired by the mzee to lead him around the highlands.

"We do nothing, father, I promise you, except show him through the bush so that he can stop and talk to all of the people he sees."

But Kene was suspicious.

"Why would any man wish to waste his precious days doing that? Especially a rich Mzungu. And why would he pay you to do it with him?"

"No one would talk to him without us," Nabo explained. "He speaks no Maa. Only Swahili. And that quite badly. We translate and guide him. He carries a tablet of writing paper and ink, and he records everything that he sees us do. He's even grown attached to us. He takes us everywhere he goes, even into the lands of new tribes that we've never seen and know nothing about. We're of no help to him in these strange places, of course, and I pointed that out for him, but he dismissed my objection. He says that we comfort him. Truly, I believe he's afraid to encounter so many black people without at least a little protection that he can trust in. But whatever the motive, he pays, and very well at that. And," he added, "you won't have to worry about caring for the boy."

"Are you sure that this Mzungu has a place among his men for a small boy like Ngatuny?" Kene asked.

In fact, Nabo had no idea whether Ngatuny would be welcomed or turned away by the mzee. He had never seen the man show a particularly strong emotion toward any of the children that they'd encountered on their journeys. The most that he could say

was that at least the mzee seemed not to hate children; beyond that
he could only guess. But Nabo would look foolish if he admitted
that he was unsure, so he smiled confidently and said, "Of course!"

Kene considered the proposition. The idea filled him with suspicious thoughts. He was never *not* suspicious when it came to
white people. But he so seldom had to deal with them directly that
he chased their existence from his mind at all times. No, Kene
could not find a good feeling in his heart for any particular white
man. And now he was being asked to entrust his nephew to one?
But he had to concede to himself that he had no better plan. As
sorry as it was for him to admit it, he could not really afford to put
food into the mouth of another hungry child. He barely fed the five
who called him "father" and had no idea what to do with this extra
one, this new "son" of his.

Kene's cattle were sick with the foot-and-mouth disease.
Dying. Again. And for some unfathomable reason, which continued on despite his fervent pleas and prayers, his guardian spirit
had stepped away from him. Thus, Kene's pleading words had no
runner, no emissary to carry them up the cloud-soaked summit of
Mount Kulal and place them respectfully, one by one, at Ngai's
feet. Season after season, the work of Kene's hands yielded a bitter,
faltering crop. He had never been remotely as successful as either
of his poor dead brothers.

Kene weighed his options gravely over the next two days, and
in the end the one that outweighed all the rest was this: payment.

So Ngatuny left on the third day, carrying his father's rusted
flint, two gray camel-hair blankets, and a heavy calabash cradled
across his shoulder in a slim leather holster, filled with blood-milk.
He did not cry. He did not pretend to smile bravely for their benefit or wave. He did not even crane his neck to catch a last glimpse

as his home and family receded farther and farther away, cocooned within the timeless, endless monotony of the plains. Ngatuny simply walked, his shoulders slightly hunched and his eyes trained on Nabo's heels. Warrior and child marched silently through parched brown weeds and bushes that whipped viciously at their ankles and burrowed tiny spikes deep into their calves. Nabo glanced over his shoulder repeatedly, wincing as the child's bare foot caught on a thorn or stubbed a sharp rock. He waited for the boy to complain or perhaps even cry, but Ngatuny never slowed, and his eyes never shifted from Nabo's feet. The warrior sighed softly and wondered exactly what it was that he had done.

In late afternoon the two travelers joined up with the five morans that made up Nabo's small company. He introduced the boy, and the other warriors, after hearing his sad story, did their best backslapping and name-calling to make their new boy feel welcome. But Ngatuny gave no acknowledgment to his new companions and, eventually, they left him alone.

They passed the night in an empty warriors' hut, being fed from the steaming stew pots of the women in the neighboring manyattas. The women had seen the young warriors when they'd first happened by. Later, when time came to share the evening meal for their own families, they went to the warriors' hut and, from a respectable distance, inquired, "Is this house empty?"

"No," came the reply, and so the women rushed home to fill big bowls full of boiled goat and cabbage and ugali, which they brought back to the secluded hut and left outside the entrance. Only when a respectable amount of time had passed and the women could be assumed to be far enough gone did Nabo step out to retrieve the evening meal.

Warriors wandered from hill to valley, from plain to river's end and never had to fear the swelling voice of hunger or the silver silence of rejection, because a moran was the son and protector of the whole tribe. Each person, no matter how much or how little they had, had the obligation to feed and make welcome a much-loved son.

Early the next morning, the warriors trekked to the distant road, which would lead them south to Nyahururu. They bartered a ride from a lorry driver, who agreed to give them space among his sacks of cabbage and onions in exchange for some of the food they had left over from the night before. So the warriors grudgingly parted with their lunch and settled into the back of the truck. They perched on top of the rough, soiled sacks, being hurled up into the air each time the lorry bounced over a crater in the dirt road. They arrived in Nyahururu in the late afternoon covered in red dust, cramped, sore, and angry.

Ngatuny had never seen as many people as he saw that day rushing by on their way to places that only Ngai could guess at. He was a bit awed in spite of himself. The town teemed with long-distance buses, lorries, and bicycles. He could see at least five stores and restaurants dotting the wide, dusty road leading away from the intersection in which he stood. He flung his little head from side to side, staring at the buildings made of concrete and wood that were three and even four stories tall. The fact that he had never been inside such a place made him feel very foolish and insignificant—especially since it was to just such a place that Nabo was leading him and the others.

The building was a hotel. Ngatuny reckoned as much because of the piles of baggage that they passed on the rickety wooden front porch. A green sign with red lettering teetered at an uneven angle over the doorway, announcing the name of the place, but Ngatuny hadn't a notion as to what the lettering stood for. And he wouldn't ask. Nabo led them up two fetid flights on a staircase so narrow that they had to walk single file. At the second landing, it spilled open onto a large room filled with long wooden tables and benches. Weak, urine-colored sunlight trickled timidly in through the streaks and stains on the window glass. People crammed onto the long rows of benches, pressed against other sweaty bodies to the left and to the right, in front of them and behind. The men chewed, cursed, swallowed, and belched in a symphonic rhythm with no thought to the cringing handful of women scattered about the room.

Of all of the women, only the waitresses moved with ease and indifference about the room. As far as they saw it, the crowd today was altogether unremarkable. Quiet for the most part. Tense? Truly. But that was to be expected with that strange white man sitting in the corner. He was not police or government. That much could be told from the demure curve of his back and the way his eyes dropped when he caught someone's gaze. The police and the government whites were much more aggressive and feral, always wanting to be seen and deferred to. This man dressed rather badly, too. His dark blond hair looked dusty and clumped full of oil. And furthermore, he was skinny as a bush snake. Not a very official appearance at all. He seemed to be watching for something. And he was also fully aware of being watched.

Nabo squeezed his large frame through the rows of benches, weaving like a snake through low grass and, heedless of the burrowing stares that followed him, stopped at the bench next to the window directly in front of Wilheim. He waited in silence for the man to speak. Wilheim chewed his meat slowly and delicately, taking long moments to suck at stringy goat flesh trapped between the slender gaps in his teeth. He swallowed, paused, and then picked up his bottle of beer and took a long draft. Nabo stood, tall and thoughtful, eyes raised slightly above the mzee's head, and waited. Wilheim searched Nabo's body with that intimate and yet glassy gaze that always made Nabo feel as if the mzee meant to own him. As usual, he pretended not to notice. Finally, the mzee let loose a long, deep, smelly belch that caused the other men in the room to turn and stare in appreciation.

"You're late, my boy. Quite late," he said softly in halting Swahili.

"We could not find transport for quite some time," Nabo answered, never taking his eyes from the space between the rafters.

"For two days, there was no transport?" Wilheim asked, baiting him. "Well, speak!"

"We did get held up in another matter," Nabo conceded.

"Ah. Now we get down to business. Come, you dog! What was her name?"

"There was no woman involved, mzee. There was a fight. Cattle raiders attacked a manyatta. Pokots. They killed a whole family."

"Did they?" Wilheim sat straight up immediately, his eyes wide and questioning. "Sit. Tell me everything you know."

"Well, I know that the family that was killed was his," Nabo said, pointing back toward the doorway where Ngatuny still stood with the other morans, blocking the traffic into and out of the tiny cafeteria. For the first time, Wilheim noticed the skinny little boy peering out from behind the legs of Lpisi, the brawniest but, unfortunately, also the stupidest of his men. Wilheim motioned him over to the table, but Ngatuny did not move. Nabo called to him also, patting his thigh in a "come here" gesture, but still Ngatuny refused to respond. Finally Nabo jumped up, walked over, and grabbed the child by the ear. Ngatuny didn't struggle, but he didn't go willingly either. Nabo sat the boy down across from the mzee. Mzee Wilheim looked at Ngatuny and then said to Nabo, "What's his name?"

"Ngatuny."

"Why is he here, and why doesn't he speak or acknowledge me? Is he dim? Can he answer my questions or can't he?"

Nabo took a short breath and then charged straight into the matter.

"The boy is very bright, but he grieves, sir. There was no one left to take care of him when his parents were killed, so I suggested that he come and work for you. You are always complaining that you need more assistance. Well, this boy suits you. And being that he is a child, his upkeep will not take over so much of your money. Half a man gets half a man's wages. He has an uncle close by to Maralal, and you can send the money directly to the Maralal post-master general. The postmaster is a friend and trustworthy, the uncle claims. The money will reach him safely."

Wilheim was silent. Nabo chanced a look into his eyes, but the mzee's thoughts left no prints to be tracked across the porous surface of his face. Nabo turned to Ngatuny, whose little face was also camouflaged by a heavy mask of indifference. The warrior clucked his tongue in disgust, wondering testily whether he really was the only one who cared.

"*Hapana!*" Wilheim shouted out in a sudden heat, and Nabo's stomach curled up around his heart. He had been mistaken.

"If this child can work, he will get all of his wages, just like any other man. I won't shortchange him, and neither shall his money line some other man's pockets. That is the problem with you Africans now," Wilheim ranted. "Everyone is corrupt. No one wants to give a man his due. So the man wants to take it. By Christ! What's this place coming to?"

AND SO BEGAN NGATUNY'S service with Mzee Jonas Wilheim. Under Nabo's tutelage, Ngatuny learned how to care for the
mzee's camels, how to use a compass, how to read maps, and how
to find water in the bowels of the forty-foot Candelabra cacti in the
bush, which they stored in canteens for later use. When there was
cleaning or washing to be done, Ngatuny did it. Everyone seemed
thoroughly pleased with his work. The mzee even bought him a
suit of clothes and a pair of shoes for their numerous trips into
Nairobi and Mombasa. It was a worn light brown suit with tan
pinstripes. Stains the color of coffee grounds dotted the sleeves,
and it had a small but easily noticeable cigarette burn on the lapel.
However, Ngatuny vigorously enjoyed his new suit anyway. The
shoes were not as absolutely thrilling as the suit—at least one size
too big—but one still couldn't walk through the streets barefoot,
could one? Ngatuny decided at once that he would pay the mzee
back for it out of his wages, so that the clothes would be fully and
completely his.

The day that he finally had enough to pay for his own suit was
a great one. The company stopped along the outskirts of Nairobi
on their way to a conference in Mombasa, and the mzee insisted
that they spend the evening in a hostel. The men, weary and bel-
ligerent, searched far into the evening for a place that would allow
blacks to enter. When they finally found that place, it turned out to
be a dingy, roach-infested two-floor inn with the toilets in wooden
stalls out back. Wilheim took three rooms somewhat grudgingly.
But so long as he and his men weren't split up, poor accommoda-
tions could be tolerated. As incomprehensible as some of his ways
were, the man was, generally speaking, of a fair mind. His warriors respected him for it and were loyal.

Ngatuny lay on his cot in the corner of the dark room and counted out forty-five shillings in coins and notes and another thirteen shillings (all coins) for the shoes and then poured the money into the front left pocket of his trousers. (The other pockets had holes, slight holes, but holes nonetheless, and he didn't want to take the chance of losing even one pence.) And then he did something that he had never done before. He ran down the hall to the mzee's room and turned the handle to the door. The mzee's voice stopped him.

"He is your responsibility, Nabo." Wilheim paced in front of the room's only window, taking anxious puffs from one of those thick, stinky foreign cigars that Ngatuny so desperately wanted to taste. "Well, out with it. What is your thought on the subject? It has been more than nine months now. Why does the child still not speak?"

"I cannot know, mzee," Nabo admitted glumly. The boy was a perfect worker in every other way, but not one of them had heard a word uttered from his mouth in the entire time that he had been in service. Nabo was the only one who ever addressed him directly, and he did so in Maa.

"I would like to be able to carry along a steady conversation with all of my boys."

Nabo said nothing.

"I know your history, so I understand your desire to help this child. But I'll be damned if he doesn't unnerve me. His voice may be still, but his eyes never are."

"What do you want me to do, mzee?"

"I can't tell you that, Nabo," the mzee sighed. "But I can tell you that something has got to change. If the child is that devastated by his loss, then perhaps he belongs at home with his relations. Maybe they can help him get over it."

"No one can help me," Ngatuny said quietly through the crack in the door, his lips perched tightly around a thick pearl of perfect Swahili. "I must help myself. I help myself by being here, with you."

He opened the door scarcely a few inches wider and slipped his tiny frame through into the sliver of pale light that fell from the bulb dangling in the center of the ceiling.

"Here, mzee, I brought you the money that is owed toward my suit and my shoes," Ngatuny said to the men, who stood confounded in the middle of the room. This time, Ngatuny spoke in perfect English. "Please accept this with my thanks." The child poured the handfuls of coins and the few dirty, torn notes out onto the mzee's bed, and then he turned to go back out to his own room. His tiny hand hovered for a moment over the handle of the door.

"I do not wish to go back, mzee," Ngatuny whispered as he stood at the door with his back to them. Skimming the surface of his voice was a sorrow, a deluge of regrets that in all the time the two men had known him they had never once glimpsed in his face. "I am without family or home. I have an uncle that I call father now, but I am not a child or a fool. I know that he is too poor to feed and clothe me. Don't send me back."

"For Christ's sake, wait, boy, *wait!*" Wilheim called. "How? How can you—"

"Just because I do not tell does not mean I cannot hear," Ngatuny said slyly. "One will say things in the company of mute children that would be left unsaid under the shadows of grown men. My ears have never needed to hear a thing twice to call out its name and meaning. My yieyio said that it's the storyteller's gift. Good night."

From that evening forward, Wilheim took over the care of

Ngatuny, teaching him to read and write in English and French. Being that Wilheim could not read or write Swahili sufficiently, he entrusted the task of teaching that language to Nabo, who was the best educated of any Samburu that Wilheim knew. Ngatuny learned geography and mathematics and was always allowed to accompany the mzee into his meetings and conventions. In this way, under the guise of innocent childhood, Ngatuny penetrated boundaries that a grown African man would scarcely have attempted and most likely would never have been allowed to enter.

Wilheim found that Ngatuny's claims about his ability to learn and remember had not been at all overstated. He never had to review with the boy, and at times Wilheim found himself being corrected. Though he never admitted it to anyone else, Wilheim quite often caught himself dreaming of taking Ngatuny home with him or plotting which London universities would be most likely to have him. The boy would be a sensation! And the best of it was that he was Wilheim's own discovery.

As for Ngatuny, his world exploded around him in a vibrantly colored spectacle of new ideas and desires. Knowledge held for him the glittering power of promise that before had only been available to him in his imagination. Understanding dulled the cutting ache in his soul that welled up uncontrollably every so often, like the muddy, sweeping waters of the Ewaso Ng'iro River. He was, at last, comforted.

And so Ngatuny passed season after season scarcely noting the time. He begrudged his field work, quickly forgetting that this type of work had brought him to the mzee in the first place. If at all possible, he snuck books and pamphlets out of the mzee's travel bags and brought them with him to read as he washed and sewed and fed the animals. After a long while, it got so that he barely thought of his home, and he even succeeded in blocking almost all memory of the vicious days and nights directly following his parents' deaths. So when he got word while on a trip to the small town of Marsabit that the time of circumcision was approaching and he was required to come home immediately, his spirit filled with panic. How would his people react to him? Would they even know him?

It shocked him to realize that the time that had passed, which seemed in his mind like a haphazard smattering of months, had actually been more than five years.

Ngatuny walked alone through the dry town, so dusty and lifeless at midday, on his way back to the hostel where the other men waited. The decision over what to do tore at him. With all honesty, he knew he didn't want to go back. He realized, however, that his life would never progress beyond the point that he was at now if he didn't. He wanted to be a warrior, to hold his head high wherever he went, to be deferred to and respected, but he was afraid. Purely afraid. The years, the distance, the tall, strong new body that he possessed, the impressive new command of words (written, spoken, unspoken but understood), none of that could dislodge the bitter fear that pressed constantly at his back. And despising fear utterly and entirely as he did, he packed his bag the moment he returned to his room at the hostel. He refused to even wait to say good-bye to the mzee. Wilheim was out spending the night in a hut with a young woman, her family, and the man whom she was about to discover would soon be her husband.

Ngatuny left word of his departure with Lpisi and gave him strict orders to assure the mzee that he would be back within four months. As uncomfortable as he felt about leaving such an important message with Lpisi, Ngatuny had no other choice. He trusted no one else. Nabo had moved on by this time, taking his rightful place within his clan and passing out of the world of warriors and into the sphere of marriage and ownership. From what Ngatuny knew, Nabo's wife was expected to give birth to their first child at any time, if she hadn't already. The couple lived in his uncle's manyatta on the outskirts of Maralal. In fact, the only one left from the original group was the beleaguered Lpisi, who had passed out of the moran brotherhood as well but who, for some oblique reason, had also passed over the proper marrying time. The next time that it would be proper for him to marry a first wife would be with Ngatuny and his age-mates. He could possibly do so before, but the union would not be blessed by the elders and would automatically incur a heavy fine of at least fifteen cattle. Ngatuny had always looked on Lpisi with pity, but also with more than a fair share of disgust. In truth, Lpisi's life was one to abhor, if for no other reason than the nothingness of it. Ngatuny refused to be that way. He went home.

CHAPTER *Eight*

. . . .

MY FATHER'S RETURN

(A PRELUDE TO CIRCUMCISION AND OTHER RITES OF PASSAGE)

Fearsome. Fearless. Fear. Fearsome. Fearless. Fear. Fearsome. Fearless. Fear. Fearful eyes clamped down against rising, violent sky, bruised, puffy-lidded sky; twisting, churning, unraveling sky, sky seeking retribution. Black and bloody purple sky undulates, falls down, arouses, then cools; the soothing depth of its caress stroking feeble restitution.

He waits alone along a passage, neither sand nor rock, neither steep nor tranquil, neither home nor hell, baiting Death with shallow, hot, and lovely breath.

Death answers. Death stalks. And the heavens shatter. He looks neither left nor right but straight ahead as sleepy-eyed Death rounds the bend and the trees on either side shiver and bow in reverence, their thorns trailing plaintively in dawn-filled dust.

He rises like a radiant black phoenix, charging. Fear-some. Fearless. Fear. Fearsome. Fearless. Fear. Fearsome. Fearless. Fear. Feeling the heat of Death's embrace and smelling the stench of rotted flesh trapped desperately between angry yellow fangs, he strikes and is countered. Death dances and leaps, clashing ferociously against the mercurial lips of fate, unwilling to be sucked under, his tawny head thrown back in the ecstasy of the kill.

But he is struck down. Death has been struck down in his prime by the cruel, raping blow of youth.

And the phoenix takes flight, his battle won.

NGATUNY ARRIVED BACK at his uncle's manyatta in the cool hours of the morning just after sunrise. His small cousins saw him coming first and ran in to tell their father.

"Does he bring it?" Kene asked excitedly, his brow suddenly wet with sweat and his large hands trembling.

"He brings it, father. He brings it. We could see it from where we stood. Come. Come to greet him," they all shouted, one voice over the other, all clamoring to be the first to tell of Ngatuny's homecoming.

Kene gave a quick prayer of thanks to Ngai for the boy's safe return, and then the entire family rushed out to greet him.

Ngatuny walked like one in a trance. His shuka was torn and disheveled. From the crown of his head to the small of his back, Ngatuny was painted in blood. Maroon stains cracked on the front of his thighs, congealed in the creases of his knees, were embedded in the crevices under his toenails and crusted to the soles of his feet, so that Ngatuny even walked in blood. On his chest just below his collarbone were two long, deep gashes that had already swollen a furious and profound shade of purple. In one hand he carried the tall, splintered shaft of his father's spear. In the other hand, trailing behind him in the dirt, was the matted, gore-streaked head of a full-grown male lion, its eyes still wide and glassy with hate, its pointed fangs exposed.

The children stood in quiet awe of their older cousin, shuffling their feet softly to make way for him as he crossed through their midst and stopped in front of his uncle. Kene masked his dancing eyes carefully to conceal the joy and pride that he felt.

"Supa, apaayia," Ngatuny greeted his uncle in a dazed voice.

"Supa, layieni," Kene replied. "And what is this that you bring me?"

"It is a token, revered uncle," Ngatuny said formally and dropped the lion's head at his uncle's feet. "I have lain and waited in the bush and roamed without ceasing under the silent, brooding eye of the forest. I have watched seventeen suns rise, and only on this last did I find what I sought. It is proof that I am ready and able to defend my clan and my people. There is the proof of my courage lying at your feet. You may now tell the lpaiyani that your nephew Ngatuny is ready to become a warrior. My circumcision is at hand."

With that, Ngatuny strode slowly past his family and into the manyatta, where he settled down into the sleeping hutch of one of his small cousins and immediately dropped into a sleep so still and deep that he did not stir (or even dream) for the next two days.

WHEN NGATUNY AWOKE, he found the preparations for the circumcision well under way. Having been away for so long, fully one-third of his short life, he walked through the days that followed, through the lives of his people, like a stranger. More correctly, he moved like a ghost of his former self, forced suddenly to rediscover the long, dark passage to the land of the living and finding himself unsure of the way. Nothing felt the same to him. Everything seemed small and insignificant, even the swelling, grassy hills that he'd so long ago loved. He walked alone across the plains, smelling the honeyed, godlike scent of thunder rolling around in the pregnant underbelly of the clouds, and he felt nothing. He now knew that the clouds were called cumulonimbus and the fearsome thunderbolts were no more than electrical currents. There was no god or spirit, benevolent or otherwise, involved at all in the temperament and timing of the seasons. Somehow harboring this knowledge made him feel hollow inside and ashamed. He was a fraud. He no longer believed in the ways of his people or, for the most part, the people themselves. Ngatuny wondered if this restlessness was a gift that came with perception or a scythe that blinded him and struck him from his true path. He could not decide and so he chose not to choose. Instead, he stole liquor and he drank.

No one expected Ngatuny to do anything, so he spent the remaining days before the start of the ceremony hanging around with some of the other boys, drinking from the gourds of nalanga wine that he stole from his uncle and telling stories about friends and strangers they had heard of who hadn't made it through the rituals.

"I am telling you all, I know for a fact that Lngeso never made it back," said Ngatuny as he turned up the gourd and drained the last of the bitter wine quickly, before any of the other boys could snatch it. The foamy residue spilled across his cheeks and dripped down his neck. He wiped it away with a woozy hand, careful to let the other boys see him directing the liquor away from the angry wounds on his chest. He belched proudly and continued on.

"The full thirty days passed and then five more before his father and uncles went to search for him. The lion must have feasted well, or the hyenas that came after, because they never found anything. Not a bone or a piece of cloth. Nothing. With these very ears, I tell you, I have heard his mother wailing. Ei! Pity."

"That is nothing. Who has heard the story of the one called Ge-kine?" asked a small, wiry boy whom they called Tepero.

Ngatuny and the others shook their heads.

"Ei, ei, ei! Where to begin with this wretched story? The boy was from the Lukumai clan and was supposed to be circumcised in the last ceremonies seven years ago. All was well with him at first. He conducted himself like a man up until the moment when it really counted." Tepero paused dramatically, and the others boys leaned in, holding their breath, biting their lips, and drumming anxious fingertips against their knees.

"The lamuratani had his foreskin right in the palm of his hand, like this," he said and snatched his dark fist closed with a mighty jerk that made all of the boys wince and grab their crotches. "No movement did Ge-kine make. Not then. He sat, eyes straight ahead, shoulders high like a stone-carved god, and waited. But when the lamuratani sliced the foreskin with his knife, Ge-kine jumped back—"

The boys leapt up in startled disbelief.

"You mean to say he moved?"

"Ei! Lies!"

"Ah! Tepero is spinning in the web of an invisible spider. He just likes to be the center of the action."

"If he says the boy flinched a little, I can believe. Some do. But jumped? Eh, Tepero is telling women's tales again."

"I tell you truth!" Tepero insisted, slamming his fist against the ground. "I will fight the next one who says again that I am not! Now, would you like to hear the finish of what happened?"

"Is he dead?" asked Ngatuny. "I don't want to hear anymore if the boy isn't dead."

"In fact, he is dead," said Tepero.

With that, the others sat back down without a word and listened.

"As it was, his own uncle had been chosen by the lamuratani to be the Watcher. He stood over all the boys with his spear ready in his hand, never moving. When Ge-kine took his turn and jumped up like that, his uncle had to be the one to spear him."

"And he did it?" asked one of the other boys with awe in his voice. "He actually killed his own nephew?"

"Of course he did. That is the duty of the Watcher—to keep cowards out of our midst," Tepero said, looking meaningfully around at the small group. "He didn't even hesitate. They say the boy squirmed and flopped on the sacred ground like a fresh-caught fish, and when it was over, the uncle wiped his blood off the spear, took his place again without a word, and began to watch the others. I hear the uncle cried like a scared woman at home when the circumcisions were over, but ei! I tell you every boy that came after that spectacle sat up tall!"

The boys sat quietly, letting the weight of the story settle over them. They were all sure that Tepero had exaggerated on some portion of it. He always did. But the story sank down deep in the center of their stomachs. Every boy secretly feared the Watcher. Despite all the prayers and the rituals that supposedly dulled their senses to the impending pain, there was always the possibility that fear would take over and they would make a bad showing. If it wasn't too bad, then the family would merely be ostracized and would most likely end up moving to another district. If the boy did something unforgivable, however, like try to run away or scream or cry, then the Watcher would take over. But it almost never happened. To Ngatuny, it seemed to be a contradiction to frighten a person into bravery, but theoretically, to be a moran, one must know no fear, no pain. If pain and fear are not known, then the Watcher is inconsequential—merely a safeguard and quite unnecessary.

But he would still be there. Just in case.

A site was chosen for the ceremonies, and after the lmasula clan elders built the sacred fire and prayed over it, the clansmen constructed a manyatta on the spot to house the boys for the next two months. Then all of the instruments that would be used during the course of the rituals—the knives, spears, paints, and the like—were prayed over as well. Only then were all of the lmasula boys of the district finally called together to have their heads shaved and begin their transition.

They entered the manyatta one by one, shedding the garments of childhood in favor of identical black aprons made of bull skin. All of the boisterous, raunchy talk of the previous days ceased. Each boy walked solemnly as he followed the footsteps of the brother before him, stepping soberly out of the sunlight and into the deep, smoky shadows of the circumcision hut.

For Ngatuny, the ceremony passed in a haze of confused, clouded thoughts. This part of life was inevitable, like the sprouting of grass in the fields after the rainy season or making love to a woman. And yet he was afraid. He sat on the floor of the circumcision hut crowded elbow to elbow with his age-mates, all of whom looked pasty-faced and gloomy, swallowing back his fear and feeling a sharp, angry storm brewing in his belly. This tempest turned into a rage that mounted higher and higher the more pronounced his fear became. Ngatuny bowed his head, burrowing his chin into his chest so that no one who chanced to look at him would be able to see his eyes. So preoccupied was this boy with hating the fear inside of him that he could not bother with anything else.

The few times in his life since the Incident when he had been unfortunate enough to encounter this type of creeping dread, he had looked far within himself to find the strength to overcome it and had instead found a cowering, sobbing ten-year-old too terrorized to even speak. Ngatuny needed to kill that child, needed desperately to crack that little neck and close those bulging eyes for good. He knew that regardless of the warped, splintered image of tribalism that had presented itself, in actuality it was fear that had killed his family on that distant day. And it was the fear of fear that had killed him, little by little, ever since.

This is it, Ngatuny warned himself. *No more. Never again. That child is gone. Dead.* He shook his head as if he were shaking off a persistent chill. *He's dead.*

It was this thought that went sliding through his head as he bent his tall frame, stepped out into the early-morning light, and sat on a short wooden stool opposite the seated lamuratani. Even sitting, Ngatuny towered over the lamuratani, whose scrawny body fit quite comfortably under the girth of Ngatuny's shadow. The whites of the man's eyes had already gone yellow with age. He looked elderly and exhausted, although Ngatuny knew him to be one of his uncle's age-mates, barely of middle age. Perhaps thirty-five or so. Ngatuny stared at the curving lines and crevices that flowed across the man's face like the markings of a river on a map and he thought, *This is life?*

He felt the child inside stirring, groaning, struggling slowly back to life. Ngatuny turned a blind eye to the lamuratani in front of him and the Watcher standing directly behind him and focused all of his energy on murder.

The shaft of Ngatuny's penis shrunk hastily under the pressure of the lamuratani's hot, slick hand as the man reached roughly underneath the apron and grabbed hold of him. Pulling the foreskin up over the tip and with a quick, underhanded slice, the lamuratani severed the loose skin, leaving the head exposed. Then he carefully lifted up what little remained of the hood, cut a small hole through it, and gently brought the head through the hole.

Ngatuny did not flinch. His eyes did not waver. He looked through the lamuratani as one looks through a twisted sheet of rain searching for a break in the clouds. With every deft movement of the razor-edged knife, Ngatuny felt the child shrink and shrivel, a carrion to soon be cast away like the useless foreskin, a quick morsel for scavengers. It was well worth the pain.

What was left of the foreskin hung down from the front of Ngatuny's penis in what the men called a "tie." Finally, with three swift strokes, the lamuratani trimmed the tie into a sharp, acceptable shape and told Ngatuny to stand.

It was over.

Ngatuny stood, and the length of his adolescent body dwarfed the lamuratani. He bowed his head respectfully.

"Thank you, father," he said and walked back into the circumcision hut.

For a month the boys stayed inside the hut, being scrutinized for any signs of sickness or infection. Ngai had been good to them. All of the boys had done relatively well, and none of them had been inflicted with the pus-filled sores or fevers that sometimes came with the circumcision. So with much thanksgiving, the elders organized the celebration that would officially carry the boys over the threshold from childhood to moranhood.

An elder donated a large, healthy brown bull. The men brought it into the manyatta, tied it down, and then slit open the skin of its throat. Then another one of the elders punctured a vein, and rich, hot blood spurted out into the pouch of flesh. One by one the new morans and their fathers, uncles, and elders sipped at the thick, salty blood of the writhing animal. When every man in the compound had gotten a taste, they killed the bull and roasted its body over an open fire. The feasting and dancing and singing continued throughout the entire night, so great was their joy. Ngatuny could hear the proud, insistent voices of his aunties and their daughters singing and rejoicing outside of the fence with the other mothers and sisters. Though he was not allowed to see their faces, it comforted him tremendously to know that they were there.

For one more month, the new morans lived in the circumcision manyatta. Having nothing better to do, they tramped through the bush, searching out small birds and shooting them down with bows and arrows. The boys brought the carcasses back to the manyatta, where they amused themselves by making large, colorful headdresses out of the feathers. Ngatuny made his headdress out of red, green, and golden feathers of varying shades and sizes. All of the other boys made a fuss over his headdress, most of them agreeing that it was by far the best, but Ngatuny waved the compliments aside, assuring them that the feathered headdress was nothing. The one he was making out of his lion head would be by far the most impressive thing they had ever seen.

At the end of the second month, the lpaiyani came to the manyatta to pray for the safety, health, and well-being of the boys, their families, and their livestock. The new morans sat cross-legged on the ground, their eyes cast humbly to the floor as the lpaiyani walked between them, sprinkling them with a mixture of milk and water meant to bless the young warriors in their travels and future battles.

Then they all went home.

Ngatuny stayed with his uncle long enough to finish his head-dress and have the new growth of his hair plaited with the fat and red ocher that is the signature mark of a moran.

On the morning he left, his family gathered together to wish him a safe journey. He stood before them, smiling, transformed from the child that he had been into a strong, confident young man. In his new red shuka and blanket, with his hair plaited and glowing a fiery red, he looked almost exactly as his brother Kemi-nin and their father before them had looked. Kene thought this but kept it private for fear of stirring up old spirits.

"You have made us so proud, Ngatuny," Kene finally told him. "Your own father could not have been more pleased with you than I am. The entire district spoke of your bravery. You did not cower. You did not falter. Your age-mates will now seek you out for guid-ance and counsel because you have proven yourself worthy. In the future, you are sure to prosper. I only wish I had more than one bull to give to you—"

"The bull is not the thing of importance that you have given me," Ngatuny interrupted him. "After my family died, you pro-vided me with the one place that I now have to return to. And when I do return, your sons and I will work together to build you a bigger manyatta and make sure that your herds are plentiful and healthy."

But even as he spoke these words (which he desperately wanted to believe), he wondered to himself whether they all knew that he was lying.

So Ngatuny returned to service with Mzee Wilheim, and things continued on almost exactly as they had for the previous five years. Only the seasons and the towns changed. Ngatuny grew even taller and his body began filling out, becoming less gangly and awkward and more manlike as each day passed. His studies also progressed greatly, and he had even taken to helping the mzee collect his data. Wilheim had already completed two books comparing and contrasting the pastoralist tribes of the plains with one another and with tribes from neighboring countries and the coastal areas of Kenya.

He and Ngatuny were hard at work on the third part of his series when the first stirrings of change began to take place.

It started innocently enough, with a stopover in Nairobi en route to Mombasa. The mzee gave Ngatuny the afternoon off, and he decided to do a little browsing in the city market. Kenya had been locked in a state of emergency since 1952, so anytime Ngatuny went out on the streets of Nairobi alone, he was always alert and exceedingly careful to look over his shoulder in case he should be followed by any soldiers looking for trouble. He kept his hand on his waist pouch, where he stored the perfectly folded identification card that the mzee had managed to get for him.

Though he'd decided not to wear his traditional dress while staying in the city, his red hair (which continued to grow more rapidly than even he expected) gave him away as a moran and, as such, he was a prime target for fights. Everyone knew the reputation for bravery and defiance that the Maasai and Samburu warriors held. So, of course, many also wanted to test him out to see if the talk was just talk or if he was really made out of different stuff than everybody else. More than once Ngatuny had been called out of his thoughts by the striking cries of "Baboon!" and "Hey, blackie!" coming from a group of white soldiers standing on one street corner or another. They invariably wanted to know if he really drank blood and killed babies and whether or not that was a spear he was carrying in his trousers. He never turned around, but their loud, derisive laughter followed him no matter where he went after that.

That particular afternoon, Ngatuny felt good. He walked leisurely through the small wooden stalls of the city market, squeezing past other pedestrians and hawkers, who sold everything from sweets to sugarcane to matches. Ngatuny bought fifty cents' worth of sugarcane. He gnawed on the warm, syrupy pulp and continued weaving his way through the narrow passages and gutters, looking at cloth and jewelry and cooking utensils. He wasn't searching for anything in particular, but he hadn't bought himself a real treat in quite a long while. He wandered unhurriedly through the crowds, examining, haggling over, and ultimately discarding item after item, dodging the hordes of men and women as they tried to get their shopping done before the evening curfew caught them out of doors. The delicious smell of grilled goat mixed with the odor of tightly packed, sweating bodies and the scent of burning leaves, which wafted over the market from somewhere off in the distance.

Ngatuny stopped at a jewelry stall to price a strand of red and gold beads that he thought would go quite nicely around his senior auntie's neck. He was about to ask the price when a man bumped him from behind. As he spun around, the other man also spun around, with a curse already hanging from his lips.

"You—" the man started, but then, all at once, his eyes grew wide with recognition. "No! No! This can't be. Not little Ngatuny.

Ha ha! But yes, I'm sure that it is! My small one has finally become a man!"

Ngatuny stared at the man coldly. He still didn't recognize him.

"I know that the time passed has been too long, but please don't tell me that you don't recognize your faithful friend Nabo?"

As he said that, Ngatuny's eyes opened as if for the first time and he saw his old friend and benefactor looking totally different than he had ever seen him before. The plaits and the red ocher had been cut out of Nabo's hair, as must happen when a warrior graduates out of moranhood. Nabo's black hair was cropped very close to his head, and he wore a rather expensive-looking blue suit and a pair of spectacles. His long earlobes were rolled up and tucked behind the top of his ears and he wore no jewelry. Ngatuny broke out into a delightfully sheepish smile.

"Supa! It is my benefactor! Ei! What could I have done to deserve this bit of good fortune?" Ngatuny laughed. "Please forgive me for not recognizing you straightaway, eh, but I am not used to seeing you look such the gentleman!"

The men laughed, joined hands, and began walking happily from the marketplace.

"Come, brother, let's find a shop and buy something to eat. I'm starved!" Nabo said, slapping Ngatuny across the back. "I shall buy you some samosas and maybe some cake for that sweet tooth of yours, and we can catch up on old times."

Ngatuny was about to answer his friend when a thundering *crack!* tore through the air directly above their heads. Immediately, the crowd began stampeding in all directions through the narrow streets. People ducked and screamed, running anywhere they saw even a tiny bit of open space.

Then again the noise burst through the throng of people: *crack crack crack crack!*

"The soldiers," Nabo yelled. "Keep down! They're firing at someone over there."

As they tried to run in the opposite direction, a group of black soldiers cut off their escape and began to randomly strike people in the crowd with black rubber clubs.

"What are they doing?" Ngatuny shouted.

"Who knows. No! Not that way. Quick, follow me."

Nabo led him through an alleyway and they came out onto Loita Street, but the moment they stepped from behind the small gray office building into the street, they found that the chaos had spread. It seemed that soldiers and now policemen were streaming in from every direction. They grabbed men and women out of the stampeding crowd seemingly at random, beating them and then throwing them into the backs of waiting police vans.

"It's not safe to stay here. You must come with me," Nabo said and, with that, the two men ran, Ngatuny barely dodging a wild blow from the baton of a black officer.

They ran past the little shops and stalls on Kimathi Street, some of which stood dark and empty, their windows shattered and the wooden doors broken in. They came up to the roundabout that led to Limuru Road and hopped onto an idling city bus whose route would take them out toward Karura Forest. Almost immediately, the bus jerked to an unsteady start, leaving the noise and chaos behind them, shrouded in a rising screen of foul black smoke.

"What could that have possibly meant?" Ngatuny panted as he slouched down into his seat and turned to watch the city fade from his sight.

"Who knows." Nabo shrugged. "Most likely nothing. Another witch-hunt. Forever searching for the invisible 'Mau-Mau.' "

"So for the sake of a few men, they are willing to trample over hundreds?"

"But of course."

"Those devils!" Ngatuny was incensed. "They call us animals and savages, and yet I saw one of them just now stomp on the neck of a small boy—impossible that the child could have been more than nine or ten—and beat him in the head with a baton."

"Don't forget, my friend, one of those batons almost came crashing down on top of your head, too. And the hand that held it was black. Our nation is divided."

"What nation?" Ngatuny countered testily. "Who but these white men says that this patch of land and all of the peoples that populate it is a nation? Kenya will only be a nation so long as its richness can be plundered."

"You are wrong, Ngatuny," Nabo whispered. "There are other ways. You will soon see that."

Ngatuny looked over at his friend, but Nabo's eyes were far away.

"What has been going on with you, friend? Really?" he asked. "It has been close to three years since my circumcision, and I hadn't seen you for more than a year before that. How is it with you?"

"I can't tell you that here and now," Nabo replied with a heavy sigh. "There is too much to say. But look, this is where we get off."

The two men jumped from the back of the bus seemingly in the middle of nowhere. They stood at the roadside until the bus had turned out of sight, and then Nabo led them by way of a tiny foot trail into the forest. The land here was much richer than in Samburu. Ngatuny could see this easily from the diversity of the trees and shrubs that they walked among. He hurried to keep up with Nabo, because even at just a few meters ahead, his friend disappeared into the thick foliage. On top of it all, it was almost fully dark by this time. *What of the curfew?* Ngatuny thought and then immediately cursed himself for thinking like a woman. Since when had he started letting any man, much less some foreign man, run him? Those bloody Mzungus had him all turned around.

Nabo stopped underneath a huge palm tree in a small clearing and said simply "We wait."

Since he didn't volunteer any information about what it was exactly that they were waiting for, Ngatuny did not pry. He trusted his friend. But the events of the day had worn on him. He was tired. He lay on his back, surrounded by a soft carpet of short grass, with his head propped up against a gentle mound of moss at the base of the palm tree. Slowly, slowly, slowly, the image of Nabo receded in his mind until there was nothing but blackness.

When Ngatuny awoke, Nabo was gone. He waited for a few moments, letting his eyes adjust as much as they could to the blackness that surrounded him. He listened carefully to the night, to the crickets and sausage bugs at play, the screeching of monkeys above and behind him, and the occasional flutter of bat wings as they circled the tree trunks and lowest branches sniffing for food. There was nothing in these noises to fear. No large animals lived in these woods. Not anymore. He tried to pick up any human sound, or even a scent that would tell him in which direction he needed to go. Nothing.

Worry seeped into Ngatuny's heart. What could have lured him away? He didn't want to leave his clearing and become lost deep within this foreign forest, but the thought that Nabo might need him gave him his legs, and he began to hunt out his friend.

He walked almost timidly at first, on the balls of his feet like a prowling cat, feeling for the vines and branches in front of him with the tips of his fingers. After some time, Ngatuny heard a faint sound coming from behind the bushes to his right. Not wanting to be given away before he was ready, he crawled over to where he'd heard the noise, letting his limbs slide slowly through the loose, fertile earth so as not to upset any twigs or branches that lay in his path. As he got a little closer, he detected a faded light coming from a lantern and heard the almost imperceptible sound of voices. Ngatuny approached the flickering yellow light cautiously, listening to the voices grow steadily louder. But he could still not make out what the men were saying. He crouched behind a bush and peered out. What he saw made him gasp so loudly that he was sure that the men standing around the lamplight must have heard him.

There was, almost directly in front of him, an arch about six or seven feet tall made from two banana stems joined at the top and plaited with beanstalks and the leaves of the mugere bush. A group of four men, Nabo among them, had just finished walking through the arch in single file. On their left lay a pile of shoes, watches, and jewelry that they had dropped haphazardly into the dirt. Presumably the men weren't allowed to wear such things as they took their secret oath. And that is exactly what Ngatuny was witnessing. He knew it instantaneously and without any doubt. The secret initiations of the Mau-Mau.

Ngatuny watched the resolute faces waver in and out of the feeble light with a mixture of shock and awe. Nabo was a freedom fighter! But how could it be that his dearest friend was now an enemy of the state? A Mau-Mau. Ngatuny didn't know what to think. The mzee had made sure that he had little to no contact with that world. Did one have to renounce his own tribe and take up with the Kikuyus in order to become a real Mau-Mau? He would have to ask Nabo later. It struck him that this was something that he was definitely not supposed to be seeing. That is why he had been left so far away. In fact, if not for the rioting in the city center, he would never have been here to begin with. He strained his ears to hear exactly what was going on. Two men stood facing the initiates. One held the sickly looking gray lungs of a goat in his right hand and a piece of raw goat's meat in his left. Nabo and the others bowed their heads to the ground, and the leader circled each of their heads exactly seven times with the meat. Next, he had each of them take a large bite out of the juicy, dripping lungs. Then he ordered them to repeat slowly after him:

I speak the truth and vow before God
And before this movement,
The movement of Unity,
The Unity which is put to the test
The Unity that is mocked with the name "Mau-Mau,"
That I shall go forward to fight for the land,
The lands which were taken by the Europeans
    And if I fail to do this
    May this oath kill me,
    May this seven kill me,
    May this meat kill me.
I speak the truth that I shall be working together
With the forces of the movement of Unity
And I shall help it with any contribution for which I am
    asked,
I am going to pay sixty-two shillings and fifty cents and a
    ram for the movement.

If I do not have them now, I shall pay in the future.
And if I fail to do this
May this oath kill me,
May this seven kill—

Ngatuny was so engrossed in the revolutionary magic he was witnessing that he did not hear the soldiers until they were almost upon them.

At the very last second, Ngatuny realized that the rustling leaves behind him were pushed not by the wind but by the heavy leather boots of armed government men. Out of the side of his eye, he saw (too late) poorly camouflaged hunched backs shimmying through the giant fern bushes. Jumping up, he shouted frantically to his friend:

"*Kwet!* Nabo, run!"

A soldier grabbed Ngatuny's collar, meaning to knock him out of the way, and the young warrior whirled around, enraged. The first thought that entered his mind was *Pokots!* and instinct overwhelmed reason. He punched the man in the throat, knocking him breathlessly to the ground. Ngatuny hit him with such force that he lost his balance and fell as well, pinning the rifle between them. He pounded the man viciously across his cheek, gashing the skin under his eye in two furious blows, all the while struggling for better leverage to get off a clean punch. The man, still gasping and wheezing for air, raised a hand to protect his face, and Ngatuny snatched his rifle right out of the other hand. He hoisted himself up to his knees, flipped the gun around, and smashed the soldier in the nose with the butt. Blood spurted across his thighs and, without thinking, Ngatuny raised the butt of the rifle once more, this time stretching it high over his head as he aimed for the space between the man's eyes.

Then something hit him, something sharp and hot, and he flew back through the air and landed with a heavy thud at the base of a tree. Ngatuny's entire body went numb. He looked around and noticed that there was blood on his trousers and a black, bloody stain spreading rapidly across his chest. His head spun in wide, dizzying circles, and the last thing he muttered before he fell into unconsciousness was. "Nabo. friend. I have been killed . . . "

IT TOOK NGATUNY more than eight weeks to recover from his gunshot wound to the point where he could be transported to a detention camp. There was no trial. Ngatuny was allowed no defense. A magistrate arbitrarily sentenced him to serve three to six years for being a terrorist and an enemy of the state who had plotted to take the life of an army soldier. Ngatuny knew that his nkai had been working steadily for his protection because the soldier that he had injured was black. If he had done the same thing to a white soldier, he could easily have spent the rest of his life in prison. Then Ngatuny, like Nabo and the others before him, was shuttled between camps until he ended up at the Langata Detention Center.

At the beginning of his confinement, Ngatuny wrote to Mzee Wilheim, explaining what had happened and pleading with him to intervene on his and Nabo's behalf. The mzee wrote back a curt missive stating that, as he refused to allow himself to be drawn into any perverse or subversive acts, from the current moment on he disavowed all knowledge of Ngatuny. Moreover, he would never associate himself with anybody who would be involved with an organization that murdered decent, innocent white men, women, and children—people who were just as much citizens of the nation of Kenya as any African. Ngatuny should have had enough sense to realize that with all the problems that the Kenyan government had, government was still government. Those who stepped outside of the boundaries of said government must expect to pay a steep penalty, even if the penalty meant the loss of one's freedom. Wilheim ended the letter with . . . *and furthermore, you are hereby terminated from my services effective immediately. May God have mercy on you. Yours sincerely, Mzee Jonas Wilheim.*

Ngatuny was dumbfounded at Wilheim's reply. Was this the same man with whom he had shared his life, his thoughts, his passion for words and for knowledge, his hopes for a future different from any that his father could ever have dreamt of? This was indeed the same man, Ngatuny reminded himself bitterly. The same *white* man. Obviously that allegiance took precedence over any that he might have thought they shared.

The worst thing about this rejection was that it alerted the prison guards to the fact that not only could Ngatuny read and write (the guards read all incoming and outgoing letters), but he was actually quite learned. His status as a detainee immediately jumped from a Y-2, which they called "whites," past Y-1, which were called "grays," all the way to Z-2, which was the code for "black." The only way his status could be bumped up any further— or, in other words, he could be considered any more dangerous— was if he moved up the last rung on the ladder to Z, which was code for "hard-core black" and generally reserved for the unredeemable Mau-Mau leaders.

The first and most vivid memory that Ngatuny had of Langata was being forced into white prison suits, lined up outside in the rain, and then told to repeat in Swahili "Mau-Mau mbaya," which meant "Mau-Mau is bad." Then a fat, stupid-looking black officer from the Kikuyu Home Guard forced them to repeat, "We Englishmen will rule this country forever." Some of the men laughed, but the irony of the officer's words was lost on him, and he ordered the laughing men beaten.

The next phrase was "Jomo Kenyatta is a dog." When the men hesitated, the Europeans and the Tribal Police officers who prowled up and down the rows began lashing out with fists and sticks. They ordered the men to lie down in the mud, while freezing rain pelted the backs of their necks and heads and soaked through the thin jumpsuits, and yell at the top of their voices "Jomo Kenyatta is a dog!" Some clever man turned the Swahili word *dog* (mbwa) into the Kikuyu word *Creator* (mba). The rest of the men followed suit, shouting as hard as they could that Jomo Kenyatta was a Creator and laughing inwardly at the stupidity and childishness of their captors.

The camp was filled with dingy cloth tents and surrounded by Dannert wire. Every morning and every evening, the home guards forced the men to squat in rows with their hands on top of their heads while the soldiers strolled back and forth doing the head count. Just for fun, they finished off each row by giving sound blows to the man unfortunate enough to be caught at the end of the line. Langata was supposed to be a place of transition where the detainees were classified and then, based on that classification, sent on to other camps. However, Ngatuny, Nabo, and the other five men that had been involved in the ceremony were never sent on. Neither were they given any explanation as to why they had to stay. They watched other prisoners come and go while they swallowed down ever-increasing amounts of bitterness and resentment. Langata was known to be among the most vicious, corrupt, and dreaded holding camps that the British had built.

Almost anywhere would have been better. Almost. Every time Ngatuny felt himself sinking into a hollow of despair, Nabo gently reminded him that, as impossible as it might be to believe, things could have been worse. They could have wound up at the Kwa Nyangwethu camp near Bahati like poor Kanyoi. Kanyoi was one of the men who had been recently transferred to Langata; Ngatuny shared a tent with him. He was a stoop-shouldered, golden-brown half-caste of about thirty years whose blinded left eye drooped miserably from its socket. His deformity had come as a result of too many beatings for writing letters of protest to the district commissioner about poor conditions at the camps. Kanyoi never spoke. It was said that he had stopped speaking (and writing) when a frustrated prison official at Kwa Nyangwethu had had him beaten and castrated.

All told, it took four long years for Ngatuny's number (No. 56605) to be called, for them to say that he could go home. In the final days before his release, the lmuget le ngarna ceremony was held in his home district. He could tell because he knew the time of the year, if not the specific date. Ngatuny knew that the elders would soon be slaughtering a bull, if they hadn't done so already. All of the age-mates that he had been circumcised with would be taking new names to go along with the new lives that came with the end of moranhood. But Ngatuny's release from prison came weeks too late.

So he never got his new name.

CHAPTER *Nine*

. . . .

IN SPITE OF HIS DISAPPOINTMENT over his ill-timed homecoming, Ngatuny did arrive back home at the start of the second ceremony, called lmungo le ngeema, after which he and his age-mates would be allowed to take brides. He went through the motions of slaughtering and celebrating like a puppet yanked by a fraying string. He talked to no one. His family worried about his brooding, worried about what he planned to do with his life besides drink, worried that he would never grow into the smiling, handsome man that he should be.

But Ngatuny took no notice of their shy advances and hints. In his mind, he was still at Langata with Nabo and the others, being overrun by rats during the day and roaches and fat black bedbugs at night. He was still fighting to choke down the cold maize gruel and stiff porridge, because one never knew when the next meal would arrive.

In his mind, Ngatuny was still in Shimo.

The Hole.

He dreamed of it almost every time he went to sleep. The vision came at the darkest part of the night, and immediately whatever dream he was having would suddenly go black, the different shades and shadows of blackness slowly shifting and growing tall. Once more he found himself trapped at the bottom of a ten-foot pit, immobilized with fear, as the mud walls began melting down on him. The closer the oozing mass came, the more he felt a hysterical terror rising in him, crawling out of his bowels and into his throat. Then Ngatuny's feet began to freeze and slip out from underneath him. He looked down in a panic and found them covered in half a foot of icy mud. He turned away for a moment, searching desperately for a way out, but in the next second, when he glanced back down at his feet, the mud had turned to quicksand. And before he could open his mouth to scream, the thick whirlpool of black sand had sucked him in. It lapped at his chin, inviting him to simply fall asleep. At first, the impulse seemed beautiful and welcome. But then—face of all faces that should come before his sleeping eyes—his father arose before him. Ngatuny quickly turned his own face away in shame, mortified that his father should see his only surviving son trapped like a rabid animal in a pit. When he looked back, he found his father gone. But then he raised his eyes, and there was his father's face, peering down at him in disgust from between the thick steel grates in the lid that locked the top of the Hole.

Father! he yelled. No sound. No answer. *Father, please . . .* Ngatuny reached his frozen, filthy hand up toward his father's face, which still stared motionless through the grate. But then his father smirked. His face cracked open in a demonic, sadistic grin quite like the faces of the more vicious members of the Tribal Police, a look that had never once crossed his face in life. Every night Ngatuny forced himself awake, his heart thumping wildly against his ribs, and he lay panting and cursing until dawn, listening to

the swells of wind crashing against the walls of his hut. He wondered each day when he would stop seeing that place in his sleep,
stop smelling the waste and decay of five thousand men on his
breath and under his arms. Langata had nestled itself comfortably
underneath the soft layers of his skin, burrowed into his bone.

The only peace of mind and happiness he felt came from the
knowledge that his best friend, Nabo, was due to be released from
Langata at any time. Ngatuny did not know what to expect from his
friend. But he hoped and prayed that Nabo would fare better in his
return to life than Ngatuny himself had.

The rest of the time, Ngatuny's thoughts were flooded with
anger and resentment for the people who had stolen all those years
from him. The commissioners, the magistrates, the Tribal Police
(those black bastards), the soldiers, the mzee . . . no, Wilheim. The
man's name was Wilheim. He was no mzee.

Of all of the people that he was angry with, Ngatuny was
the most infuriated with that man Jonas Wilheim for making
him doubt the wisdom and the worthiness of his own people. Ngatuny's callow mind had never stopped to question the all-
powerful views and knowledge of the white man. He had never
stopped to wonder, for all of their information and reports and sta-
tistics and technologies, what did they really know? It had taken
Ngatuny almost half of his life to come to the realization that in-
telligence can't be automatically equated with wisdom. Or true devotion. No. He had allowed the . . . Wilheim to be the agent that
had corrupted his judgment and perverted his loyalties. The worst
of it was that, for a time, Ngatuny had really tricked himself into
believing that Wilheim cared for him as a person, as a true human
being with rights, needs, and desires as strong and as valid as his
own.

Ngatuny the child had compared his world to the mighty, insistent world of the whites, and he had agreed with them that his people were shameful and backward. He hadn't even wanted to come back and live among them when it was time for him to leave the moranhood and settle down.

Well, his stupidity be damned! He had finally completed his journey through their so-called heart of darkness, and he'd found that, indeed, he was one of the savages hooting and hollering from behind the painted masks, running up the twisted banks of a native river. He didn't have anything whatsoever to do with the suave, "heroic" white man who traveled comfortably up the same river on his sturdy European steamship looking down haughtily on what he believed to be a primitive, prehistoric world.

And that was just fine with him.

Months passed this way, and Kene became afraid that Ngatuny's nkai had failed him and he would never amount to much after all. Though many families of eligible young women had inquired discreetly about his return, he had never returned the interest. Kene decided to try one last time to set his beloved nephew on the straight path. The two sat early one evening in the shadows of a huge tamarind tree playing a spirited game of ntotoi. The tree was flowering with fragrant yellow-and-red buds, and the wind gusting around their heads showered them with sweet smells and silken petals. Ngatuny was winning.

"You know, son," Kene said in a carefully light tone, "if we were really playing this game, we would be wagering cattle. You see, if we were playing for stakes like real men, well, then I would have the incentive to whip you properly."

"Eh? You think so?" Ngatuny asked mockingly. "Well, what I say is this: You are an old man who can no longer move your stones correctly. To speak truth, you would probably fare better if you allowed the stones to move themselves. Surely it would be faster, eh? Besides, if we were playing for cattle, then right now you would be about three or four head in arrears. So, ha! Isn't it lucky for you that we're playing the way small boys do?"

But Kene's meaning was not lost. Ngatuny shook his head in silent agreement that, indeed, he was a man acting as a boy. He had no responsibilities, no honors, no respect. He had grown tired of waking up every morning after only half a night's sleep and smelling the sour odor of stale wine on his breath. Ngatuny sighed deeply, heavily, trying to release at least part of the bilious cloud of disgust that coated his heart and mind.

I am a man, he thought. *I have to be.*

But he wasn't. Not really. Not in the eyes of his people. He looked like a man, though. The last traces of his moranhood were gone. He'd cried for the first time in seven years after the lmungo le ngeema ceremony, when the plaits had been shaved from his head. They had grown down past the center of his back and were his pride, even though the faded color remained only on the bottom half. There had been no red ocher with which to dye his hair in the camp. His scarlet shukas had been discarded for more proper robes and blankets, a staff to replace his sword and spear. Ngatuny uttered all the proper words and attended all of the appropriate ceremonies. He was a man.

Then why did he still hear the laughter of the home guards and the Tribal Police and the soldiers bubbling up from the bottom of every full gourd of wine he drank? He always drank them down quickly, but (or perhaps because) by the time he got to the bottom of the gourd, the laughter mysteriously stopped. For the very first time, as he sat under the tree cradling the shining black stones in both hands, it occurred to Ngatuny that he had become exactly what all of those people, including Wilheim, had wanted him to be. Nothing. His splintered soul had been cut off from the wellspring that had given it life in the first place. And he, in years' worth of recklessness and stupidity, had shunned its cooling, revitalizing waters, running instead, with eyes closed and arms outstretched, toward the blazing valley sun.

Suddenly he was furious. A great realization came to him like a swift and painful blow: *That is how they mean to subdue us.* The thought sputtered into his head, and the rage that followed it welled up in him pure and unfettered. *Freedom and independence are meaningless if we are cut off from the earth, the God, the ancestors, and the convictions that bred us. That nurtured us. Finally and forever we will be their subjects because we will be them. We will never remember ourselves and our fathers. It will always be their laws, their greed, their ways.*

We Englishmen will rule this country forever.

"Ngatuny?" Kene ventured quietly. He was not sure what to do. This thing that had caught fire in Ngatuny's soul had sparked seemingly out of nothing in a mere second of time. Kene sat confused and a bit frightened at this sudden change, but he decided to let it run its course, whatever it was. When Ngatuny finally spoke, he said this:

"Father, I would very much appreciate it if you could tell me the whereabouts of the money that I have sent you while I was away these past years."

"I have it, son. All of it, almost. It is buried in the courtyard near the goats and the prayer fire."

"Please, sir, I must have it to secure the cattle that I will need for a proper bride-price," Ngatuny said softly, with ingratiating formality. "Then we will begin to build our homestead and we will prosper, and the number of Kene's cattle that will graze on these plains will increase tenfold. I promise.

"Your sons will grow into men of consequence." Ngatuny nodded his head yes, reaffirming his belief, making plans. "They will be men of strength who know and love the ways of their fathers. I promise you. I promise."

Kene sat with his head bowed and said nothing. Nothing needed to be said. He was greatly, greatly blessed.

~

KENE MADE THE ARRANGEMENTS for Ngatuny to take his first bride. The two families negotiated throughout the entire rainy season. Negotiations could have taken much longer and the outcome been much more costly had it not been for the fact that the girl, Kedua, had discovered that one of the suitors her parents were considering was the one called Ngatuny. The girl ran directly to her mother, begging and pleading with her to interfere.

"But these are men's dealings, girl. What have I to say?" came her mother's response.

"I don't know what, Mother, but please, you must say something," the girl persisted. "This is the one that I want. I know it. I have known it since I first saw him at the firestick ceremony.

"Oh, Mother!" The girl began to weep. "I know that Father prefers Nayapre. I can tell by the way he laughs and teases him when they meet on the road to town. What can I do, Mother? Tell me what I can do."

"Nothing, my heart, nothing."

The mother soothed the daughter the best that she could and told her that things of this nature were best left in the hands of Ngai and their men. But that night she slaughtered one of her fattest goats, under the pretense that a feast was called for in honor of her husband's friend who was visiting the manyatta. She chopped the head off the goat and boiled it until it was tender while she set the rest of the animal to roast. When the meat was all prepared, everyone gathered round as the husband and his friend broke the skull of the goat in half and began to strip the meat from the bone. When the two men had picked the bones clean, they passed one half of the skull to Kedua's mother, who was the first wife, and the other half to one of her co-wives. The women deftly plucked the eyes out of the skull, scooped out the irises, and ate them. Then they daintily chewed at the creamy whites, Kedua and her mother sharing, until the eyes were all gone. After that, the feast began.

At the end of the night, when all of the laughing, singing, and eating had been done with, Kedua's mother approached her exhausted husband. He was curled up in her sleeping hutch, full of food and praise for his good wife who had made him look so generous in front of his friend.

"Husband, I must speak to you about something that is very important," she began timidly. "It is about Kedua. You know that she is my only child, and I suppose that is the reason that I am wont to give in to her whims. You see, husband, I happen to know that, well, she desires to marry the one called Ngatuny—"

"What! The drunkard?"

"No, my husband, he is no drunkard! Not at all. Well, I suppose he was—in the past. But not now! Right now he has gotten himself to work and is doing very well. People speak of him all the time. He will one day be quite prosperous. I am sure of it."

Her husband was silent, and she knew that she had crossed a line. She wondered if her little talk had done more harm than good.

"Well, I suppose I won't be bothering you anymore with this foolish woman's talk," she said in a gentle, soothing voice, not unlike the one she had used with Kedua. "My husband is strong and smart. I know that he will do what is right for his daughter's happiness. He could not do anything else. Sleep well, my husband, sleep well."

But Kedua's father had only feigned surprise when his wife brought up the subject of Ngatuny. In fact, he had been searching quite diligently into the young man's past, looking for clues as to his character and that of his family. He had actually been leaning toward Ngatuny, and the fact that his daughter actually preferred the man clinched the deal. Well, that and the two extra cows that Ngatuny was going to have to pay. After all, he didn't have the best reputation in the world. He had been known to drink more than his fair share of wine and beer at times. Ngatuny was in no position to quibble, especially when one kept in mind what he would get out of the deal. People from all over considered his daughter to be one of the most beautiful, even-tempered young girls in the district. On top of it, she had been circumcised at eleven years and had since been untouched. She would come to him fresh.

Ngatuny lived up to his future father-in-law's expectations without exception. He paid the bride-price gladly, like a real man, and threw in some extra camel-hair and woolen blankets for the girl's uncles and cooking utensils for their wives. So on the appointed day, the two families and all of their friends got together and cut open the throat of a black-and-white spotted bull that Ngatuny provided. The young couple got the first hot, rich taste of the blood, and after all of the guests had their turn, the animal was slaughtered and placed over an open fire to cook. When the people tired of eating roasted bull, they feasted on spicy cabbage stew, sweet rice, maize, goat, and fowl.

The dancing and singing continued all day and throughout the night. Ngatuny was highly praised in song and word as a generous man who would never let anyone's wine gourd go empty, nor their stomachs go unfilled. The guests praised Kedua as a stunning bride. Her dark skin glowed with pride as people continually complimented her beauty, the gorgeous red dyed goatskin that she wore, and the brightly colored enkarewa that swung from her neck, telling all the world that she had just taken her husband. She watched her cousins and all of the other young girls eye her beautiful new husband jealously, and their discomfort fed her heart.

The new young couple came to live with Ngatuny's uncle, and at first all went well. Every one of Ngatuny's promises to his uncle came true. Kene no longer had to struggle. Under Ngatuny's careful management, the size of his herds grew dramatically. Kene's own sons, who were now morans themselves, kept the cattle and the camels grazing out on the plains because there was no longer enough room in the manyatta to house them. The women welcomed Kedua warmly. Their hearts filled to see the newness and the joy of life sweeping through her large black eyes as her gaze followed Ngatuny's confident stride everywhere he went. *Ei! She's like a fat little puppy trailing after its mother's milk!* they all laughed behind her back. But Kedua's need endeared her to the women, and they cooed over her and coddled her like she was a sweet little girl instead of a grown woman of almost seventeen years and a soon-to-be mother. For her part, Kedua taught the other women her mother's tricks for breeding sheep and goats, so even the women's animals grew plentiful and fat.

Like any good wife, Kedua settled down almost immediately and happily to having children. She had a boy each year for the first three years, and everyone that saw her agreed that she radiated good health and womanliness. Motherhood fit her better than did her own skin. Ngatuny took on a new status as a man with large, prosperous herds and beautiful, healthy sons. Urged on by Kene and some of the other elders, he took on another wife, a scrawny but good-natured girl called Nkaina who was from a very well regarded family. Shortly after that, Ngatuny took on a third wife, called Nangai, whose family was not so highly esteemed but whose beauty was well known all the way to Maralal.

As the other two women settled in to having their own babies, Kedua tried to take consolation from the fact that although she was forced to share her husband and her world now with these outsiders, she was still the first wife and the mother of Ngatuny's eldest sons. At first, nothing significant changed in Kedua's outward attitude or appearance. But Kene's wives noticed that the light in her heart that had endeared her to them so quickly was flickering and faltering. They clucked their tongues at her in private. They warned each other that if this foolish young wife didn't learn that her duty and responsibility was to her entire family and not just one man, well, there would be trouble for all of them. The kind of jealousy she had hold of now, the silent, sneaking kind, could eventually bring ruin to even the strongest household. After some time, even the men became aware of the tension between Ngatuny's senior wife and her two young co-wives. But just like a man, Ngatuny thought, *Oh, well. All she needs is another child to make her feel her womanhood again. She's been rather long without one.*

The birth of Kedua's next two sons did alleviate some of the pressure for a while, but Nkaina had been hard at work making her own new son to go with her young daughter. Nangai, the heifer, had the nerve to follow up her baby girl with twins! She had one boy and one girl, two shriveled-up, scrawny-looking things no bigger than rats and the same gray, washed-out color too! Kedua thought for a moment that they might not survive, but no, her husband's seed was too strong. How she ground her teeth together and choked back bitter tears when she overheard Nangai say gaily to her husband, "Look at this! There is one for you and one for me!"

As the seasons passed, Kedua began to resent even her own sons, because they seemed to get more attention from their father than she did. Where had the days gone when she had been the only light to shine on her husband's strong, dark face? On the nights when he slept with his other wives, Kedua lay awake crying, smelling the scent of his body in the smoke from her fire, touching her neck and her cheek and her breasts, pretending that her slender hand was his large, competent one. She cried out to her nkai over and over again: *Why was I picked to have this love? I didn't ask for it. I didn't even want it!* She was trapped. Had anyone ever told her in her young days that she would not have a husband successful enough to afford many wives, she would have laughed and dismissed the person as a loudmouth and a fool. And, indeed, she did get the prosperous, handsome husband that she had always felt herself worthy of. But now that she had him, she couldn't bring herself to share him, not even with her own children.

Late one night, when her husband had gone off visiting a friend of his, Kedua snuck out of the manyatta and kneeled on the ground, her body cloaked by the mist from a cold, lightless sky. *Ngai,* she prayed, *hear me! I cannot go on like this. Something must change. My husband's life is so crowded with these outsiders that he scarcely has room for me. I cannot do anything myself because I would be called greedy and jealous and unworthy of a man such as Ngatuny. So you must be the one to avenge me, my God! Avenge my pride! Get me my husband back. Please.*

Her answer came almost immediately in the sudden rumbling sound of men in the distance.

NGATUNY RETURNED the following evening to find his home decimated.

Kene could not speak for himself, so his second wife explained it: A band of about twenty-five or thirty Somalis carrying torches, knives, and machetes had descended on the manyatta late in the night after everyone had gone to sleep. They roused the women and children from their sleep and forced them to watch as Kene was beaten. One of the men stepped forward and demanded in sign language that Kene tell them where his animals were being kept. Kene gestured back that unless they at least let the children go, he would die from their beatings before he revealed the whereabouts of his animals. The leader pushed Kene's senior wife toward the children and then pointed with his torch towards one of the huts. She ran about the manyatta, grabbing screaming babies and carrying them or pushing them into her hut. But the children were too many. They could not all fit. So the woman snatched the first children that her hands landed upon and threw them into a second hut. By sheer chance, she grabbed Kedua's second son, Lolorok, one girl from Nkaina and two from Nangai, three of her own children, and two from one of her co-wives. Then she ran into the first hut and sent Nkaina into the second. Kedua was nowhere to be found. After the children were inside, the men blocked the entrances by wedging in wide thorn branches quickly chopped and pulled from portions of the fence.

Now, the man demanded in his strange language, *where are the animals?*

I don't know. Kene shook his head and shrugged his shoulders.

Two of the men stepped forward and gripped his arms. A third man emerged from the crowd swinging a thick, jagged-edged leather baton around and around in slow, deliberate circles, coming ever closer to Kene's face. Then, with a heavy grunt, he sent the baton sailing in a crisp, fluid arc directly into Kene's jaw. Kene sagged under the weight of the blow, but the men holding his arms would not allow him to fall. He struggled feebly to raise his head, but when he did, the women began screaming and wailing even more pitifully, clawing at their own faces and arms. At first he couldn't figure out why, until he felt the chill, rank air pounding against his teeth and his gums. The spikes at the end of the baton had ripped through the side of his mouth, slicing through the skin halfway to his cheek. Blood flowed in a sticky mess down his chin, puddling in front of his knees as he knelt in between the raiders, looking like some terrible parody of a warthog.

Kene couldn't stand the thought that his face could so terrify his women, and he dropped his head again, this time in shame. It might have been the abrupt movement or the cold wind or, perhaps, the weight of fear, but the numbness that protected him wore away the instant he let his head fall. Suddenly Kene's whole face felt like it had caught fire, like someone had taken a branding iron and seared through the flesh all the way to the bone. Pain pulsated inside his head like a drumbeat, blinding him until tears dribbled across the bridge of his nose. But Kene refused to scream. He knelt silently on the ground, panting and cursing in his mind.

Where are they? the leader growled, circling and taunting him.
I don't know.

I know what will make him speak, yelled one of the men at the back of the mob.

The leader turned around. *What?*

A young man ran up to the front, anxious to impress his age-mates with his clever thinking and strong spirit. From his waist belt he pulled a canteen full of petrol, which he had been using up until then as a quick way to start campfires. The boy popped off the lid and doused the wooden planks in the entrance of the children's hut. Snatching a torch from one of the men, he waved it in front of Kene's face, then held it up to the beams.

Where are they! the boy screamed.

Kene just stared, his own bloody wounds and pain forgotten. *Somewhere to the east. My sons have them. I really don't know. You . . . you wouldn't dare . . . you can't . . .*

But the boy could not understand his words. The only word he recognized was *maiyolo: I don't know.*

Before Kene or any of the other men could stop him, the boy struck the torch against the plank closest to the doorway and dragged it all along the wall and across the entranceway. The dry beams ignited instantly, the flames sucking greedily at the splintered wood and cracked mud. The torch passed over the branches from the fence and a rough, woolly camel hide that hung behind them like a curtain in front of the entrance. The hide smoldered for a pregnant instant, and then the flame burst to life with a resounding pop. Thick, greasy diesel fumes coated the air, and black smoke billowed up into the night sky. Unsure of what was happening, the children inside began to cry even louder. The hungry flames found their way through the cracks in the mud walls. They latched on to the rafters and beams on the inside of the small hut, flowing easily and rapidly like the waters of a rising stream.

The boy leapt toward the second hut, but one of his own men tackled him and grabbed the torch. He flipped the boy over and held the torch so close to his face that the skin on his cheek began to peel and blister.

Have you gone mad? the man shrieked. *What have you done to us?*

I . . . I . . . I only . . . I thought . . .

But no one was listening. Everything turned to chaos. Men held Kene down as he feverishly clawed at the earth, trying to get free of the many hands, his own screams melting into the shrieks of the wives and the children. The entrance was already covered in flames, but Kene could feel his wife reaching out from behind the wall of fire. The women surged forward, now heedless of the men, beating them out of the way, screaming for their children. Some struck feebly and desperately at the flames with their lessos, ripping open their hands as they grabbed wildly at the burning thorn branches. Others ran to their huts for water. But in the seconds that it took to move the men, to find the water, the fire had already escaped them. The mud burned hot and fast as coal. The parched wood split itself open wide, inviting the fire inside.

The leader of the party was at a loss. He stood there being shoved around, hemmed into the chaos like an ignorant mute, while disjointed thoughts collided in his mind, no one taking any distinct form or shape. Then, for no reason at all, out of the din and confusion, he heard the tiny voice of his youngest sister:

Do not go, my brother. This is not the time for raiding, nor is it the will of Allah. You cannot succeed in this. You will bring ruin to us all.

But he hadn't brought ruin. That stupid boy—he did it. That stupid, stupid boy. That child killer. He hadn't intended for anything like this to happen. They could have had the animals they needed if not for that stupid, ridiculous boy . . . Because of him, these strong men were now divided. Some were running through the manyatta, pulling at the smaller, useless stock animals, mainly sheep and goats, trying to get them free from the bomas. Others fought among themselves, screaming and pushing one another, unwilling to concede blame. A couple of brave men were standing beside the women, dousing the fire with the water from the women's huts. Some had already run away.

The man walked over to the boy, who was still holding his face and struggling to get off the ground.

Look at the ruin you've brought us to, he screamed, yanking the boy off the ground by his hair. *We could have taken what we needed without setting fire to babies. You have no patience, boy. You never did. Do you truly expect Allah to bless those who would murder children? This is not what we came for. For your part, you will be the one to stay behind and explain to their fathers and brothers exactly how this happened.*

The man snatched his own baton out of the waist of his trousers and, with a stunning blow to the temple, knocked the boy unconscious.

HOW DOES ONE DEFINE the ending of a life when the dead man still walks and breathes? When the passageway between worlds has spewed back an empty soul, where does that soul find refuge, being neither of that world nor of this? And what does the soul do when it is not even sure that an actual world exists at the other end of the passage? When it does not care and even the bitter taste of oblivion has become sweet?

Ngatuny was such a soul.

No words could touch him; nor could anger, nor sadness, nor grief.

It had not even brought him any pleasure to slit the throat of the man who was responsible. The morans had been called and had arrived at the manyatta in numbers exceeding two hundred, a sea of red and black sitting silently outside the fence, waiting for

Ngatuny's word. They had questioned the Somali youth momentarily, just to be certain that he spoke no Maa. He didn't. The only
word they understood was *Garissa,* which was of no help. Garissa
was the only Somali settlement near the Samburu district, so it
was obvious that the raiders had to have come from there. The boy
could tell them nothing that they did not already know. So they
turned him over to Ngatuny.

"With the hand of my father Kene, I kill you. With the hands
of my dead sons and his, I kill you," Ngatuny whispered.

The boy struggled and screamed, pleading to his foreign god.
Ngatuny turned his head and spit in the dirt. It disgusted him to
see such cowardice. Gripping his knife with one hand and the
sweaty, slippery curls of the boy's hair with the other, Ngatuny
sliced the boy's throat with no more concern or spectacle than if he
had been slaughtering a goat. The fact that he had never before
taken another man's life was not enough to give him pause.
Ngatuny watched for a brief moment as the throat opened up and
grinned at him, gurgling and spouting blood. But he did not wait
to see that the boy was fully dead before he dropped the knife in
the dirt and turned wearily back to his hut. Ngatuny was so, so
tired. He had nothing left in him that could rage.

A few of the morans were chosen to take the remains of the
children out into the bush. They made sure to carry them very
carefully, because the tiny bodies were falling apart. The fire had
reached most of them within a matter of moments, catching onto
their clothes and their hair, hopping from one to the next, since the
tiny hut afforded them no space to move or dodge or run. The wife
had shielded three of them with her body for as long as she could,
but even though the toddlers had survived the fire, they still did not
survive the night.

The morans began their trek to Garissa, leaving Kene and

Ngatuny to see to the burial of Kene's senior wife. The women seemed incapable of tending to the body, especially Kedua, who lay in something of a waking coma, unwilling to be roused by anyone. Ngatuny expected nothing else from her. After all, she had been among the most respected of women—prosperous, beautiful, with five strong, healthy sons. Now four of them had been snatched from her in the cruelest possible way. She had only one son left to live for, and Ngatuny wondered if that one would be enough.

The days that followed passed without acknowledgment. Kene began to heal somewhat, but the biting flies and fat black gnats that buzzed about the raw meat of his face bothered him constantly. He hadn't even the energy to swipe them away most of the time. Ngatuny looked at him and pitied him—a broken man made old so quickly. He hated the thought that he was planning to leave this uncle who had nurtured and loved him so well. But in truth, Ngatuny felt himself cursed. He did not know by what manner of witchcraft or deviltry he was being pursued, but he admitted to himself that something had to be following him. Something had to have been hunting him for sport since he was a small boy. He had never been let alone. Not ever. His uncle was a good man who deserved to be left in peace to live out his older years with respect and dignity. He did not deserve Ngatuny's capricious fate. (At that moment, Kene was having the same thought, and if Ngatuny hadn't announced that he was leaving first, Kene would have.)

So the two families parted ways, keeping close as neighbors, but no longer sharing the same homestead. Ngatuny continued to provide for his uncle. But nothing, not their quiet afternoon games of ntotoi and long talks, not even the frequent visits from the faithful Nabo, who had heard about the tragedy and vowed to stick close with his friend and be his support, nothing could bring back the desire that had driven Ngatuny.

Ngatuny's eyes closed shut against the relief of grieving and healing.

More than three weeks passed between the time of the raid and when the morans finally came home. They could be heard, hundreds strong, marching toward the manyatta from a considerable distance. The sound of the distant approach swept Kedua up in such a confused and furious haze of terror that she pushed her little son Lolorok underneath her sleeping hutch and squeezed in after him, coiling herself around the child's small body and crushing him against her chest until he gasped and begged to be let go.

Ngatuny heard them as well, but his heart did not flutter. He had no fear. Not anymore. As he stepped out of the safety of the thorn fence he chuckled to himself at the irony of his life's battles. What confronted him as he raised his eyes to the hillside took his breath away.

"My wives! Kedua! Nkaina! Nangai! Come quickly!"

Two of the women stepped fearfully out of their huts. Nangai stared at Nkaina from across the courtyard, her eyes glassy with tears. Nkaina motioned to her co-wife, and the two ran together and clutched each other around the neck.

"Wife," Nkaina whispered, "we should not fear every sound we hear. What will become of us if we do, eh? Let us go and be brave. Our husband would not call us to our deaths. Eh?"

"Eh," Nangai answered, but her voice wavered and the tears in her eyes fell forward.

The women grasped hands and walked slowly to the entrance of the fence.

Kedua did not come out.

When they saw what their husband saw, the women dropped to their knees and began to weep uncontrollably.

The warriors surrounded the manyatta. Behind them, another

group of warriors drove a herd of cattle so large that Ngatuny could not guess at the number. Behind the cattle was a herd of camels about half the size of the first herd. Farther still, Ngatuny could make out goats and sheep and a row of people being led up from the back of the ranks with thick rope tied around their necks.

"My father," said one of the morans to Ngatuny, "we cannot hope to replace your loss, but at least you and your family have been vindicated. These Somalis know well, as do the other tribes that seek to steal from us and defame us, that if they kill one, we kill ten. And if they steal ten head of cattle from us, then we will take one hundred. They will not soon forget again.

"These animals are going mostly to your neighbors, who lost their own animals to those same raiders who defiled your home. But please feel free to take as many as you want. These animals cannot take the place of the sons you lost, but you will have many more sons. To ensure that your line is continued, we bring you a gift. What one people stole from you, they will also give back—"

And with that, the young warrior reached behind him, grabbed hold of a girl, and shoved her forward. The girl lost her balance and went sprawling into the dirt at Ngatuny's feet. He eyed her suspiciously. She was young. No more than thirteen or fourteen and absolutely fragile looking. Ngatuny wondered how she had survived walking for the entire journey with little or no food. He sighed sadly as he studied her. These people were so different. Her nose was straight and thin, her hair hung past her shoulders in thick waves and curls, and her skin was the color of copper. Not at all like the shining black skin of his own women. He wondered remotely what fate could have led the child to this. Perhaps her people also believed in personal guardians, and perhaps hers was as errant and neglectful as Ngatuny's. At least she was modest. She wore a dark, finely embroidered and rather costly looking hijab, which now hung across her body in dusty, shredded rags. But still, she kept trying to pull the ripped veil up over her shoulders and head. Curious little thing she was, truly. Though her head was bowed, her back was straight. She did not tremble. She did not cry. This girl was somebody.

"Who does she belong to?" he asked the warrior.

The young man laughed. "You, father. At least now she does. She is the new wife that will replace for you your lost sons. Before she was the daughter of their Imam and sister to the one who led that party against your house. Nima is what they called her before, if I remember right. But her name is at your discretion."

CHAPTER *Ten*

. . . .　. . . . . .　. . . . .　. . . . .　. . . . . .　. . .

A ND SO MY MOTHER came to my Father humiliated, hungry, and alone.

They shared no words, they shared no history except one filled with death and displacement. So my mother learned his ways and eventually spoke his language. To the best of my knowledge, she never uttered a word in her own tongue again. When she did not know the proper words to make my Father understand her, she remained silent. And eventually, my Father learned to read the shapes and the sliding colors of her silence, the meaning behind the shift in her eyes.

Nima accepted her fate as one that had been chosen for her by her God, whom she had also been forced to abdicate. She clung to this fate like a drowning man grabs hold of the same glittering, jagged reef that lashed out and caused his boat to capsize in the first place. But her thoughts lay hidden, as though the translucent veil had never been lifted from her face. Nima settled into her new home without judgment or complaint. And if she happened to cry a bit each night, well, her face was always dry by morning.

Luckily for Nima, my Father never considered women to be part of the wider world of hope and loss or the politics of war. So against her personally, he never held any grudge. He was never cruel or neglectful, and he never allowed her to be beaten by his other wives (who held no such lofty notions about the separateness of women). As time passed, he even stopped seeing her otherness. No longer did he find the sharp bridge of her nose odd and disturbingly European. Slowly, he began to allow himself to enjoy her.

In those early days, the smooth, untouched feel of childhood lingered across her skin much like the powdery silk of pollen being kneaded between one's fingertips. Her eyes were cast in the wide, slanted shape of an upturned willow leaf and were so heavily fringed with lashes that they always appeared to have been lined with kohl to make them stand out. Mother used to giggle and whisper with me like a little girl about those early days when Father made up excuses to touch her lips and the high arch of her cheekbone under the pretense of rubbing away some grit or dust that she could tell from his eyes wasn't really there. *Your father loves,* she said, *but cannot say "love."*

For her part, Nima never blamed my Father for his role in her abduction. Nor did she blame the headstrong brother whom my Father occasionally mentioned but whose name never crossed my mother's lips (though it often crossed her eyes, and she would cry). But Mother did not cry, she said, because of regret. She cried because the flow of life was what it was and, being such, the experiences of her life lived on in and of themselves. For the most part, she loved and respected them.

When you cease to will and you allow God's spirit to expand around you, it eventually becomes you, she often told me. *So no matter where you find yourself, no matter what the circumstance, it becomes right and fitting. You need never be afraid.* In her my Father found a confusing mix of childishness and wisdom, independence and submission, as though she submitted to him not because she had to but because she was absolutely gracious and she wished to make him feel more at ease. It made her smile easy and her laugh light and full. It took years, but even the hostility of her co-wives collapsed under the careful caress of Mother's concern. Kedua's case was hard and could never be won, but Nkaina and Nangai eventually grew to love her, and by the end, no three sisters could have shared more devotion for one another.

For Father, Nima became his solace. My very first memory of this life was waking up in my cradle, shivering, feeling the wooden slats pressed against my back because I had knocked the scratchy blankets off in my sleep. As I reached up to slap the cold away, I heard my Father cry out in the darkness. His own sleep had been disturbed by some unimaginable evil that scared me terribly because it was bad enough to scare him. I remember being hardly able to see him through the bare light of the snowy-white embers of the pit fire. I reached out my little hand, trying to cover the distance between us so that I might pat his head and make him feel well. He continued to twist and struggle and cry out, but I couldn't reach him and began to panic, until Mother leaned over in her sleep and placed one of her tiny hands on the center of his chest. Immediately my Father stilled. Nima was the only person whom Father ever told the content and the cause of his dreams, dreams that would stay with him in one form or another for the rest of his life. What's more, Mother was the only person who could make the dreams stop.

I wandered the forest for three days and nights, dreaming of the two of them, dreaming of myself. My grandmothers Xana and Cosa protected and watched over me until early that fourth morning. I awoke to the rich smell of bygone rain, the sound of doves weeping, and the trembling of sodden, prickly leaves crashing against loam. And I was alone. It was their way of saying *Go home*. While I understood that my grandmothers were right, I felt dejected and miserable at the thought of having to go back to Lolorok and the others without some kind of revelation, some deeper, more stable understanding of where I had been or what I had seen. I wasn't even particularly positive about what I had been searching for. The only thing that kept coming back to me was my mother's admonition not to will. But hadn't her own passing been the most extreme act of will possible? And hadn't Father's whole life been nothing but his will overriding, overpowering, and overcoming?

The only thing I was capable of understanding at that point was that their lives and their spirits defined my own and only through them would I find my way out. But what did that mean? And if I was really to find a way out along the route that I planned, didn't that mean that I would have to leave them far behind? None of it made any sense to me. If at that moment I could have actually laid my hands on the desire and fear that seemed to have overpowered everything else in my mind (except each other), I would have crushed them, broken them in two. Just like Mother had done.

But something told me that the only reason she had been able to do what she did was that there was no contradiction within her at all. There never had been. It always seemed to me that everything she did came from a place of peace, understanding, and total involvement. She walked as if there were no past and no future. The only moment that existed was the moment currently being shared, and it commanded her fully. But me, I tended to be afraid, to hang back, to ruminate. Didn't her kind of quiet wisdom beat my book learning on all counts? How, then, could I have lived with her, loved her beyond all rational thought, and still never learned the one thing that she'd set out to teach me, the thing that had made her life not only bearable but beautiful and radiant? It just made no sense.

Finally, after walking through the morning, I stepped out from underneath the cool canopy of dusky leaves straight into the glaring afternoon heat to face the trail that had led me to this place to begin with. Just a few paces from the tall line of trees, the ground had once more turned powdery with dust, the late-night rain already dead to memory. I began walking slowly at first, because the muscles in my legs and shoulders were still very stiff and I was limping. Too, the thought of what awaited me from Lolorok frightened me now that it was actually time to face it. I knew I would be beaten, but wondering how severely plagued my mind and cracked open old fears just as the white sun cracked my sore, dry lips and the skin on the back of my neck. If it was too bad, I wouldn't be able to start back to school as soon as I had hoped. That is, if cousin Lalasi was not so angry with me that he would deny me the offer that had previously been made.

The closer I got, the faster I walked, fear and worry nagging at me, whispering in my ears and laughing. My family probably thought I was dead. At that moment, I couldn't think of a single reason why I should not be. I had no real ties to hold me here. All I had were foolish dreams that seduced me, kept me awake at night while they made love to my insecurities and ignorance, telling them to hush now, all would soon be well. But there was nothing tangible for me to reach out and grasp hold of, nothing to tell the world that I was a serious and worthy individual, someone who deserved respect. I thought, as I stumbled over the short thorn bushes, of having children like Lolorok said I should. If I had at least one or two babies, then people wouldn't look down on me the way they did and laugh behind my back. Then even if I didn't make it to the heights that I dreamed of, at least I would be able to call something mine, something sacred that commanded respect of a certain sort.

All good women wanted children. My education meant next to nothing in the eyes of my people if I did not settle down at some point and become a real woman. Even the few other girls that were still in my school at my level were at least circumcised and had prospects waiting for them from respectable, professional men who lived in relatively busy towns like Maralal and Nyahururu. A couple even had boyfriends in Nairobi. I had nothing.

I stopped where I was, right in the middle of the path, and forced myself to admit to something that I found so shameful that I had never said it to another person in my life. Every so often, when I got to feeling worse than usual about the choices I was making, when I felt as though I must be ruining my life for sure, I would secret myself away somewhere, preferably somewhere dark and silent, and I would make myself say out loud as I did then on that path: "Well, I really don't want any of those little bastards anyway. No, I don't. *Nasarian does not want children!* They whine, they nag, and they stink, and quite honestly I just don't want them!" Shocking as it was, that pitiful little act of rebellion made my heart light. It made me giggle. But in the next moment I began to worry that I was some sort of reprobate. Could I be one of those delusional perverts that I'd read about in the *Home Journal* magazines that my teacher had sent to her from home? I wasn't sure of anything, including what one had to do to become a delusional pervert, and as I neared Lolorok's manyatta, I began to cry.

TAISERE SAW ME FIRST. She had been hanging her wash out to dry on top of the fence near the entrance. I watched her as she sang, her voice twisting sadly through the air like the soft trill of a long-tailed bird. She sang:

> *Maape booki mapelai netii Yeso. Maape pooki.*
> > *Kara apa napurusho*
> > *Kara apa namenisho*
> > *Kara apa nandekisho*
> > *Kara apa nalolotoi!*

> *We all go where Jesus is. Let's go all.*
> > *I was once a thief*
> > *I was once jealous*
> > *I was once one who abused people*
> > *I was once a prostitute before I met the Lord!*

I listened intently to the somehow disturbing clarity and conviction in that small voice. She used simple words. But it was not so much the words as the piercing melody, which nursed a complexity of understanding that defied structure and rule. I wondered how Taisere could know anything at all about defiance when her life was the picture of compliance and propriety. I, however, never did anything by the rules my family and my people set forth, and yet I could never have sung the way she did nor understand where she came by the fortitude to believe so strongly and yet so peacefully. Just like Nima. Taisere had her back to me as I approached, still straightening out the wrinkles in the old clothes and faded blankets and humming. Suddenly, her song stopped and her body tensed.

"Nasarian?" she called quietly over her shoulder.

"Yes, sister. Supa! How is it with you?"

Taisere turned to me with tears lighting up her wide eyes. When she saw the condition that I was in, she gasped and then quickly covered her mouth with her hands, ashamed of her rudeness. I suppose I looked much worse than I thought I did. My sister dropped her washing in the dirt and ran to me, wrapping me in her arms.

"Oh, my poor sweet sister," she cried, pressing her warm body against me, rubbing my back with wet fingertips. "How is it that you are not dead? Where could you have gone? We considered going to the Maralal police, but husband said to wait, and at first I thought him very cruel and heartless and I told him as much, but look at this, for once he was right!"

My sister laughed and cried and her soaring voice became, for me, the ringing of a sea of tiny brass bells. In that moment, I thought her so beautiful, so much like Nima, that she made me forget my predicament. I laughed with her and cried too, hugging her hard, wrapping my arms around the slim indentation of her waist and breathing in the sweet scent of smoke, soap, and milk that clung so gently to her skin. I felt her tears slide down onto my neck, slipping underneath the knot of my lesso. Very quickly, I bent my head and kissed the soft, unprotected skin of her collarbone, licking very delicately the warm pool of my tears that had collected there. She started. I heard her suck in her breath and I froze, panicking, sure that I had done something terribly wrong. Slowly, her body relaxed, and I felt her run the tip of her finger down my neck and the center of my back, and she leaned in to my ear and she sighed.

"Nasarian!" one of the children shouted, peering from behind the entranceway. "She is here! Mama Nkaina! Mama Nangai! Nasarian has come home!"

Taisere and I jumped back, doused in the icy water of little-boy laughter. We looked for him to tell him to keep quiet, but the child had already darted off, scampering delightedly into one of the huts.

"You must go, sister. Lolorok will be very angry if he hears that you stayed here instead of coming to see him immediately on your return," Taisere whispered, pushing me away.

I grabbed her outstretched hand and rubbed it, wanting to kneel down and kiss it too, but not daring. Instead, I stroked the long, curving lines that crisscrossed her palm and gently, achingly put my lips to the tips of her fingers.

"I'm so sorry," I breathed. "I should have died rather than worry my sister so. Maybe I shouldn't say this and I don't know whether you will be able to understand, but I feel like I must tell you that you may very well be my only friend."

"I understand that, little sister," she smiled. "I . . . I understand you. Now go! They are coming. Lolorok is with Lalasi in the grove right where he was the other day. Hurry. When you get back, I will take care of you."

I knew exactly what she meant. The knowing of it hung between us, heavy and unbreathable, like the air that waits between the first flash of lightning and crack of thunder that calls forth a summer storm. I limped away as quickly as I could, and Taisere ran inside to head off the others. Their urgent voices mingled with one another, trampling each other, calling me out from the far side of the fence, but I didn't answer. I rushed head on to meet that bastard of a brother of mine, not sure of whether to curse myself for allowing these traitorous thoughts or let them run free. Again, I chose not to choose and instead let the thick pall of invisibility fall over my eyes, trapping them in blankness and stupidity. Where had I been? I wouldn't know. Why had I gone? I couldn't be sure. After all, what was I except an emotional, temperamental woman-child? No amount of book learning could change that. What would make him expect to get a straight answer from one such as myself? Nothing. I knew I would get by without being forced to give a truthful account, without revealing my real self, my questions, or my searches, and it sickened me.

He was right where Taisere had said he would be, he and Lalasi dwarfed beneath the massive shade of a baobab tree, its magnificent, swaying branches stretching up and out like a soul in supplication. The fragrant greenish-gray pods of fruit hung low, ripe and ready to drop. The plaintive calls from a dozen darting, red-winged warblers reached out to greet me, all the while questioning and answering each other in a richly woven baluster of song that held the very sky in place. I came upon the men from the side, so I heard them before they saw me.

"Come on, foolish man," Lalasi chided, "we here both know that you have a flask of nalanga wrapped tightly under that robe. Pass it now. The sun is burning me up, and I must drink. Bring it fast-fast or you will come upon some serious trouble from me!"

"Have your eyes gone bad, man, that you cannot see that my hand was just now reaching for the flask?" Lolorok countered, a wicked grin eating up his face. "Ach! You shame me. My own flesh has the audacity to call me stingy! As though I were about to jump into the bushes and hide so I wouldn't have to share. However, in truth, you are rather greedy. Perhaps—"

"Ei! There is no winning with you! What is going on in this world when the elders no longer get their respect?" Lalasi laughed.

"Quick-quick! Pass the flask, man. My hair has turned white waiting on you."

"It was already white, old man—and, of course, I say 'old man' with the fullest of respect! Oh, well then, here," he said and passed the wine to his cousin. "Ei, ei, ei! I just can't believe it. I am getting insults from you, you old goat! Ha! I must have sunk to a new low."

"Eh?"

"Eh."

"And only now are you just realizing it?"

"I refuse to be so insulted!" Lolorok played up his injured pride, slamming his fist into the dirt and stirring up a soft cloud of dust. "We shall settle this difference at once!" He pounded on the ntotoi board that sat between them. As he produced the polished stones from his pouch, Lolorok smiled again. The beads of sweat and oil that dotted his pimply face gave him a shiny and rather freakish look.

"You know, of course, that if I win," he challenged, "you must reward me with a full flask of nalanga."

"Don't bother yourself with 'if,' " Lalasi laughed. "It's a naughty little word that will never lead you to something that could actually happen. But, in the case that we are going to throw the word 'if' around, *if* you ever dared to beat me, I would catch you in your sleep, just when you weren't expecting me, and I would throttle you good! I'm a terribly bad loser, I admit!"

"Hmmm. You are saying that you would treat me as if I were a roguish Pokot caught loafing in your wife's hut, eh?"

"Now you have understood me!"

"And you would know all about that, wouldn't you?" Lolorok poked Lalasi in his side and laughed uproariously at his little joke, which I didn't find funny in the least. In fact, their bulky, sweaty, brutish presence made me ill. It was then that I announced myself, ready to take my beating and wanting to get out of their way as quickly as possibly.

"Supa, brother," I said softly, casting my eyes at the floor.

The death of laughter draped the air like a filthy curtain. It echoed helplessly, mournfully under the sudden crushing silence. Lolorok stood, staring at me from underneath black, fleshy eyelids exactly like his mother's. He walked forward slowly, circling around me, coming ever closer, so close that I could hear the unevenness of his breathing, see the twitching in his arms and smell the hot, bitter wine on his breath. I closed my eyes and thought of Nima. She smiled.

I heard the thundering clap of the first blow before I felt it. Then I was on the ground, lying on my stomach, being pummeled, choking on bits of dry grass and sandy pebbles. My skirt flew up around my waist, exposing my bare ass, and he beat me there too, rocking me with a scorching blow of humiliation so deep that the pain of his fists couldn't touch it. I screamed in impotent rage, trying all the while to claw my way out from underneath him, but I wasn't heard, my mouth being filled by torn, uprooted spears of grass. The stale, spiny stalks cut into my lips and nose, suffocating me. He rode my back, curses falling down in torrents as fast and jagged as his fists, pressing himself tight against me and, I think, laughing.

Then he was gone, dragged off by Lalasi. I curled up on my side, too tired, too sore to cry, my lungs throbbing in my chest, beating in the same uneven rhythm as my heart, unable to breathe. Why, I wondered, why didn't he even bother to ask me where I had been?

I WASN'T ABLE to make my way back to the manyatta until well after nightfall. I lay there in the dirt, feeling the shadows from the baobab tree fall down around my legs, cooling the furious purple bruises and gashes until, finding more and more bruises and gashes to cool, the shadows lengthened and covered every piece of me. Then it was dark and the hyenas began to cry and moan, following one another and the warm scent of blood wherever it could be found. Following it to me. A timid moon peeked out from behind wisps of silver clouds as they flapped across the sky on the twilight wind. Along with this wind came the spicy, robust smell of cabbage, goat, and sweet basmati rice from someone's hut nearby. The aroma of good, hot food smacked me in the face and told me to stop being stupid and get up. I listened, grudgingly, and began to make my way to Lolorok's manyatta.

I walked as quickly as I possibly could, dodging the glowing eyes of a pair of hyenas that followed close behind, not knowing quite what to make of me. They had surely been hoping that I was dead underneath that tree, but since they could now plainly see that I wasn't, they had to consider whether or not I was a snack that would be worth the trouble of hunting for themselves. I hoped not. I still had a ways to go. Each time the moon went behind the cover of the clouds, I lost sight of them. It comforted me not to have to see them prowling, but then I became afraid that when the moon next came out from behind its sheath, there they would be, directly in front of me, blocking my path. My legs itched to run, but that would just give them the proper excuse to make chase, and I had to keep in mind that I was damaged. I wasn't going to go anywhere fast. So I walked on steadily, trying to disguise my limp from the predators, praying for someone to come for me, anyone, even Lolorok.

I sensed my way through the blackness, wondering if perhaps I had missed my path. The hyenas hung back some, pacing and yawning, exposing the yellow edges of their fangs in the quick, ir-regular glints of moonlight. I was about to give up, head back the way I came or turn off toward the lake, for I knew the manyatta to be close to the lake, when I heard:

Maape booki mapelai netii Yeso. Maape pooki . . .

There was no mistaking the voice, and I laughed out loud— a startling, broken cackle that made the dogs inside the manyatta growl and bark. The singing stopped as suddenly as it had started, dropping me back into the dark, alone. I hurried toward where I heard the sound coming from, the hyenas forgotten, holding my leg to stop it from cramping and locking up. I was almost upon the manyatta before I could finally distinguish the faint outline of the fence from the rest of the night. She waited at the entrance.

I could just barely make out Taisere's slender figure leaning against the frame of the fence, but the darkness stole everything else from me. I couldn't see the eyes that watched over me or the lips that sang, and I searched for a light or a fire of some sort that would show her. She grabbed my hand and stroked it the same way I had stroked hers earlier. But then another hand, this one chapped and wrinkled, took hold of mine, and I knew that my mothers had been waiting up too. No one spoke. The women led me to a small niche behind Taisere's hut where a pot full of boiling water already waited on my arrival. It was an ancient cast-iron pot that someone, somewhere, somehow had managed to crack so that the water could be filled only halfway to the brim. Taisere leaned over the pot, her hands wrapped round an old woolen scarf for protection, and grabbed one end while Nangai leaned in over the other end, and together, grunting and heaving, they lifted it off the fire. Nkaina waited with a plastic Mickey Mouse bucket filled with cold water. I watched as she poured the water, checking every so often to see if the temperature was satisfactory. Each time she leaned over to stick the tip of her baby finger in it, some cold water fell from the bucket onto the outside of the old black pot, making it sizzle. Finally, when she was satisfied that I would not be scalded, Nkaina stepped forward and began to strip the bloody rags from my body and, one by one, she dropped them into the fire.

My mothers sang softly, sadly under their breaths as Taisere unwrapped a heavy brown bar of soap from some waxed paper and dipped her rag into the pot. She scrubbed my body in tender circles, going over the bruises and cuts with her fingertips as though the simple acknowledgment in her touch could heal them. When she was done, my body shone in the deceptive firelight, looking like it had never been touched. While I was still wet and dripping, she applied layer upon layer of watery, pink lotion to my skin, massaging it into the muscles of my legs, skimming lightly over the swell of my backside, and kneading the knotted-up muscles in my back and shoulders.

When that was done, my mothers rose, lessos draped over their arms, and dressed me. Nangai slipped a beautiful red skirt trimmed with black roses over my legs; it fell in a wide circle just below my knees. Then Nkaina wrapped a sheer golden lesso twice around my torso and tied it in a delicate knot over my left shoulder. Finally Taisere stepped forward. In her hands, she held string after string of beads in every size and color imaginable. She first draped over my head the largest strands of white, red, and pale blue, which came out wide, almost to the edges of my shoulders, and fell halfway down my chest in a swooping arc. The strands got thicker and smaller the closer they came to my neck. The smallest ones, made of orange, turquoise, white, and yellow, fit almost like chokers around my neck. Then she wrapped a maiden's band of red, black, yellow, and blue beads around my forehead, with a silver pendant hanging between my eyes. Around my ankles went bangles of silver, and on my feet, brand-new Firestone sandals. The black rubber of the sandals looked almost exactly like leather in the dim light, and I marveled at how well these particular ones were made. It was almost impossible to tell that the fashionable lines that crisscrossed the bridge of my feet were really the tread marks from the tire of an old army vehicle.

My mothers left me then to the care of my sister. Taisere led me to her hut, where a steaming cabbage stew with rice waited, covered with a wooden bowl to keep it hot. Her young sons and daughter already had adjoining mud huts of their own behind hers, so Taisere and I ate alone, sharing a bowl of cool water with the meal. I sucked down the stew, heedless of manners, and Taisere discreetly refilled my bowl three times before I could ask. After the meal, we snuggled up together in front of the embers of her fire and drank tea with milk and sugar out of chipped porcelain cups that held the figure of the Virgin painted in red, her head bent in prayer, on two sides.

"Lolorok is so bloody cheap, I tell you," she whispered in my ear. "He acts as if we'll go hungry if I spend money on housekeeping when I know quite well the way he hoards what he really has. I never know when I'll get enough to get to the general store for some real shopping. That's why I save my tea and sugar and stuff for special treats. Like tonight."

"What's so special about tonight?" I asked. "Am I leaving tomorrow? So soon?"

But that was a stupid question. Had I not run away, I most likely would already have been gone.

"You go at first light," Taisere answered, lowering her head and blowing at her tea. A slim whisper of steam floated from the top of the cup, encircling her nose like a little wreath. I laughed.

"Exactly what is it that you find so amusing, sister? I would have thought that you didn't want to leave." Her eyes narrowed, and her voice became very soft.

"Oh no! It's not that at all," I babbled, starting up too quickly and spilling hot tea on my leg. "Damn it!"

Taisere raised her hand to her lips and giggled. "What else did they teach you at that missionary school?"

"Stuff that I wouldn't dare repeat in front of a delicate little rabbit like yourself," I answered, giving her a mock half-bow. "And I wasn't laughing at you, or the thought of leaving. I was just laughing because, well, ah, well, you're just very pretty."

I felt my neck and the sides of my face grow hot, and I plunged my head down into my chest so as to hide my embarrassment. In the failing light, we could barely see each other, and yet neither of us made any move to rekindle the flame in the pit. The darkness cradled us safely above an abyss of revelation that at any other point might have been too frightening to cross.

"I am very fortunate to be thought of as pretty by one as beautiful as you."

"Ha! I'm beautiful, eh?"

"Yes, of course you are!" The tone of her voice rose as though she were suddenly upset, and I reached my hand through the smoke and darkness to touch her shoulder.

"I'm so very sorry, my sister, I did not mean to upset you."

"You are quite serious, eh? You truly don't realize how you look and what a commotion you cause."

"You thoroughly confuse me, you know. It is nice that you wish to make me feel better, but you needn't exaggerate—"

"Ach! I wouldn't. I am quite vain, I'll have you know. Normally, I wouldn't appreciate the competition." Taisere's teeth struck a light in the darkness as she smiled and laughed. "But you must know that, with the exception of complexion—you are a shade or two darker—you look exactly like your mother. I remember your mother. Your father used to drag her behind him practically everywhere he went, at least to places where she was allowed to go, and on many different pretexts. But all these various reasons, they were all phony. Everyone said so. The real reason that he took her so many places was because he loved the attention she got. That skin of hers—the way it glowed—and those eyes. Ha! The first time I can remember seeing her, when I was a very small girl, I ran straight to my mother afterward and talked her ears off about this lady with the eyes that took up half her face. 'Half her whole face? Is that so?' said my mother. She was kind enough not to laugh at me. 'Yes, yieyio, like this,' I said and stretched my eyes." Here Taisere pulled her lids back on top and on bottom so that the curve of her eyeballs showed.

"Well, miss, I walked around like that for days, determined that I should grow into your mother and have eyes that shone like twin moons and curved round like a cat's. In fact, quite a few of us little girls did. We also greased up our skin to make ourselves shine, although the effect was hideous, I assure you. And we would poke out our lips to imitate that pretty little pout of hers. When your father brought your mother round these sides, we would follow her around, calling after her *Abiae,* meaning our Somali queen. She must have thought that we were the most ill-mannered, wretched little vagrants that ever lived, because each time she turned around, we all had our hands to our eyes, pulling them all the way back with our lips poked out. I'm sure she thought that we were teasing her, for she never answered.

"And here you are, baby Nima, little Nasarian, just as beautiful and doesn't even know it. And on top of that, you are learned too. I must be honest and say that, in spite of the fact that you don't have any children, I wish I was more like you."

I choked on the sip of tea I had just taken.

"Like me? Impossible!" I sputtered. "Now you really are having me on. Your life is perfect."

"No, no, no. It's not. Living with Lolorok is sometimes not so easy. He doesn't hit me or anything, like some husbands do their wives, and aside from being miserly, he takes care of his responsibilities, but, oh, I don't know. The only way I can put it, I suppose, is that it's just him. He has been my husband now for—" She counted quickly. "More than eight years, I believe, since just after I left school in any case, and he is still a stranger to me. I never admitted this before to anyone, so please, don't be impatient with me. It's hard to get it out. I'm simply stuck. Yes, I guess that is what I mean to say. Stuck. However you, my sister, you have choices."

"But, Taisere, you're very intelligent. You have choices. You've had schooling too. You just said so."

"Only up to form five. And my father was grudging about that. He wanted to know from my mother why he should waste his money on school fees and what good history and arithmetic would do me. He wanted to know if all of this wonderful knowledge would pass itself down to all of the children that I was going to have, through my breast milk. But she persisted, and I went. I loved it, really loved it, you know. The hymns we sang, the old books from overseas that smelled like leather and the ocean, sitting up late at night on those hard, smelly old cots and reading love magazines by flashlight while we plaited each other's hair . . . " She shook her head, lines burrowing their way across her forehead and the bridge of her nose, the far-off look in her eyes retreating.

"Eight whole years of schooling is a long time, longer than most get, I suspect. But of course, in the end Father was right. After all, what did it get me besides a husband who insists that I should read him the fine print on his bills and duty statements but that I shouldn't read anything else?"

Taisere sighed and felt the bottom of her teacup with her finger. It was cold, so she threw it back into the pot and began groping around the floor for her slim, metal blow-pipe and found it lying near her feet. She dug one end of it into the fire pit and blew air down the tube from the other end. Immediately, the embers danced to life, revealing the stinging red heart that had lain unseen underneath the white ash. Without looking, she reached over and grabbed a handful of kindling, dropped it into the pit, and placed the pot back on top of it.

"I may not leave this manyatta very often," she went on without looking up, "but I know that so many things are going on in this world. When I go to market, sometimes I sneak a newspaper just so that I can find out about some of it and feel as though I am really a part of it and this country, that I am really living. It is the best I can do. I do have my children to look after. Their welfare comes first, and since their life must be here with their father, then this is where I must be too. It is my fate. My children are my life now.

"You, on the other hand, not only finished form five, you're going to complete your A-levels. Who can tell what will come next? You might even get to university after that—if you do well. Most of our men don't even go that far." She laughed for no reason that I could tell, and the sound rained down on my head like a thin stream of water over smooth rocks. "Nineteen years," she sighed, wiping tears from her eyes with the back of her hand. "My sister has nineteen years, is not even circumcised, has not had even one child, and still has somehow managed to surpass our men. Ei, ei, ei!

"When I was your age," Taisere said, turning to me, all of the laughter gone out of her eyes, "I had my third child already. And I am only a few years older than you. Nasarian, my sister, what shall become of you?"

"I am going to write," I whispered fiercely. I leaned in and grabbed hold of her elbow, though I was not even aware that I had done so. "I'm going to the States and I am going to write. Books, essays, articles for the paper . . . anything they'll let me. I am. I don't know how just yet, but I am. I'll send for you if you want."

For a moment, Taisere's eyes lit her face. She caught my fire. Finally, someone knew my dream. It was something that I had never dared tell another person, not even Nima. *Especially* not Nima, who I couldn't believe would've understood. Now Taisere knew. But just as fast as the spark caught, it died, leaving doubt and suspicion mixing round on her face. Fortunately, she was gracious enough and understanding enough not to give voice to these fears. Then again, in a way, it didn't matter whether she said anything or not, because I could see her thinking, *But who will take care of you?* Instead, she held my face in her hands, caressing my swollen lips, and she murmured, "Nasarian, for good or bad, my place is here with my children. When I first brought a child into this world, into this clan, my options were buried out there in the bush with the afterbirth. But I pray for you, my sister, I pray that you discover what it is that you seek. Oh, my heart, for all of your confusion and your silly tears, I do believe that you will find it. I only hope that what you find is truly what you sought."

CHAPTER *Eleven*

. . . .

THE SUN ROSE, stretching and yawning, breathing fresh scarlet rays across the dusty backs of the zebras and baboons as they loped along the plains, in search of shade and a cool drink of water. Lalasi and I were already on the road. The sun bore down on me, massaging its heat into my scalp and conjuring up small, maddening rivulets of sweat that trickled down the middle of my back and my chest and between my legs. That insane, dry heat so frustrated me that I almost started to cry. But I dared not complain out loud, not with Lalasi walking straight and proud, his sweat-drenched head still held aloft, looking very important and purposeful. The only concession my cousin made to the heat was that he wore Firestones on his cracked, blistered feet instead of the shabby gray dress shoes he'd come in. Other than that, he had on the same wrinkled, dark blue trousers and white shirt, which hung across his spare frame as though it dangled from a wire hanger. There were large rings of dried sweat underneath each of his armpits, and the suffocating morning heat made new ones appear rapidly.

Lalasi had insisted before we left that I change out of my lesso and put on more appropriate town clothes. When I'd told him that I didn't have any, he'd ordered me to wear my school uniform until we had the chance to buy me something decent. So I itched and sweated, constantly tugging at the high white collar and the gray woolen vest that cleaved to my body, sucking the life and the energy out of me like a synthetic leech. I struggled all the way to the road, choking on hot dust and sunshine, with my little vinyl suitcase wavering precariously atop my head. When we finally got to the main road and were able to flag down a minivan, a dingy old white jalopy with a picture of a red, green, and yellow marijuana leaf pasted in the center of the back window, Lalasi hopped up front and left me to fight with his bag as well as my own. So I packed our belongings under the ripped cushions of our seats. Well, mine was ripped anyway. Lalasi made sure that he got a good seat, one where he wouldn't be squished, right up front next to the driver.

A sweating, bearded man in the first row got up and helped me push the bags all the way under the sticky tan seats, wedging them between his stained green canvas bag and the metal peg that was bolted to the floor to hold the middle seat in place. I squeezed myself in by the window and, being conscious of the foul, sweaty odor of my body, opened it wide. We bumped and jumped and sagged along the road at a pathetic little pace, stopping every so often to stuff one more person into the cab. There were four rows of seats in the van, each designed to fit three people, but the tout wasn't satisfied until he had crammed sixteen people, a baby, plus himself and the luggage in the back and two more up front with the driver. It didn't matter. He snatched up our money with relish, comfort not a concern, even though he spent much of the three hours of the trip crouching against the door in the little step that was meant to help people get into the van. We were on our way.

The pockmarked, dusty road opened up and swallowed us whole and we rode on, oblivious. Wrapped in crumpled wool with the sun-bleached road looming endlessly ahead, I thought I was about to faint from the heat. There are days like that here, where nothing, not even the sky, can stand against the thunderous, crashing waves of heat that threaten to batter down every stronghold, every hiding place. Mother Earth is struck dry just as we women, her guardians, are struck dry of every life-giving wellspring that lies buried under our skin, save for sweat and milk.

We lumbered past more zebras, obstinate and sullen, too hot to be afraid of our approaching vehicle and barely budging as we rumbled close by them, moving onward and no concern of theirs. I spied, directly ahead of us, two vultures squatting obscenely on the carcass of a buffalo, its ribs poking through the hole in its gut where its entrails had been neatly excavated, probably by a hungry lioness or perhaps a pack of them. A thick, black swarm of flies circled relentlessly above the body like a demented cyclone, but the vultures paid no heed. They perched with their claws dug deeply into the haunches of the buffalo, waiting for whatever it is that tells a vulture that it is all right to give thanks and partake of the morning meal.

I studied the birds intently in the few seconds before the van puttered by, dropping them back out of sight. The black wings were dusted over gray. The spots of red that marked the backs of their heads seemed to ooze and run, as though they were actually open wounds. For some reason, even after we had passed, those two birds stayed in front of my eyes or, more correctly, they perched menacingly on either of my shoulders like two black devils, digging the claws in deep, waiting. I waited too, wondering which of us would give in and disappear first.

Maralal was not what I'd expected. The minivan finally pulled into the Maralal depot sometime after noon. I dragged out our luggage while Lalasi laughed with the driver, slapping him meaningfully on the back. For his part, the driver fairly doubled over in laughter, his hard, protruding belly heaving up and down, so that the striped engineer's cap he wore fell off his head and into the dirt. I hauled the bags over to where Lalasi stood and waited silently behind him. Eventually he noticed me, and after a few more minutes bid his new companion good-bye, promising to meet him later on for some beers.

As we walked slowly toward my new home, the spirited chimes, plinks, tings, and jingles of lingala drifted over my head from someone's transistor radio inside the whitewashed liquor store next to the depot. We passed the center of town, and in the middle of the long, unpaved main road there stood a small roundabout with two dreamy, swaying eucalyptus trees in the middle of it. Clusters of dusty leaves drooped straight down from the branches like the heavy, hurting raindrops that pelt your head during the first windless evening storm after a drought.

Directly in front of the trees were two pathetically dry little bushes that never flowered once during the entire two years that I was to live in Maralal. In between the bushes stood a yellow wooden sign with the letters NCPB painted in green between what looked like two identical coats of arms. As we got closer, I saw that the coats of arms were only two half-peeled ears of maize plopped inside the outline of two shields. Underneath, it said, NATIONAL CEREALS AND PRODUCE BOARD, and directly below that, someone had pasted a black-and-white sign that said MARALAL DEPOT, with a little red arrow pointing in the direction from which we had come. It was the only sign I saw welcoming me into the town, and I wasn't impressed.

The roundabout island was surrounded by tiny posts striped in green, white, red, and blue, from which barbed wire was strung around its circumference. I almost burst out laughing. Who were these people expecting to keep away from their precious little sign when the barbed wire only came up to one's knees? If anything, I reckoned, that paltry little defense was nothing but an invitation for the area kids to come vandalize the place. It was a small thing, but it stuck in my mind because it didn't seem to make much sense. However, I knew better than to point it out to Lalasi. He was one of those government officials whose job it was to create stuff like that. For all I knew, he was the one who had ordered it built in the first place.

On either side of the wide main road there were rows of towering eucalyptus trees, with a third row running straight down the middle. These trees, Lalasi informed me, had been planted by the British a long time ago, in an attempt to spruce up the town. I nodded and raised my eyebrows with the appropriate interest, but to me the trees looked sad and out of place, and I preferred not to speak about them. We passed by the shops and restaurants, most of them made out of concrete or wood with sloped, rusted tin panels for roofs. Many of the storefronts were painted a beautiful sky blue that would have been quite cheerful if they hadn't been so dusty and dirty. Others, like the tobacco shop, were painted a mustard yellow that always made me hot when I looked at it because I immediately thought of the sun.

People passed us, many of them staring and whispering to each other. I checked their faces to see if I knew any of them, but I didn't. I turned to Lalasi, who had noticed also and was smiling.

"They are wondering whether or not it is a new young wife that I am bringing home," he snickered, even though I hadn't come out and directly asked him.

We walked on, occasionally dodging the white government-issued pickup trucks, which, besides one or two army trucks and some bicycles, were the only vehicles on the road. When the trucks rumbled by, belching and spitting black exhaust and kicking up screens of dust, some of the people on the road darted away, hiding behind trees or in the gutter until the truck passed.

"You see," Lalasi snorted in disgust, "our people are stupid like animals. A foolish little thing like a truck wanders by, and they scatter as though the thing were not a machine to be controlled but some sort of beast with a mind of its own. When will we learn?"

Again, I shut up. In truth, the trucks seemed sort of loud and scary to me too. But I was too used to seeing them at school to be really afraid. My friends and I hitched rides every now and again to get to the store or somebody's house. But still, I never got too close if I didn't have to. Why court trouble?

Finally, we turned off the main road and headed across a wide, grassy field toward a row of almost identical houses. Past those houses were more identical houses, all of them connected to one another. I panicked. This couldn't be it. I couldn't live here. I'd never find my way home. I had horrible visions of myself standing outside in front of these shining duplications and yelling, *Kaji ngang ang! Kaji namanayi!* Hey! Hey! Where is our house? Where do I live? And then Lalasi would charge out of one of the doorways and beat me across the head with the heel of his crusty gray shoe for embarrassing him with my uncouth behavior.

"Certainly, cousin, we are not going into one of these?" I asked quietly.

"And if we were?" he said slowly, raising an eyebrow and staring at me out of the corner of his eye.

"Well, uh, then I would probably shut up as I am doing right now."

"Good girl."

But luckily we did bypass the little houses, continuing on the dusty road up a long, steep hill. On one side of the road, large, skinny trees and short, spiny bushes the color of dried nuts ate up the hillside, crushing one another, leaning out toward us, waving a gentle hello in the breeze. The other side of the road had been cleared for as far as I could see, and a barbed-wire fence ran alongside the open space. Groups of ostriches dotted this side of the hill. Some of them strutted slowly, posturing arrogantly for all the world, their long white, tan, and brown necks held perfectly straight, their eyes brimming with reproach. Most, however, stood still, looking tired and grouchy, the sun wilting their beautiful feathers and their pride. Finally we reached my new home. It was a white house with tan tiles for the roof set far back from the road and surrounded by a crying cloud of huge, sleepy-looking willow trees. We walked up the drive toward the front door, but at the last second Lalasi turned to the left and went round the concrete walkway to the back.

The back of the house wasn't nearly as nice looking as the front. Next to an old rusted water pump, a heap of garbage and dried leaves lay strewn about, rotting away as it waited to be burned. It made the whole back of the place stink of old meat, moldy vegetables, and bitter smoke from previous burnings. Beyond that, a few timid rosebushes peeked out from between the willow trees, yellowed from dust and age and sun. They hunkered down close to the earth, crouching like a woman does if she is about to be beaten. No bush dared show a bloom, because any new flower would be peeled of its beauty within hours, the heat of the sun leaving nothing but a withered, sighing stamen to mark the place and time of death. I wondered what had possessed Lalasi's wife to plant rosebushes here knowing what the climate would do to them.

We came to the back door, and I found it decrepit as well, with the white paint chipping off in the middle and on the sides, exposing the gray wood underneath. Lalasi paused for a moment, his hand raised as though he thought he might knock first. But then he shook his head, grunted, swung the door open, and strode into the house. I followed quickly behind him, through the wide blue kitchen and into the sitting room. Lalasi had picked up his pace so much that I had to sprint through the kitchen to keep up with him, and in doing so, I tripped on the threshold that joined the two rooms and my bag flew off my head and through the air, barely missing Lalasi's shoulder before it splattered on the floor. The cheap brass clasp clanged open and, just like that, everything I owned went sliding across the tiled floor, the vinyl squeaking like a trapped mouse.

It stopped directly at the delicate slippered feet of my new benefactress. I stood there mortified, wanting to glide right back through the door and down the road. Lalasi didn't even turn around and look at me.

"Nasieku," Lalasi said dryly.

"Yes, apaayia," came a sad little reply. I looked sharply at the woman on the sofa. Surely that baby voice couldn't have come from her. Then I noticed the faint outline of a tiny child who waited curled up in a ball, hiding behind her mother's back on the sofa.

"This is Nasarian," Lalasi continued. "She is your new sister. She's here to look after you, and you must always mind what she says unless I tell you differently. She goes to school as you do, so she will help you with your homework and also the chores. She will call you when you are needed. Otherwise stay out of her way. If I hear that you have pestered her with any of those foolish questions of yours or—*and mind this carefully*—any more of those nasty stories, you will have some bad trouble from me. Are we clear?"

"Yes, apaayia," the child whispered. I still couldn't see her face.

"Good. Now show her where to store her belongings—besides on the floor."

"Yes, apaayia."

Without so much as a word to his wife or a second glance in my direction, he strode back out the way we came in, leaving me stranded at the center of an ocean of silence and resentment. Hearing the door slam shut and heavy footsteps receding along the concrete walk, the child finally peeked out from behind her mother's back and stared at me unabashed from underneath a row of thick black eyelashes that curled up delicately at the ends like a closing fist. She was the deep, sweet color of a cocoa bean, and when she smiled, which she did then, she showed two rows of perfect tiny teeth, all ivory and shining, with a minute gap between each and every tooth. Her pudgy face lit up slowly, tentatively, exposing dimples in both cheeks that looked almost exactly like my own. I couldn't help but smile in return.

"Will you braid my hair?" she asked.

"Right now?"

I could tell by the surprised look on her face that she hadn't thought of that, but since I'd brought it up, she said, "Uh . . . er . . . yes! Let's do it right now! Yup. Let's go!"

She bounced from behind her mother, and it was only then that I noticed the stony look on the woman's face.

"Yieyio, is it fine with you if we braid hair now? Or is there something else for me to do?"

"My husband does not find me capable of caring for my own child. Imagine."

I looked from mother to daughter, trying to find a clue as to what response might do the least damage, but the mother refused to look at me. The little girl had also dropped her head at the acrid sound of her mother's voice, every trace of smile extinguished. She hugged herself, rocking back and forth on her heels. I wasn't sure how to proceed.

"Ngoto Nasieku," I said humbly, using her formal name, which meant "Mother of Nasieku," trying to win points with her. "Your sister Taisere has asked me to say hello to you."

At the mention of her sister's name, the woman's eyes took on some life, and for the first time, she really looked at me.

"Taisere, eh? And how does she do? And what of her children?"

"She is quite well," I answered. "And all of the children are healthy and happy and they send love to you."

"Is it so? Well, that is fine. Yes, yes. Come on, girl," she said and eased herself up out of the folds of the overstuffed red sofa. "I'll show you to the loo. You are absolutely filthy. And you need some fresh bandages. Lalasi didn't do that, did he?"

My breath caught, and I stepped back. Why would she think that Lalasi had been the one who beat me? I shook my head no and looked away, at the ceiling. The plaster was discolored and chipped, thin tendrils spreading out from little vortexes, the fissures reaching across almost the entire length of the ceiling like a huge, stiff web.

"Tell me more about my sister, eh?" the woman said, slipping her rough, cracked hand into the crook of my elbow.

"Ngoto Nasieku," I started, but she interrupted with a laugh and said, "Ketigile. That is my name. I am not as old as I look. Not even half of Lalasi's age. These proper terms are not appropriate. I am but a few years older than you, only three years older than Taisere. So you see, in truth, we are age-mates."

I gasped in disbelief and then once more immediately afterward, because I couldn't believe that I had been rude enough to gasp. It seemed impossible that this woman was barely into her late twenties. Taisere had never told me her sister's age, only that she was older, but from the way she had talked and from the way Ketigile looked, I'd assumed that there were at least fifteen years between us. Her skin was ashen and wrinkled around her eyes and mouth. Her cheeks puffed out as though something were stuffed inside of her mouth, choking her. Ketigile didn't have all of her teeth or her hair. She had put one of those chemical relaxers in her hair at some point, so it was very fashionably straight, but it only brought more attention to the fact that she was balding. The hair that was left was pulled into a small knot at the back of her head. Scalp laced with woolly fuzz peeked through the fine strands at regular intervals, and her fingers strayed nervously to her head, patting, rubbing, straightening, but only making the deficiency more apparent. I looked at her and it struck me all at once that her hair hadn't fallen out; it had been pulled out. That was why a few stubborn spots kept trying to grow back in.

"Yes, Ketigile," I said, looking away quickly. "I do in fact need to wash. Please show me the way."

She rounded the corner to a small loo. The door was jammed, and Ketigile had to put the entire weight of her body against the splintering wood before it would give way. Inside, next to the toilet, was a stall shower set against the far wall. The tiles surrounding the stall had once been pale yellow with pink and blue (or perhaps purple) flowers, but now they were streaked with mildewed stains of black and gray. Ketigile handed me a faded red towel and closed the door behind her. I stripped my clothes off and turned on the ancient faucet. After the water started running hot, I stepped into the stall, being very careful to avoid the loose tiles and their sharp edges as they bobbed and slid underneath the pressure of my feet and the rushing water. Gently, I began scraping the crust off my body. But after only a few minutes, the steam from the water, mixing with the almost unbearable heat of the day, began to burn in my lungs. The vapors rose, covering my face like a mask, and I couldn't breathe.

I hurried from my bath, dizzy, panting, and sweating, and almost fell over Nasieku, who hadn't left the front of the door.

"Guarding me, eh?" I said and tried to smile.

"Don't try to fool me, sister," she said solemnly. "You are sick. But don't worry." She took my hand and patted it. "I will take care of you. Come here."

Ketigile had laid my things in the top two drawers of the heavy wooden bureau in Nasieku's room. My books sat neatly in a pile on the nightstand next to the large bed. The covers had been turned back, and a white cotton dressing gown lay spread out at the foot of the bed and, on top of it, a bottle of iodine, bandages, and some pins.

"This is where I sleep, and now you shall sleep with me," Nasieku informed me. "Only get some rest. I shall come with your dinner shortly."

She slipped away silently, smiling, and closed the door softly behind her. I stood for a moment, deciding whether it would be proper to go after her, but my aching body cursed and screamed for some attention. So instead, I bandaged myself up and, when I felt satisfied that I wouldn't bleed all over the pretty white flowered sheets, crawled into the dressing gown and collapsed onto the bed. It was the most comfortable bed I had ever slept in, big and soft, with barely any dents at all in the thick mattress. I slept immediately and so deeply that I didn't even dream of Nima, nor did I wake until the following evening, except for once when Nasieku brought me dinner.

She waddled into the room loaded down with a tarnished silver tray piled high with goat and rice and cabbage and salad. She walked with her total concentration focused on delivering her food to me safely. The open bottle of Coke on the tray wiggled fearfully as she rounded the corner of the bed, and just as it was tipping over, I grabbed the neck of the bottle, barely saving it from spilling all over the bed. The smile on her face as I set the soda down on the night table was filled with such naked gratitude that I dropped my eyes. I hadn't done anything.

"Oh, thank you so much, eh, sister," she giggled and then nervously lowered her eyes. "My father would have strangled my neck if I dirtied the bed like that." Her voice dropped to a whisper as she set down the tray. "I'm not supposed to be doing this, but Mother is sleeping. She will sleep until my father comes home, and if he doesn't come home, she'll sleep through the night. So as long as there is no mess and we're quiet, it's all right, eh?"

"Eh," I whispered and reached out to grab her trembling hands. Stupid jackass that I was, I finally understood.

"Well, eat!" she commanded.

"Yes, miss!" I saluted her and she giggled again, happily this time. Her laugh warmed the air like yellow sunlight, and it reminded me of Taisere's laugh. I made a mental promise to myself then to make her laugh as often as possible. To begin with, I burrowed into the food, as she watched eagerly, taking a huge bite of the goat, with my face set to smile. And I was immediately assaulted by the most wretched flavor I'd ever run across my tongue. I gagged and tried to hide it behind a fake cough, but she wasn't fooled. The food was so horribly foul that I just didn't know what to say. But I had to say something to get out of having to eat it. The meat was charred to the point where it tasted more like smoke and charcoal than animal, and the rice had been burnt brown and black. The cabbage smelled so strongly of salt that I dared not try it. The salad seemed the least evil, so I started there.

"Very good salad," I lied, trying to talk around a huge mouthful.

"Yes, sister, but how is the meat?" she asked, staring at me with grim insistence. I almost laughed.

"Don't you know, girl, that the mark of a truly good meal is the salad?"

"You hate it, don't you?" she sighed, and her little face fell so completely that I thought for a moment she might be having me on. But she wasn't.

"I don't hate it one bit," I said quickly, trying to make up. But she was smart, and I couldn't get away with an outright lie. "I just think that Ketigile must have been very tired when she prepared this. That's all."

"Mother didn't prepare this, I did. I did it for you because I knew that she couldn't. She's . . . she's having a bad day today. I just thought that you'd be hungry, and I suppose that you really do hate it. I knew I couldn't do it right."

She turned her head away from me and pulled her feet up onto the bed. Her tiny body folded up into a ball again, a small dark stain on the white blankets. I set the tray carefully on the floor and pulled her close.

"My heart, please don't cry," I soothed. "Please tell me what is wrong."

"I only wanted you to like me," she whispered. "And now I've fouled it all up. I shouldn't have cooked. I'm so bad at it. But I hoped that you wouldn't be able to tell the difference. Father never can. At least he never says anything."

"Do you do all the cooking?"

She hesitated. "Most of it. But only because Mother sleeps so much that Father would never have his dinner and then they would fight."

"How often do they fight?"

She shrugged and refused to look at me, so I decided not to push the issue.

"How is this?" I said, wiping a tear from the hollow underneath her eye. "When I wake up again, we will start to cook together. I will show you everything I know. But that's not so much, I warn you!"

Nasieku smiled shyly. "I would like that very much. You promise?"

"Absolutely."

"And will you cook for my birthday? It's coming up very soon, you know. In a couple of months. Father said that I could invite some of my schoolmates over to play games. But I told him no because, well . . . " She hesitated again and looked away. I followed her gaze out the bedroom door and across the hall to the closed door of Ketigile's room.

"But it's no matter what I said before," she continued cheerfully. "Things are different now. Right?"

"Surely. So, will you tell me how old you are going to be on your birthday?"

"I'll be eight years old. Practically grown up."

"Practically? Why, you'll be married and moved away even before me!"

Nasieku laughed and laughed.

CHAPTER *Twelve*

. . . .

NASIEKU AND I SETTLED comfortably into each other and created a routine that seldom forced us to cross paths with Lalasi or Ketigile. In the morning, I would sit her down at the small white table in the kitchen and feed her sweet, baby-sized pancakes and eggs. Luckily Lalasi didn't take breakfast and was usually gone by the time we got to the kitchen. Ketigile never woke until long after we'd all left. When Nasieku was done eating, she would slide down onto the floor and sit between my legs, fingering the hem on my long blue skirt or pounding on my toes with her fat little fist, while I plaited her hair in small braids going round her head like a wreath or sometimes straight back in rows. As her hair grew longer, I saved up my pocket change and bought pink and blue and gray and yellow ribbons to tie into the ponytails in the back. After her hair had been done, her teeth washed, and her little face scrubbed and greased till it shone, we would walk hand in hand all the way down the hill to school.

First I walked her to the Catholic primary school. The three-room brick building sat at the end of a long, winding path surrounded by tall, skinny jacaranda trees that showered purple blossoms onto the rooftop and the pathway, right up to the front door. We were usually the first to arrive, and I would see Nasieku all the way into her classroom and sit her down at her desk, then together we would wait for the teacher to arrive. She was always impatient for me to leave, tapping her foot loudly against the hard wooden floor or drumming her ruler and pencils across her desk and tossing her hair clips at the chalkboard. When that didn't drive me away, she would open up the top of her desk, reach inside, and pull out a tiny brown frog or a cricket or a lizard or one of those huge and hideous, incredibly noisy sausage bugs.

Sometimes her plan was foiled because the thing would be dead, having suffocated during the long, airless night. Then she'd pout like the world had just ended. But usually the universe worked against me and her captives lived. She loved to torment me with the sausage bugs the most because she knew how I hated them. Having been trapped all night long, as soon as she let the insect go, it would fly around in vicious circles, its long, striped body vibrating and giving off the most awful buzzing noise. The sound echoed menacingly through the whole room, coming closer and closer while I panicked and, invariably, the bug would finally smack me in the face or try to climb down my dress or some such nonsense.

But not even the sausage bugs would drive me away until the teacher arrived. I knew that if I left before then, the little elf Nasieku would never be seen in the class. I would come after school to pick her up, as had happened a handful of times in the beginning, and the teacher would be waiting for me at the door of the schoolhouse, her round, dark face as wrinkled and sweaty as her black nun's habit. She had preached and preached to me about how wicked my baby cousin was and how her end was bound to be one full of misery and ignorance because she had managed to skip yet another day of school. Only after her tirade was done, usually in front of a crowd of snickering seven- and eight-year-olds, would she finally yell, "And you, miss, don't have to hide anymore. You may come out now. It's time to go home!"

As soon as the teacher turned and went back into the building, Nasieku would peek around the back corner of the building and wave at me. The other children would fall over themselves with laughter, and I would have to drag the child home by her ear while she explained how a poor, innocent little white puppy dog with big black spots (so cute she just couldn't resist!) had followed her into class. He'd told her that he was lost (after I'd told her I was lotimi, she'd insisted that she was too, and, in the absence of elephants, she swore she could talk to every stray dog and warthog in the district) and she'd helped him find his way home. What else could she do?

And if it wasn't a puppy dog, it was a fuzzy little pink-nosed, long-eared hare. Or she had been picking flowers (for me, of course) and lost her way, only to rediscover the right path when the final school bell sounded. Ei! How could one small girl be so unlucky? Where, then, I would ask, were these incredibly beautiful flowers that she had spent all day picking? She'd give a fiendish little smirk and shrug her shoulders. Who knew? On some days the dog got them. Since her devilishness brought her constant admiration from her classmates and made her the most popular girl in her class, she had no thoughts about settling down to actually do some work.

"Sister," she complained, flouncing her little body around in a tantrum, "I will never be as smart as you. Why force me into it? Remember when you told me ignorance was bliss? Well, don't you want me to be happy?"

So I waited her out, enduring her torments and constantly being late for my own classes.

After school, we'd take the same dusty path back into town, walking in the shade of the eucalyptus trees, many of them bent over like old men or leaning at a precarious angle out of the earth, the roots creeping like backward vines up out of the soil, toward the vibrant arches of sunlight.

"Supa, ntito ai," we were greeted at practically every corner by the old men who sat around all day discussing things. Even in the heat of the afternoon, they had dark blankets slung across their bony old shoulders and sometimes even knit hats on top of their heads. Carved walking sticks lay at their feet or propped up against trees as a sign of respect for their age.

"Entaa supa, apaayia," we always replied and kept walking.

We were supposed to go straight home, but we never did. Instead, we stopped each afternoon at a restaurant called Quicksand's for cake and pop. Nasieku adored the place. It made her feel very grown up to patronize such an establishment. As soon as we got up to the concrete front steps, Nasi would start to swagger and shake her hips like a movie star. She'd glance back at me, and in an atrocious English accent, she'd say, "Come, dahlin'." And we'd enter, both shaking our bums like there was something bad caught up back there and we were trying to turn it loose. Occasionally, someone was standing on the wooden porch and we'd have to dodge by them, laughing, in order to get through the front door. But usually the porch was empty, because creeping ivy vines hung suspended from wires at regular intervals made sweeping green arches across the porch. It looked very pretty, but if you were taller than an average twelve-year-old, you usually got slapped in the face by the swinging green arms.

Inside, the air was cool, the lights dim, and the tables draped in red-and-green checkered cloths, which were topped with glass panes that kept them from getting dirty. The proprietress, a heavy-set Kikuyu lady called Mama John who wore a red wig and false teeth, waited on us every day. Very solemnly, she'd hand over our menus, which Nasi could only partially read because they were printed in English, and she'd wait with her hands clutched behind her back while we discussed which meal we would take. In the end, Nasi always said in a very deep and dignified voice, "Mama, I believe I shall have one of your wonderful somosas" or, "If it pleases you, Mama, I would like a mandazi."

"Very good, my daughter. And would you prefer tea or pop to drink?"

"Ah, I believe I'll have a pop, thanks so much. Fanta orange, my dear lady, if you will."

At some point almost every single day, Mama John would run back through the dining room, huffing and groaning, shifting her considerable weight from side to side, and grab her homemade iron-handled broomstick from the far corner. Then she'd turn right around, wig pushed way back on her head, sweat dripping off her second chin, and make for the kitchen again—all the while mumbling, "Those bloody zebras! I'll show them what! Imagine the nerve. Showing up day after day at my back door. The bloody beasts do everything but knock on the door and beg breakfast!"

Nasieku always dropped her head on the table in the crook of her arm and laughed until she cried.

Chores waited at home afterward, which I didn't mind because Lalasi gave me money for doing them. Soon after I'd arrived he'd begun giving me all of the household money for shopping and supplies. Ketigile said nothing to me, but she kept to her room more and more. I paused in front of her door a few times, thinking to knock and finally speak with her, but the dry, heavy odor of old whiskey wafting under the door stopped me. Sometimes, though, the sound of her sobbing quietly, trying to muffle the noise under a pillow or a blanket, was what stopped me. But the house ran smoothly, and at the time, that seemed more important. The dinners were cooked at the proper hour, and if they weren't gourmet, they were at least edible. Nasi and I ate when the chores were done, leaving out two plates for Lalasi and Ketigile but never knowing when or if they would be eaten.

All of the money that was left over went to me. After I paid for our afternoon excursions and gave Nasi a couple of shillings to save for herself, I hid what little was left inside of a ripped seam in my battered old suitcase. I was already planning.

After chores came homework, which Nasi complained and whined all the way through. But much to my surprise, when I could get her to give an answer it was always the right one. Over time I realized that the girl had the potential to do exceedingly well but just preferred getting attention over good grades. I swore I would work on that with her, make her see the value of education. But even as I thought about it, poor Taisere popped into my mind, Taisere and all of her children, and I wondered if I was not the stupid one.

Basically, we were left to ourselves in the evening hours to tell stories, sew, or read late into the night. Nasieku complained bitterly that her father was the meanest man in the world because he refused to buy her a television set so that she could watch the love stories off the BBC and *Family Matters,* as her more affluent friends at school did—the daughters of the men who worked with her father. She and the other girls in her class had their very own Urkel fan club. But, she whined, she was being cheated because she had never really even seen the show and she hated pretending that she knew what her friends were talking about. Me, I loved the calm and the quiet, but I commiserated anyway so as not to seem like I didn't understand her angst.

The only thing that interrupted the peace of these days was the early-morning hours that brought Lalasi stumbling through the house screaming drunkenly for Ketigile to get up and get him some food. He was always loud enough to wake us, and we lay huddled together, breathing softly with our heads touching under the blanket, while he pounded on her door, belching and crying, finally breaking it in. Ketigile never screamed or fought back when he got on top of her and bit her until blood flowed from her shoulder or her arm or her thigh onto the bright blue of the freshly mopped tiles. She didn't run or dodge when he threw picture frames at her head. Usually he missed, but once he hit her dead on, and, having nowhere else to hide, she burst through our door, stumbling and muttering under her breath about there never being enough left for her, with a shard of glass as long as my index finger dangling from the center of her forehead. The doctor had to be summoned, as embarrassing as it was to have to fetch him at that late hour. He solemnly informed Lalasi that the next time his wife should drink herself into such a stupor, it would be best to tie her down to the bed. In his opinion, if she should ever again cause herself such a vicious accident, it would be very unlikely that she would live. Lalasi paid the man without comment and the doctor, disgusted and appalled, especially at the sight of Nasieku cowering in her mother's doorway, stalked out into the red onslaught of the dawn without another word.

These episodes almost always happened in the non-hours of the day, the time set aside for dreaming, so by dawn we were usually able to convince ourselves that none of it was real. We barely saw Lalasi and Ketigile and never knew what these conflicts were about, if there was any reasoning behind them at all. In truth, neither her parents nor their struggle was very real to us. They fought their battles on an old dreamscape in which they were the prowling, spitting, pointy-eared, green-eyed predators. We, though destined to be the prey, were crafty and slick, never getting caught, never seeing more than two dueling shadows.

Nasi often tired of our dreams and our games, which was the only way I could think of to keep her from wallowing in fear, and those days would be bad. On those days she sought her mother and attempted to hold her tight or comb her hair for her. Sometimes Ketigile responded with clear eyes and a shy smile, and in those moments I could readily see that her lips had once been very beautiful.

But other times she stared at Nasi, stared at us both like we weren't there, her mind, her eyes, confused and tangled as the rotting roots of a dead weed. But the worst was when she talked. Like the time Nasi went to her and held her hand the morning after a particularly terrible row and Ketigile started talking to her, saying things about herself and her love and the feel of a man's hands between her thighs that terrified the child. She desperately needed to be heard by someone, anyone, including a horrified eight-year-old, so she crushed Nasi against her sweaty, stinking chest and talked, every dry sound a flurry of condemnation.

But then Ketigile started screeching, and keening, and slurring her words, all the while drooling old whiskey down her chin. Nasi shook so badly that she couldn't breathe. She mashed her eyes shut and she began mouthing *Nasarian* over and over. So I slipped in through the open door and grabbed Nasi's arm, knowing that I had no right to come between mother and child but not caring. Ketigile grabbed Nasi by the collar so hard that her school shirt split open at the neck and she clutched the child violently, stroking her hair and her cheek, where the skin had turned purple from fear. Then Nasi took one heaving gulp of air and let out a desperate howl that startled Ketigile into loosening her grip. I braced my foot against the bed and pulled Nasi's arm so hard that I thought I might have injured her, but she still screamed and clawed and fought her way free.

On days like that, to drown out the wail of Ketigile's crying, I told Nasi stories of Nima and Ngatuny and their incredible love that was even better than the BBC soapies. She listened, never taking her eyes from mine until I had finished, and then she'd shake her head and promise that one day she would be in love like that and someone would be smart and daring enough to make a soapie about her life.

One day she asked hesitantly, as though it had been on her mind for a while, if we might not go live with my parents. She was crushed but not surprised when I finally told her the truth—that my parents were dead and that was the real reason I had come to stay with her, not only to go to school. Her parents had never thought to fully explain my presence in their home, and I hadn't had the courage to talk about it until then. So when Nasieku had talked about my parents in the present tense, seeing them in her mind still walking and breathing and laughing and loving, I hadn't the heart to correct her. Hearing the real truth so disappointed her that I had to make up a new method of distraction. I invented a system of asking Nasi, just at the point when the fighting had reached its pinnacle, to whisper in my ear the things that made her happiest. So, much like Nima, she immediately gave back to me the things that I had first given her.

Pierrot, she'd whisper, and I can still, at certain times, feel her breath singing against the tip of my ears and the wet spots on the downy pillow that let me know that she had awakened long before I.

> Pierrot
> Took his heart
> And hung it
> On a wayside wall.

> He said,
> "Look, Passers-by,
> Here is my heart!"

> But no one was curious.
> No one cared at all
> That there hung
> Pierrot's heart
> On the public wall.

> So Pierrot
> Took his heart
> And hid it
> Far away.

> Now people wonder
> Where his heart is
> Today.

I had no words of my own to offer, none to quell the misery that seeped fear from the sediment of her heart like poisoned water, and it shamed me. So I answered back the only way I could,

feeding her love through a middleman. She gave me Langston and
I gave it right back, hoping that beauty might win.

> *You are like a warm dark dusk*
> *In the middle of June-time*
> *When the first violets*
> *Have almost forgotten their names*
> *And the deep red roses bloom.*

> *You are like a warm dark dusk*
> *In the middle of June-time*
> *Before the hot nights of summer*
> *Burn white with stars.*

And eventually, she would sleep.

Almost a year passed this way. Sometimes we would sing or
tell stories or recite poetry to drown out the sound of blows. Sometimes, on very rare occasions, we'd even sleep through it, so ac-
customed had we gotten to the nighttime ritual. It was like being
tucked into bed. We only became aware that it had happened again
when one of us woke to go to the loo in the morning and found
blood smeared across the tan wallpaper and pooled in little spots
on the floor.

"When Mother dies," Nasi once said to me, "will you take care
of me?"

There was nothing in the world I could say but yes. No dream,
no poem, no metaphor on a page could stand against the truth and
the need in the eyes of a child. Which is precisely why I never
wanted children. It never occurred to either one of us that her
mother wasn't going to die sometime soon. In our two minds,

the idea took on the certainty, the imminence of the next good drought. No one ever wants to see the bloat of death clinging, like an abscess, to the faces and bellies of their cattle or, God protect us, their children. But to question disaster, to question death, is to question God Himself, and who, who among us is willing to do that? However, what is curious is that neither of us ever assigned a cause or a blame for that death. It was as though we thought that Lalasi's hand left no print and so, with no evidence readily found, no permanent misdeed could have occurred. (Of course there was plenty, plenty of evidence everywhere—even deep down in us, in the folds of our skirts, in the cool, wet grip of our clasped hands, in the creases of our minds.)

But we were both wrong. We were looking for death in the obvious place, but not the right place.

The rainy season came again, slicing through the cruel heat and turning the roads and gutters into little brown gullies and sneaking rivulets. People stayed off the roads and out of the streets in general, including Lalasi, who came home much earlier and usually less drunk. Unfortunately, that didn't make him any easier to live with. Boredom preyed on him, and he paced the living room and the kitchen relentlessly, pantherlike, pulling at shaggy tufts of his hair and muttering. Occasionally, he called Nasieku to him as he sat at the small table in the kitchen sipping on one of his endless bottles of Red Stripe beer. She came slowly and stood before him, fidgeting, avoiding his eyes and glancing over at me as I stood to the side of the doorway, out of his sight but where she could still see me. He never did anything, however. He just looked at her for a few minutes and then told her she was a very good girl, reaching into his pocket for five or ten shillings, tossing it to her and sending her away.

One night he didn't come home at the usual time, and we assumed that the rain hadn't been able to keep him away from the lodge. Gratefully, we snuggled right back into our daily routine. Nasieku, perched on the edge of the dressing table, recited Frost and tapped her toes in time to the swinging rhythm of the words.

"Nature's first green is gold," she sang. "Her hardest hue to hold—"

But then the front door swung open, crashing against the side of the house, rattling the flimsy bedroom walls. And in that moment, like an egret that flees from the sweeping force of the sirocco long before the blue drips from the sky, somehow we felt, *we knew,* that the slam of that door held the completion of the change that had been sneaking around us for months. Somehow.

"Her early leaf's a flower." Her voice began shaking.

Footsteps smacking against the cheap tiles.

"But only so an hour."

The steps stopped right in front of our door. I huddled against the head of the bed with my trembling hands pressed tightly into my stomach. Nasi never moved.

"Then leaf subsides to leaf," she whispered, her body growing smaller and smaller as I watched her in the reflection of the warped oval mirror attached to the back of the bureau.

"So Eden sank to grief."

"So dawn goes down to day," I whispered back, feeling the middle of my chest grow hot with fear.

"Come out here, Nasieku," he called softly through the door.

"Nothing gold can stay . . . "

As she jumped down, her dressing gown got snagged in one of the brass angels on the bureau drawers that acted as handles. I got up to help her get free, but she slipped away before I reached her and went padding out onto the cold floor in her bare feet. I yanked the chain in the ceiling to cut off the light, jumped off the bed, and sat on the floor with my back pressed against the wall by the open door, struggling to hear what was going on in the living room. Ketigile was already out there, huddled on the sofa, I presumed. She had been waiting. I pressed my knees against my chest and rocked back and forth just like Nasi always did no matter how many times I begged her not to.

"I won't allow it." Ketigile's voice, not quite sure enough to be resolute, grated against the firmness of her words like dry leaves being crushed in the palm of a hand.

"Don't forget yourself, woman. This house is mine. This child is mine. You are nothing that my charity does not allow you to be."

"I am her mother."

"You are not!" he shouted, slamming his fist into the wall. I cringed. What did this have to do with poor Nasi? "That job was taken from you a year ago and by one who was a stranger to you.

"Now look at you," he snarled. "Nothing. You are nothing. Tell me which man in this town would condemn me for killing an embarrassment like you?"

Nasieku began sniffling and sobbing softly, and my arms itched to grab her and run. But where could we go? No one would have us.

"She is too young to be circumcised, Lalasi, please," Ketigile moaned.

So that's what this is about, I thought and relaxed a little bit.

"For the last time, you stupid whore, the girl cannot be married unless she has been circumcised! You cannot possibly be so drunk that you forget things most basic."

"But why, husband, why should she marry now?" she whined. "Even out in the bush no one makes a girl marry so young anymore. You will be shamed and ridiculed if you do not wait until she is at least fourteen. Perhaps you could get away with it at even thirteen. But not now. She is barely nine years old." Ketigile's pitiful whimpering sounded almost exactly like Nasi's.

Nobody moved or spoke for a very long moment. Misery rushed through the house, sneaking in from an open window, smelling of raindrops and heavy winds. It ground the silence into a thick pulp that lay wasted on the floor, overcome by the incessant drumming of water striking the roof and splashing on the floor from my eyes. I listened to the emptiness from a great height, hearing myself above everything else saying it was over.

"Wife," said Lalasi softly, and I heard the scrape of one of the heavy wooden chairs from the dining table as it pulled up alongside the sofa. "Ketigile. I did not tell you this before because I did not think you capable of understanding. I admit that. But I must reckon with you now before this thing is done. And tonight is the night when the moon is where it should be. Tonight I can take her to the ngamuratani. If it is not done now, it will have to wait a full month, until the next time the moon is positioned properly. And I will not wait.

"I must tell you that I went one day last month to the laa manyit," he continued. "I watched him as he examined the goat intestines that I provided, and suddenly his face soured. When I asked what was wrong, he said that death was coming. Naturally, I thought he meant you, but he said no, the death was not for one in my household but for one of my house by proxy. He then said to me that Lee Kebore must die."

Ketigile gasped and whispered, "But why?"

"He is sick, wife. Not even he understands how sick he is. He will die before six months have passed. My laa manyit has never ever been wrong about a thing like this. Ketigile, that man has had this child booked for a wife since she was kicking in your stomach. He never got over the fact that you chose me over him.

Me. Still poor and hungry back then. He couldn't understand why you would do it when you could have had a man of his property and wealth. At times I disbelieve it myself . . . " His voice sounded very faraway and gentle, unlike I had ever heard it before.

"But we were all different people then, with different ideas and . . . " He sighed, shaking it off. "Still, we must look to our child's future and our own. I understand your reservations, Ketigile, but think! He has offered to pay a bride-price greater than any I've ever heard of."

"How much?" she asked, a sly, crafty tone creeping into her voice.

"That is none of your concern. That is men's business. Just you know that we will finally have the rest that we need to buy that new car I've been telling you about and maybe even enough to send you to Mombasa. I know that you had old friends from there and you always used to talk about going to . . . uh . . . have some time to yourself and get back to the way you used to be."

"Yes," Ketigile murmured dreamily, "I did want to do that once a long time ago, when this one was still young . . . "

"Now you can."

"Husband, I just don't know. It seems so shady and unseemly. What will people say? What about her schooling? She is the daughter of the district chief. How could that possibly look?"

"I have discussed these things already with Kebore. She will attend school as long as she wants, and they will pay the fees. There is no disgrace there. And she will be cared for by Kebore's senior wife until she comes of the age to bear her own children. Only then will she be given over to Kebore as a full wife. But the beauty of it is that he'll be dead by then! However, it must be done now. If we wait too long and he dies too fast, they may send her home and ask for the bride-price back. But if she's been there for a while, they wouldn't dare. It would be shameful, and they would look very cheap and stingy. Now, I've told Kebore that I've a cousin who wants her also, and my laa manyit has said that the union would be right and proper, but it must be done in a hurry. That's how I got him to raise the price and offer to take her now. That stupid old man would sell his soul to get his wrinkled hands on anything of yours. If you had a dog it wouldn't be safe either." He chuckled. "Ironic, eh?"

I crawled around the corner so I could see what was happening, where Nasieku was in all of this. She had retreated into the far corner behind the door and stood there covering her mouth with both her hands, tears running steadily across her knuckles and down onto her chest, staining her little white nightie till it was transparent in the front.

"Listen to me, Mother of Nasieku, you must back me on this," Lalasi coaxed. "She will be home again within the year. I can almost promise it. There is a chance that she will be inherited by one of his people, but it is a slim chance. I'm almost positive that I can bring her home to you. I will discuss it discreetly with Kebore. These are very special circumstances. And then, when she is ready, she will marry again at a proper age and with no reduction in the bride-price."

They were silent again, Ketigile cradling her head in her arms. For a moment, it had appeared that she was steadily considering Lalasi's proposal. But when she raised her eyes to his, Lalasi found them glittering with hate and disgust. "This is absolutely ridiculous," Ketigile hissed. "Who has ever heard of such a thing as this? Selling your only child like she was a slave. You'd probably sell her for a bottle of beer if you were thirsty enough."

Lalasi leapt at her yelling, "Shut your filthy mouth! Shut it!" He wrapped his hands around her throat and squeezed as she clawed his face and tried to wiggle out from underneath him. But he trapped her under the weight of his body, screaming right into her face, "Look at what I've done for you! I should have killed you, you whore, but look at you! The way you sit high, doing nothing in the world but looking down on everyone else! Could Kebore have cared for you this way? Could he?"

"Yes!" Ketigile screamed at the top of her voice. *"Yes yes yes yes yes . . . "*

Nasieku finally saw me beckoning to her, and she ran to me with her arms stretched out and her face contorted in fear. But Lalasi saw the movement and leapt again, catching her just before she reached me.

"No!" I scrambled to my feet. "I won't let you do this to her. You can't. She doesn't want to go, do you, Nasi, do you? Tell him!"

But she could only whimper, her voice snatched up and away by stealthy fingers of grief, greed, and fear. She could never contradict this father of hers. I don't know what I was thinking. I wasn't thinking. I ran toward her, and Lalasi pushed her out of the way and jumped on top of me, knocking me to the floor. He wrapped his hands around my neck and dug his thumbs into the soft flesh under my chin, crushing the air out of me.

"GO!" he screamed at Nasi. "Get into your clothes. Now!"

I tried to tell her that she didn't have to and that she shouldn't, but I couldn't speak. Lalasi's face hung in the air directly over mine, his eyes yellow and dead, his mouth stretched wide open, trying to catch his breath as he spit half-finished curses into my face. He was old, too old and haggard to be fighting, but he couldn't give up. His skinny, wrinkled body writhed against me, dragging me down into his hate, shoving my head way down deep in it until I gagged and threw it back up at him, choking and gagging. The room stank of sweat, beer, whiskey, and blood, and the thought came to me that maybe I was meant to die there. Maybe the death that we had been feeling all this time was my own.

"Apaayia, please!" Her voice came at me from down a long, dark tunnel, along with a sudden rush of air. He let go of me when she came back into the room, and he rolled over onto his side, panting. I rolled over too, still wheezing and coughing, and tried to crawl toward her voice, but she ran from me, leaping over my body and crouching in the doorway, having put on the long white skirt and white shirt that she wore each Sunday to church. In her hair was the white ribbon I had given her for her last birthday.

"Come, apaayia. I am ready to go with you. Just please don't hurt her, all right?"

Lalasi rose slowly to his feet, hands on knees, back bent, breath hitching as though there were tears in his lungs. He sat carefully, almost gently upright while wiping the thick, white spittle from the corners of his mouth. After looking briefly down at me, then glancing toward Ketigile, Lalasi strode with deliberate and painful steps from the room. Nasieku followed behind him, her back hunched over like an old woman's. She didn't look fearful anymore, just terribly tired and small. I tried to catch her eye, but she never looked back.

Lalasi took her to a ngamuratani named Ge-torrono, a very old woman notorious throughout the district for shoddy and botched circumcisions. Only the poorest people went to her and those with pregnant daughters who needed to have them circumcised and married before the babies arrived. Ge-torrono was exceedingly busy that night, the fourth night after the new moon. She lined up three girls at once and lay them down on dirty cow skins streaked rusty brown with old blood. Nasieku said she found herself sandwiched between two older girls, around thirteen or fourteen, one of whom cried as her mother screamed at her from the outer room, "This is what you get when you spread your legs for every bloody Kikuyu and Luo that blinks at you!" Ge-torrono had no time to prepare and very few instruments to work with. So she did one girl after the other without stopping. There was too much money to be made and too little time. Nasi said she almost got sick all over the floor because she saw somebody else's blood streaking Ge-torrono's razor as the old woman stood over her and smiled. She passed out.

NASIEKU CAME HOME with a wad of cotton shoved between her legs and no clitoris and no labia.

Ketigile and I invited some of her little friends from class over to the house a few days later for tea. They brought gifts for her, beads and purple hair ribbons and a silver locket without a chain. I gave her a book of poetry by Whitman and told her to read one aloud every night in her new home. Ketigile was good enough to go back into her room after she finished helping me bake the cake so the girls wouldn't have to see her.

It took Nasi a few weeks to heal. I shaved her head for her as a sign that she had completed her transition, even though no one had thought to do it before she was cut. The following day, she was gone.

CHAPTER *Thirteen*

. . . .

NO WORDS PASSED in our household for nearly a year. Even the beatings stopped. It seemed as though Nasieku had taken not only all of the laughter but all of the passion of every kind with her when she left. I studied constantly for my A-level exams, reworking things that I had already memorized years ago just to be sure that nothing could escape my notice. If I did well enough, I would be in university the following January. I would never have to see Lalasi again. That thought drove me on furiously. I hated Lalasi so viciously that the image of him lying dead, his pants down around his ankles and muddy, his body defiled, his throat cut back to the bone, kept me awake at night, sometimes till dawn, feeling the pressure of the slick, liberating knife in my hand. I still got up minutes later, did my morning chores, and dragged myself to school so exhausted that my eyes felt like raw, itchy lead balls. My body shook to the point where some people who didn't like me started spreading the story that I was a glue fiend. But I didn't care. Revenge fed my body better than sleep ever could, and if the only revenge I could have was in my head, then so be it.

Lalasi finally made the long trip to a dealership in Nairobi and bought his car, a blue 1990 Mercedes with a dent in the grill.

Ketigile never went anywhere.

My exams started early in June. English literature, composition, history, science . . . I could barely keep them all straight. In spite of my frazzled state, each time I walked out of the examination room, I knew I had aced the test. It wasn't even fun anymore. The only one that gave me any trouble was science, but I didn't care if I got a B or a B+ in that subject. I'd never liked it anyway. My last exam came, the literature one, and I got stumped on a question when I drew a blank as to whether the man I wanted was Byron or Shelley. I guessed Byron, but still the question plagued me afterward as I wandered through the streets, past Quicksand's (which I never so much as glanced at, much less entered anymore), and eventually up the hill.

I walked slowly and methodically, playing snatches of poetry back in my head, singing under my breath, hoping I might find a certain rhythm to the words that would jog my memory. I walked alongside the ostrich farm, throwing the babies who ran up to the fence bits and pieces of the mandazi that I had wrapped in a napkin and stuffed in the pocket of my starched white shirt. They hopped and strutted next to me, kicking up dust and pecking at one another, each trying to be first in line for a treat. I tore the rest of the cake into pieces and threw them over the fence, where the hatchlings fumbled and tripped over themselves, stretching out their long necks in search of a piece of sweet bread.

I slipped away in the confusion and turned up toward the house, kicking the gravel out of Lalasi's pretty driveway and dropping in handfuls of tacks that I'd found in a teacher's desk at school. With any luck, they'd blow out a tire, and when he got out to see what had happened, he'd get a tack jammed into the ball of

his foot. And if God were really with me, he'd hop straight up off
that foot and land on some more with the other. I smiled at my
wickedness and giggled. I loved to see Lalasi when his car didn't
work, which was often. He'd gotten so used to driving that it didn't
seem as though he could walk anymore. When he was forced to,
he'd come in that night limping and cursing like an old man, his
brown work clothes covered in dust and filth, with big rings of
sour sweat under his arms and seeping from his neck all the way
down his back. He came directly to me on those nights demanding
his dinner, and without even looking up at him I'd say, "This is not
my house. What have I to do with your dinner? Where's your
wife?"

The old Lalasi would've broken my jaw for such cheekiness,
but this new Lalasi didn't have it in him. Greed, like a cunning old
whore, had worn him out and stolen his fire to warm her own
cracked and wrinkled hands late in the night.

I came up the walk not so much thinking this as feeling it,
wondering if I was courting the same tricky old whore by living in
this man's house, this parasite whom I loathed, all the while growing steadily stronger and becoming educated off of his charity. Did
that not make me a parasite of a worse sort? A whore myself? Did
I really have a choice? Or was it my destiny, every woman's destiny,
no matter what clothes she wore or whose bed she shared, to be a
whore? Was the difficulty really within him, where I had so firmly,
so self-righteously placed it, or within me? Certainly, he had never
lied or pretended to be something he wasn't or turned his eyes
away from wrong as though he had never seen it, just to keep
peace. What would Byron do in this situation, I wondered, and
then immediately snorted with laughter at my own ridiculous
question. Byron was a man. And from what I knew of him, he
seemed the type of man who would sooner pat Lalasi on the back

than condemn him. Moreover, Byron was a white man. What couldn't he have done?

As I rounded the corner toward the back door, pushing languid, overgrown willow branches out of my face, I was startled by the most pitiful cry I'd ever heard. It rose up over my head, hovering above the trees and the rooftop, spurring the warbler-wrens and the rabbits in the rose garden into hasty flight, somehow denouncing and bemoaning life all at once. Involuntarily, I stepped back away from the house, away from that depraved sound, my hands grasping at my own throat as if I could catch it and kill it within myself. *Ketigile*, I thought, my body suddenly trembling, *not you too*. I ran around the corner and bounded through the door, flinging myself past the kitchen, and came to a dead stop at the sight of Ketigile kneeling at the end of the sofa. Her body, wrapped in a tattered shawl as old and gray as mourning, shuddered as she cried into the crook of one arm while holding Nasieku's hand with the other.

Ketigile peered up at me, bewildered, as if she wasn't quite sure who I was. Then, showing neither recognition nor surprise, she said, "So, you've come here to see my baby die."

I looked past her at the gray, gaunt face encased in the fluffy red of the sofa, which now seemed to be a garish coffin, and said, "Nasi?" But the word came out only in a whisper, and she didn't hear me. I tried to walk to her, to reach out to touch the tip of her nose and wiggle her awake as I used to do each morning before school, but my legs shook too badly and I stumbled, sliding to the floor. So I crawled, panting and groaning, sweating and cursing, moaning and crying like I had just heard Ketigile crying moments before. I grabbed her tiny body and felt the fever burn through my fingers, her skin stretched taut over her bones.

In disbelief I ran my hands over her rough, ashen arms, all the way up to her cheeks. This couldn't be the same laughing child that I loved. The one who was ticklish under her right arm but not under her left. The one who called the roses in the garden *falas* instead of *flowers* no matter how many times I corrected her corrupted English. The one who slept with my hair wrapped up in her fist just to be certain that I would still be there when she woke up. The one I used to watch through the window of the tiny brick schoolhouse on mornings when I reckoned I could afford to miss the first half hour of my own classes to make certain that she was all right.

This child lying in front of me didn't move and couldn't speak. This child had eyes that would not open, a body almost too frail to touch, and an ugly smell, sour and hot as the fever in her blood, drifting up out of her skin.

This child, obviously, would die.

And there would be nothing I could do about it. Again. Like always. Nothing I could do.

"*What happened?*" I screamed at Ketigile. "What have you done? What's wrong with her!"

Ketigile just rocked back and forth, back and forth, drooling a little, mumbling under her breath, "He said I would have her back in my arms before a year's time. . . . He said . . . "

"*What happened?*" I reached back and slapped the stupid woman, clawing at her cheeks and breasts. But even my anger was shallow and empty. Shock had stolen my strength. I could barely make a fist. Showing rage and defiance against a woman too feeble and broken to fight back made me sick inside. But much like Lalasi, I couldn't stop.

"What have you done? What's wrong with her? Tell me right now. I'll kill you! I swear it!"

Pathetic tears, empty and bleeding, trying to reach back to

change myself into a body, a mouth, a vessel strong enough for truth and action to inhabit it. Ketigile and I both the same, fighting ourselves, fighting each other only incidentally when the self became too smoky to clutch onto. Fighting, now, for this child. But time and futility are woven tight together, like a saffron basket made for water carrying. The only indentation in its circle is the soft curve on the bottom that fits directly onto a woman's skull. Pain can't change time. There was no way to make this right.

Ketigile didn't fight back. She sagged underneath my weight, though in truth she was larger than I, and tried to cover her face with her bony, scabby arms.

"It's not me," she wailed. "It's not me. They brought her back this way. They did it."

"*Who?*"

"The Kebores," she cried. "They did. Kebore is dead. The brother and the senior wife brought her back here this morning after Lalasi left. They yelled at me and hit me and said I should never have tried to pass over a sick child to them. But it wasn't me. I swear it."

"*What else?*"

"The woman," she sobbed. "She, she hit me and laughed and she said, 'So this is Kebore's love, his beautiful flame, his jewel that none of us were good enough to be no matter how many sons we bore,' and she spit on me. And they dropped her there on the floor and said that she had been sick since the first few months after she came. They said they don't want any more death in their house. But they do want their money back. Ei! Ngai! What is Lalasi going to do to me when he finds that he'll have to give back his car?"

THE WINTER MONTHS PASSED, July melting into August without comment or complaint and only a bare minimum of rain, and I nursed Nasieku through bout after bout with pneumonia. It seemed as if every time she got her color back and put on a little weight, another, totally different infection clamped down on her chest, squeezing her in a sadistic vise until she coughed blood. Lalasi stayed as far as he possibly could from his home, quietly selling his car (unbelievably, at a profit) and making discreet payments to the Kebore family. He disappeared for a few days in late August and came back carrying a black-and-white Panasonic television, which he set up in our room just opposite the bed. If I propped enough pillows up behind Nasi's back, she could actually watch it for a while. But her attention wasn't like it used to be. She usually drifted off to sleep in the middle of the shows, and when she woke, she could never remember the parts she had seen. When she finally got to see *Family Matters,* she yawned.

"This is stupid," she complained. "Shut it off."

MY EXAM SCORES came right around that time as well. Three A's and a B. I laughed. These scores would get me into any university in the country and quite a few abroad, if I had the money for that kind of traveling (which I didn't). I threw the paper away.

September and October slid into November and December and Nasi got set to die.

Ketigile and Lalasi paced the house like two caged animals, snarling, hissing, and swiping at each other. I spent my days carefully laying clean dressings over the open sores that sprouted up, oozing, all scarlet and black, across Nasieku's arms, legs, and scalp and even in the tender, completely smooth area between her legs. When I couldn't take any more, I'd go outside to the rusted pump and vomit out all of the misery and the stench of sickness until there was nothing left in the dry heaving but pain. On good days we read poetry and told stories about yellow-haired fairies that lived in huge stone castles. And about magic countries where people lived happily and ate nothing but mandazis and sugar biscuits all day and no one ever fought and no one was allowed to be sick. On bad days I laid her over my knees for hours, sometimes all night, with her face hanging off the edge of the bed, draining the mucus and pus out of her lungs, letting it drip, drip, drip foully into the large white plastic bucket on the floor.

An odd rain, heavy and malignant, began falling late one night, electrifying the house and everyone in it, making way, clearing a wide path for Death, trying to wash away the sickness. Finally. But I refused to let it leave, to let her leave. I held her so hard she moaned in her sleep, and I swore I'd never let her go. No God perched high like a vulture on His pristine mountaintop was going to make me, either. He would have to come down here and try to wrench her from my arms Himself. And if He did, I swore to myself, for once, for once I would fight Him. I'd kick and claw and scratch and rip His eyes from His head if He dared try to take her away from me. No. She couldn't leave. I couldn't just stand by and do nothing. Not this time. I'd lost everything else, and no one could take Nasieku from me. No one would close those little eyes that had looked to me so many times in the night for the reassurance that she needed to let herself drift off to sleep. No one would still that small voice, that laugh that echoed in my mind constantly like so many fireflies caught up in a pearly, silver tide of mist and rain. I closed my eyes, rocking her, stroking her head, being branded by the fever that invaded my body through my arms as they cuddled and comforted and loved. Out in the sitting room, Death flew round and round in wide, excited arcs, catching the tigers' tails, drawing them into bloody battle.

"I told you, you filthy, greedy animal," Ketigile seethed. The lingering presence of Death had enlivened her and, for once, made her clear-headed and bold. "You should never have taken her to that place, to those dirty people—"

"Shut up, you whore! How dare you speak of someone else as dirty when all you know is filth!"

"Don't change what we are talking about. What happened for us happened long ago. That man is dead now and so, thanks to you, is the girl he loved and even the memory of love. And you seem to forget that, stupidly, I chose you! I live with you! Everything was always about you! *But tell me now, Lalasi, what about your daughter?*"

"Oh shut up, can't you? You act as though I don't care for her just as much as you do," he whined pitifully. "That child is mine. She is the only one I have to carry my name. Imagine! A whole chief with only one namesake, and a girl at that. But am I ashamed? No! I love her just as you do. Am I not the one who refused to put her in a hospital when the doctor insisted? Did I not say that we would care for her at home no matter how bad it got?"

"If it weren't for you, we wouldn't need a hospital, you bastard! Tell me, man"—and I could hear her pacing up and down in front of the sofa—"was the money worth your daughter's life?"

"Shut up! It wasn't about money. You don't know what you are saying! You are drunk as usual."

"No, I'm not. Not now!"

"Yes, you are! You are always, always drunk. You disgust me!"

"How dare you say that to me when you are the first-first one to bring whiskey into this house. I couldn't drink if it weren't for you. You know I never leave this place anymore. Not looking like this."

"Shut up!"

"*No!* I will never shut up until I die! Never again will I shut up, you pig! You black ape! You bloody child killer!"

The weight of two bodies slammed against the wall and then rolled down onto the floor.

"I will never shut up! Never!"

Lalasi howled in pain. I smiled, wondering where she'd landed the blow.

"How was I to know that this would happen?" he cried. "This thing has been Ngai's will from the start. I can't figure it any other way. There was no way for me to know, I swear!"

"Really!" she screamed. "What about your all-powerful laa manyit? Shouldn't he have known? Shouldn't he?"

That's it! I thought. We had tried every other doctor in Maralal. They'd all said the same thing: treatment in Nairobi could help for a while, but it would only be dragging out the inevitable end. But perhaps the laa manyit could help somehow. He did seem to know everything else . . .

"Sister . . ."

"Shhh, little baby. Hush, my heart, we are going for help," I crooned as I wrapped Nasi up in the white sheets and the thick woolen blanket, covering her head but making sure to leave a small space for her nose and mouth. "We are going to make this thing better. I promise."

I lifted her gently and cradled her fragile, beaten body softly in my arms as if she were an infant. Her body felt as though it weighed less than the blankets she was wrapped in, and the feel of the emptiness made frustrated tears spring into my eyes. We walked out of the room, passed right by them unnoticed, and stepped out into the driving black rain. I closed the door behind me, slowly, cutting off the sound of shattering glass and tears.

Blindly, we made our way down the gravelly path, sliding over the slick, shifting rocks. The rain pummeled my face and my arms and my legs, for I had forgotten to put on a shawl or a long coat before I ran out of the house. I'd thought only of Nasi and nothing of myself, which was quite foolish because I was the one doing all the walking. Still, we couldn't go back. So I felt my way through the night, so black and formless that, by stepping out into it, I became part of it, disappearing into nothing. The water hit my body like icy, sharpened spikes and pounded my face until I bent over, crying. With frozen hands, I felt carefully inside Nasi's blanket, making certain not to expose any part of her body to the cold, and touched her arm to see that she was still dry. Her body was damp but from sweat, not yet from rain, and I started to trot, knowing that I had no more time to waste. If she were to get wet in a cold rain like this, it would surely kill her.

As we descended the hill, I imagined the trees that I should be passing on the left of me and the markings in the fence post to the right. The murky blanket of rain obliterated everything from my view except the first meter or two directly in front of me, so I had to gauge with my mind how far we had left to go. My arms, absolutely freezing and now quite numb, refused to move or adjust when I felt Nasieku sliding from my grasp. I panicked, giving in to frightened, hitching sobs, and turned around, thinking to go home. But I was blocked on all sides by the darkness; it had allowed me to creep into it, but it refused to let me back out. I turned back around toward town and ran on, hunched over Nasieku's body, shielding her face from the rain.

Then out of nothing a jumping, flickering ghost arose in the darkness. It was a light, a lonely yellow light, from one of the duplication houses, which meant that we were right on the edge of town. We had to go through town, past the transport depot, until we came to the short hill just beyond it. That's where the laa manyit lived. We could make it. I laughed and kissed Nasi on the forehead, but not even the cold touch of my lips could make her respond.

We're now directly in the center of the field—the trees on the right are about, hmmm, one hundred meters off, the houses on the left, about fifty, which means that the little wooden footbridge should be coming up directly ahead in just a few moments. Yes, exactly here—

We went sprawling headfirst down a steep incline, tumbling over each other in a hideous collage of flailing arms, legs, clothes, blankets, and cold mud—right into the ditch just below the footbridge. Frantically, I ripped through the mud and trickling gutter water searching for her body.

"Nasieku!" I screamed. "Oh God! *Where are you?*"

I rummaged blindly through the stinking water while the rain attacked my body, pelting me with frozen accusations, until I grabbed hold of her ankle and flung my body over her, struggling to lift her out of the mud. She lay face down and I turned her over, cradling her tiny, twisted body in my arms.

"Oh, Nasi, I'm so sorry. Are you all right? You aren't hurt too badly, are you? Please don't be angry with me. Please speak. Are you okay? Nasi? Nasieku? Oh God! *Oh God! NASIEKU?*"

When had I first refused to realize that there was no shallow breath rasping in my ears? When did I first feel the fever begin to cool? I don't know . . . I don't know . . . I don't know . . .

The neighbors roused the police from their beds by telephone when my screaming and howling didn't stop. They told the officers that there was a woman being raped or beaten right down in the ditch across the meadow from the government houses. So the officers arrived, cranky and shivering, pointing their semiautomatic weapons down into the darkness just in case. And they found us crouching there, burrowed into the mud just above the foul water, rocking gently back and forth and back and forth and back . . .

And they took us home.

THEY BURIED NASIEKU in a box at the foot of some hill, where she was prayed over by a white Catholic priest in a bloody red gown that looked as though it was made of velvet. All of the women admired this gown but commented on how hot and uncomfortable the priest looked. All of the nuns from her school and her classmates were in attendance. Nasieku wore her blue-and-gray school uniform and was wrapped in a gauzy white shuka that covered all but her face. I know because I dressed her in it, but no one else saw her because Lalasi ordered the box closed. He didn't want to feed any of the rumors being spread by the Kebores about how and why Nasieku had died.

The mourners threw flowers in the grave and many people cried for Nasi. Sister Taisere was there, and she cried, too. The men all gathered round and shoveled dirt on the body after it had been lowered into the ground, and then the children joined in also, flinging fistfuls of hot, red earth down onto the coffin until she lay all covered up and invisible. The women circled the grave, moaning all the old songs, the ones they didn't sing in the church of the Catholics.

They used stones instead of leaves to cover the body in the

grave, stones piled high in a great mound (as if Nasi were going to try to get up and run away and had to be stopped), and then they left her there.

I didn't go to the funeral. I couldn't. Ketigile came home and told me all about it. Every detail. Lalasi went straight to the lodge.

Later that evening, she came back into my room to talk.

"Turn over, girl," she commanded, slapping me lightly on my bum. "Sit up. You act as though it were your child buried today and not mine."

I didn't appreciate that remark and refused to answer it.

"I understand that you cannot feel for me," she started hesitantly, fingering the black lace of her long skirt. "But I feel for you. And I love you because you loved when I couldn't. You tried to protect and I didn't. No one ever thanked you, so perhaps I can thank you now."

I looked up at her warily. She laughed and offered a bitter little smile. It was a very small one, just enough to turn up the corners of her mouth, but not so much that you could see the empty spaces where her side teeth used to be.

"Here, take this," she said, handing me a long, thick brown envelope. I opened up the seal and looked inside.

"What is this?" I spit at her. "What trouble are you trying to find for me?"

"No trouble, Nasarian, I swear it. This money is Lalasi's money. It is not stolen. He has given it freely."

"Where could Lalasi get this type of money, and why would he even think of giving it to me? What is going on with this?"

Ketigile laughed again. She looked infinitely miserable. Like a black Fate. Ketigile was the eldest of the three Fates, as far as I saw it. She was the hunchbacked crone shrouded forever in black, who kept winged Death as her faithful familiar. Her job for all eternity was to cut the glimmering threads that bound mortal life.

She answered, "Lalasi is quite well off, you see. He has many investments. I know of only a few, but I surprised him. He thought I was too drunk to know about any. He has herds of cattle and camels and sheep, and he owns part of a business in town. The government doesn't pay him much, but the bribing of a district chief is no cheap affair. Lalasi is always well rewarded for whoring himself. So take."

Her words made no sense to me. They gave me no understanding. In fact, those words stripped me of any piece of understanding I'd thought I had. The only thing I was left with was a mounting fury too deep to even feel. My fingertips, my bowels, my face, my mind went numb.

"You mean he didn't even need the money?" I whispered. "He let her go for nothing?"

"No, not for nothing, my heart," she said, looking away. "Not really for the money, but not for nothing. He was searching for something when he did it. An end, perhaps, to something that had nothing to do with my child. I do believe that he was trying to prove himself better than he knew himself to be, more cunning and crafty anyway, to someone who most probably no longer cared. He wanted to finally have a control that his money and position could never have bought for him. This is all very old business that can't possibly make any sense to you, and I'm sorry for that. But this is all I have to offer. If it is unselfish reason and logic that you want, you won't find it here. Life is very rarely that simple."

"I don't want his money," I wept. "And I don't believe for one second that he wants me to have it. He slapped me when the police brought us back, even though I still had her in my arms."

"Yes, that was very bad. I won't lie. Perhaps Lalasi doesn't give from a completely willing heart, but fear and guilt will make you do many things, sometimes even good things, the right thing, if not for the right reasons. But don't be foolish now, girl," Ketigile said, stroking my hair. "You need it. School starts in less than three weeks. You must get there early to pay your fees."

"What are you talking about?"

Again she laughed and smiled, this time without so much hatred and sadness.

"I was not nearly as drunk as everyone thought. I noticed things. Like I noticed the letter you got. The one you had been waiting for for months. And I noticed that I never heard a thing about it. So I looked. It was right where I thought it would be. Right where anger and grief would have told me to put it if I were you. So I stole it and gave it to the doctor along with your information the next time he came to visit Nasieku. He applied to the schools for you.

"I am not a smart woman, Nasarian, not educated like you or my sister or even my baby. I would not have known what to do with that letter. In truth, I could barely read it. But the doctor knew. And he kept his word to me and never told Lalasi about it. He agreed with me that at least one person in this house should have the chance to leave it on two good legs. This is your chance. You are enrolled in the private American university in Nairobi. I heard you speak of it to Nasieku. I knew it was the one you favored. I mentioned it to the doctor, and he knew it right off. He called it the best foreign university in the whole of East Africa. You must go. They want you."

I didn't know what to say or even to think. But she didn't wait for a response.

"You will find in the envelope enough to take you through all four quarters, plus a sizable amount left for pocket change, books, and clothes," she continued. "But budget. Put it in a bank, per-haps, if you can. There won't be another one of these coming to you," she said, jiggling the envelope, "for a year's time. One every year until you graduate. All I ask is that you send me the certificate at the end. I will hang it on the wall right in the center of the living room, so that if anyone should ever come to this house again . . ." Her voice fell to an unsteady whisper. "It will be the first thing they see . . ."

"Don't cry, Ketigile, please don't cry."

"The very first thing . . ."

CHAPTER *Fourteen*

. . . .

A LITTLE MORE THAN two weeks later, I slept on a burlap sack of green onions crammed into the steps of a packed south-bound Nyere bus. I dreamed in snatches throughout the night, of woolly red earth and forests that smelled curiously of mangoes and lemon-spotted butterflies. The butterflies wept from the gilded folds of their crumpled wings as I turned in circles, calling Nasieku's name. At one point, I heard her laughing but not from any specific place above or behind me. Actually, it might have been me that was laughing. I'm not sure.

In any case, I woke up trembling and cursing out the words to a song that had no melody (that was, in fact, not really a song at all).

> Loneliness terrific beats on my heart,
> Bending the bitter, broken boughs of pain.
> Stunned by the onslaught that tears the sky apart
> I stand with unprotected head against the rain.

Loneliness terrific turns to panic and to fear.
I hear my footsteps on the stair of yesteryear,
Where are you? Oh, where are you?
Once so dear . . .

The bus had barely lurched to a full stop in the depot when the men next to me began kicking at the doors and I was rushed off the steps by a thick, impatient swarm of travelers. I suddenly found myself hemmed into a cobweb of narrow, paved streets already buzzing in the purple light of dawn. The hawkers with their wheelbarrows and the vegetable women carrying cabbages and onions and tomatoes tied up in rough blankets on their heads competed with the maize vendor's bulky grills for sidewalk space. I hoisted my little vinyl case onto my head and plodded through the street with no direction other than the driver's vague instructions to catch a matatu on Moi Avenue out to Kasarani and that side of town.

Nairobi, I discovered immediately (and rediscovered daily in the weeks and months that followed), was a city of ghosts.

Not real ghosts, mind you. Not the disappearing kind, like they have in Mombasa. The kind that can walk into a green sea and turn it blue or that run at you screaming with mouths that don't open anymore once they've looked into your eyes and realized that you were not the person they sought. The ghosts in this city fanned gnats from yellow, draining wounds and wore brittle khimars that could no longer cover their hair or their tears or their children as they sat curbside on flattened Westinghouse refrigerator boxes and waited. These ghosts had trekked from parched, red places like Rwanda and Somalia and Ethiopia. They sat listlessly outside banks or post offices as though at any moment someone would walk out and hand them wads of money or mail.

I stared long into the women's vacant faces that first morning. I suppose I was half waiting for one or the other of them to recognize me, call me daughter and welcome me to my share in their misery. I would gladly, even thankfully have gone. But not one of them looked back.

So I walked along alone, sniffing at the streets which smelled burnt even though as far as I could see there was no place for a morning fire or a prayer. Only monstrously gray buildings and buses and fast-footed people. Eventually I found a matatu stop that I hoped was the right one and inched my way up toward the front of the rush-hour queue. Two or three full mats left before I got my turn. The tout pushed me into the last seat in the van and then shoved a bony, gray bearded man in pin-striped pants and a stinking white shirt into my lap. "Enough room for everyone!" the tout shouted in Swahili and banged the roof of the minivan, at which the driver immediately careened into the middle of the teeming road. The skinny man nestled himself deep and comfortably into my crotch, turned to me, and smiled.

The mat let me off at the beginning of a long, twisting dirt road. I trudged around the bends, pushing through the heat as it stopped to smile and greet me. Like an old, childless auntie, the sun kissed my temples with rough, dry lips not made for loving and caressed the soft indentation of my spine until my scalp and my back bled with sweat. Even the deep green shade from the trees that lined long stretches of the road didn't really help. However, the cows that loafed alongside me disagreed, basking in those smooth, hanging shadows as though they led to watering holes and not roots. A heifer chewed cud in the shaded gutter while her calf stretched between her spotted legs to nurse. The sight of the clockwork rotation of her jaws tapped frightened, burning tears from my eyes. I couldn't figure out why I should cry over cattle, so I simply assumed that these fresh tears of mine were just another sign of my lack of discretion and self-control.

Rounding the final curve, I came upon the tall university gates just as the askaris shoved them open. Roosters and lonely yellow ducklings scattered everywhere as a shining new BMW sagged and bumped out into the craggy road. Without warning, the driver gunned the engine and swerved toward me, forcing me to leap into the gutter with the cows and a couple of bleating goats. But then, before I could get back on the road, the guards started pulling the gates shut again.

"Hold! Hold!" I yelled; but they didn't, so I had to run and jam my arm into the gates to keep them from closing. Only the askaris still wouldn't open up for me. I stood there like a fool with one arm dangling onto university property and the rest of me held at bay. Quite slowly the guards looked over my faded secondary school uniform, the Firestones on my feet, my reddened eyes, and the cheap, torn case that wobbled on top of my head as I struggled with my free hand to hold it up.

"What is your business here, eh?" said the mustached one. No greeting. No formal welcome. Nothing. In fact, he shut the gate just a bit more, wedging my arm tighter still between the iron grates. Such rudeness deserved rudeness in kind.

Purposely and spitefully I withheld my greeting and refused to ask after his health.

Instead I briskly stated my business: "I'm to start school here this week. I need to get registered and find my lodgings."

The two men looked at each other, and the short one shrugged. The mustached man cracked the gate open just wide enough for me to squeeze my body through. I had to take my suitcase off my head in order to fit.

"Administration building on the right," the short one said but did not answer when I mumbled, "Asante."

I headed off across the dry lawn, listening to it crunch under my feet, wanting to scratch the itch where it jabbed at my heels with tiny, thirsty spears of grass. It was the first grass I had felt under my feet since the night before I left Lalasi's house, when I'd rolled through the thorns in Ketigile's rose garden, cutting myself on grief. At sunup I had fallen asleep under maroon rose roots and dreamed of my mother floating on her lesso through an endless yellow sea, her mouth covered in starfish and black sand. (I had never seen any of these things at the time so how they showed up in my dream, I don't know. Perhaps the dream belonged to my Father, who then, for whatever reasons of his own, lent it to me.) Perhaps . . .

"Don't mind them," a man whispered to me in Maa.

I spun around so fast that my case, which I had just then put back on my head, tumbled off again, onto the ground. I hadn't seen or heard him idling up beside me. As I was busy thinking, he'd just appeared in my language, in my thoughts. Out of nowhere. Like another ghost.

"Close your mouth, sis, or you'll be eating sausage bugs and gnats in another moment," he laughed, picking up my bag.

"Ei! So sorry, eh?" I stuttered. "How rude of me to stare that way. I just didn't expect—"

"To see one of us here? Well, don't worry. You assumed correctly. I'm the only one you'll find, and I'm not a student either. Me, I'm a porter."

My heart fell. Only then did I notice the mop and pail in his hand. This man was tall, his shoulders broad and strong like my Father's. Likewise, he had my Father's proud eyes. And yet here he was working for Mzungus, doing a woman's job. I wondered testily if the canteen cooks were men too (they were, I found out later, but not Samburu cooks at least).

"So anyway, where from? What clan?" he asked. He didn't bother to find out whether or not I wanted him to walk with me. He simply led the way onto the path towards the big red-brick building in front of us.

"Lpaiyani from around Maralal, Porro, and those sides. Hey, listen, how did you know—"

"That you were Samburu? Well, I saw your ears first off. But I wasn't totally sure until I spoke and you turned around so sharply. You're nusu-nusu, ya? A half-caste?"

I nodded my head, and he did too.

"Yeah. I wasn't fully sure, but now I am very glad that I spoke. Isn't it our good luck that I happened out this way? I wasn't going to, but something in me said, No, Augustin, stop being lazy and get up fast-fast for work. And there you were waiting for me to escort you from the gate."

"Yes," I muttered. "There I was. Waiting."

Augustin's sandals made no noise as we turned onto the cobblestone walkway. Not at all like the smart-looking young boys in Levi's jeans that ran past us, laughing and click-clacking in their shining, hard-soled leather shoes. My new friend's sandals were papery thin, like house slippers, and I could easily see that he wore no socks because his brown corduroy pants, which had been patched with denim around the bum and on the inseam, were at least two inches too short. Augustin's thin work shirt was clean and well pressed but, once again, his mannish patchwork job could be easily seen under the arms and at the back of his collar.

As I looked at him, a mortifying realization washed over me in a hot, stinging rush. I saw for the first time what those guards had seen when they'd looked at me and decided in an instant how I would be treated:

Unkempt. Poor. Backward. Bush.

I had no business in this guarded, privileged place. They knew it, and I should have known it too. Unless, of course, in addition to being simply unsophisticated I was also stupid as well.

Suddenly nothing in the world seemed as important to me as getting away from this man whistling and smiling next to me, this man who carried his mop in one hand and my battered, ugly case in the other. He was not my new friend. He was oafish and clumsy. Ignorant and forceful. I was nothing like him. I belonged here.

I had to belong here. There was nowhere else for me to go.

I told myself to smile, thank him, and walk politely away. Even so, as we neared the wide-open double doors of the administration building, I snatched the handle of my suitcase out of Augustin's grasp. Without a thought for civility, I practically ran through the entranceway, barreling into the crowded, narrow halls.

He was nothing. Just an uneducated porter from the bush. *But I belonged here.*

I think I heard Augustin make a sound like he wanted to call my name, but I had never told him what it was. So after an embarrassed, fidgety minute of indecision, he turned around and headed back to work.

❧

MY FIRST YEAR of school rushed by in a haze of industriousness. I never stopped moving. When the lecturers had no more work to give, I quizzed myself and read extra chapters from unassigned books. In retrospect, I realize that I was afraid of being too quiet, of sitting down and being still. Afraid of the understanding that accompanies a silent mind. It would have been too difficult for me to admit that I wasn't fitting in. It would have been next to impossible to admit that college wasn't what I had made it out to be for the last dozen years or so—since I was old enough to understand what the word "university" meant and that it wasn't impossible for me to get there.

But I knew that many of my classmates were laughing at me behind my back. They laughed at my clothes and my funny accent. They were astounded by my total ignorance of things that they considered most essential. The hip-hop that everyone else listened to jarred my ears. I hadn't heard of Tupac or Busta or Biggie. I didn't hang out when guys watched stolen British porn movies in the common room after hours. I had never been inside a shopping mall or ridden a motorbike.

One day an Indian girl named Rayna tried to stick a Magic Marker through the hole in my ear. When I spun around and snatched the marker out of her hand, she and her friends snorted with laughter.

"Oh, so sorry." She shrugged with wide, innocent eyes. "I thought that's what it was for."

By the end of the year, I decided that something had to change.

It took some time, but through a combination of craft, flattery, constant accommodation, and quiet begging, I managed to acquire my first three friends.

Lorraine, Idia, and Charlie.

I handed my schoolbook money over to Lorraine and she dressed me in stylish blouses and imported jeans. Charlie bought perfumed gels and sprays that smelled tart like green apples to make ringlets out of the thick frizz of my hair. Idia coated my lips and my cheeks with burnished mahogany and carmine.

At the end of it all, I looked nothing like the dirty, awkward girl that had come walking up the road the year before. But somehow people were still wary of me. Lorraine said that so many of the guys treated me funny because I held on so tightly to the same basketful of secrets that I had been keeping since I'd arrived. No one knew quite what to make of me. In all the time I had been at university, almost no one had been able to find out anything about me. None of my classmates even knew for sure what tribe I belonged to. Most people just assumed I was a Kenyan-raised Somali, and I never corrected them. I didn't see why I should.

What was clear were the obvious and generally uninteresting facts. My parents were dead, and I had a far-off, benevolent relative who provided my school fees in their absence. I was studious (not lonely and unwelcome), and that was the reason I took classes instead of going home to visit my family for the summer break and would continue to refuse to leave for every holiday and intersession throughout the next two years. I wrote to no one, spoke of no one, missed no one. I hated children. I had never had a boyfriend and, at my late age of twenty-two, didn't seem to want one. I made straight A's without much effort, which meant that I studied so much and so hard not because I had to but because I wanted to (hence I was also just plain weird).

And I wrote poetry.

The poetry I wrote was about love and falling, frothing mists. Mists that played out a nightly seduction with the endless fields of cold, blue, white man's wheat (roots inundated with a century of black blood and sticky shame). I wrote of the way the rising haze stroked and sucked the secret sweetness away from each shivering stalk. It turned supple and young into bent, brown, and old, then clung—heedless, shameless, and satiated—to steep valley walls. I wrote about screaming muddy rivers and dark, lonely pits of freedom. I wrote stories about death.

And I had nightmares. Still.

Most of the time it was the same one. I dreamed I was sitting alone in the back of the long blue-and-white school bus. The bus headed swiftly down Thika Road, rising and falling on black waves of concrete that had been brutally cut into an ancient sea of hills and fields. To the left and to the right, the red-and-green earth (who could not recognize herself when patriots and politicians called her Kenya, who knew nothing so banal and superficial as principalities or statehoods) watched us ride. She followed us, wavering in the heat, growing, dying, and springing back to humid life as we unmindfully passed her by.

(So, even in my dream, I wrote about her too.)

Throngs of people walked the roadside, trooping like soldier ants up and out of the safety of the mound. Men sat underneath baobab trees cutting each other's hair and gossiping. Or else they ran in place, trying to flag down speeding matatus in which there was no more room. They stood on corners hawking fruits, fish, sweets, or grilled maize. Mothers walked with babies strapped in sashes on their backs, their heads tied up in dingy, faded rags and loaded down with provisions. Toddlers ran behind, barefoot and bottomless, snot dripping down their faces as they laughed or cried for some attention. I watched those children fly past my window like little gurgling witches, hating them but loving them furiously all at the same moment. Their chubby, dusty legs and crooked little teeth indicted me, cursed me, because I was alive, they were alive, but Nasieku was not.

And in this dream each night, all these children merged into one small, lonely child, actually changed into Nasieku, and suddenly she was the one running along the roadside, barefoot and bottomless. But unlike the others, Nasieku was conscious of her nakedness, shamed by the unnatural smoothness in the places that had been meddled with, and she tried to hide herself with her small hands as she ran and ran. I looked to see to whom she was running, but the road was empty and dark. She was just running. And I couldn't help her because I was traveling alone on a big, belching school bus, going far and fast in the opposite direction. I forced myself awake every night during this dream, jumping up with my fists jammed into my mouth and tears steadily crawling into my ears.

This same dream came to me just before waking on that morning too, the morning that my misfortune began to take shape in earnest, blowing and churning like sirocco winds, squeezing bit by bit under the crack in my door. But the dream was especially terrifying that day because I woke up chanting phrases in a language that my mother had never taught me. My legs hung off the bed, jerking and twitching, as though I were planning to walk into Nima's death and confront her with her words. My stomach shook, and I smelled sour, dirty, and frightened like my sheets. I staggered out of bed and stepped into the loo, ready to plunge into a cold bath. But Lorraine, who was also my flatmate, had used the last of the water and left before I'd even woken up. So I threw on some clothes, grabbed her large pink pail, and started downstairs to the courtyard.

My rubber flip-flops slapped hard against the stairs as I dodged out into a crash of blinding sunlight. Already the farmers outside the fence had begun the day's burning. The sun stewed all the juice and spicy flavor out of the smoke, so it wafted over into our courtyard dry and brittle, seeking to mingle with the more pungent odor of sausages and honey coming from the canteen. I ran to the faucet outside of the boys' flats, turned the handle three grinding times, and listened for the water as it shuffled its way up the pipes. Cold water spurted out onto the ground, and I let it run to make sure all of the rust found its way into the tiny plot of soil surrounding the faucet and not my bucket. When the cold stream flowed clear, I put the bucket underneath it and filled it until water licked the very top and sought the edge of open space. Turning off the faucet, I walked carefully back across the courtyard, swaying under the weight of the water.

"Bring," called out a loud voice behind me.

I turned my head and saw Augustin trotting up to me. Then I shamed myself by immediately glancing around to see if anyone was watching us. I had often seen him around the campus since that first day, but I had never again spoken to him.

"Quick-quick, bring the bucket here."

But before I could move, he reached out and grabbed it without breaking stride and moved sharply toward the door of my flat.

"You know, bwana, I shall never marry you if you don't change these slovenly ways of yours. Look at this: it's halfway to lunchtime practically and you're not even bathed or dressed. Honestly! I thought girls were the clean ones."

"I am extremely clean, thank you. If I wasn't, then I wouldn't be needing the water, now would I?" I quipped, trying to make light of my embarrassment.

"How do I know what this water is for, eh? For all I know, you could be making tea."

We stepped through the doorway of the flat, and the cool air, cool like the bowels of an Arabic mosque, cool like a snaking tunnel of catacombs and dim like that too, clamped down on us. Laughter echoed up the twisting staircase, dancing in time with the morning radio tunes that snuck under the doorways to greet us as we climbed the stairs. My eyes had yet to adjust to the dim light, and when I tripped on a stair, Augustin reached out from behind me and pressed his free hand against my back to steady me. His fingertips were also cool, but cool like yellow flowers at midnight, cool like green, foamy sea spray, and firm. I appreciated that kind of touch and so let him keep his fingertips pressed in that little space where my shirt had left my shorts and exposed just a thin breath of my spine.

At my door, he set the bucket down and waited.

I wasn't quite sure what to do so I said, "Yes?" as politely as possible.

"Oh, oh, oh. Sorry, ya? Didn't mean to hold you. I was just, well, wondering what you were doing for the rest of the day. I reckon you must be rather busy but I thought I might accompany you on your errands or what have you. Sawa sawa?"

Again, I found myself at a loss. On the staircase I'd discovered a strange, rather shocking truth—I liked having him near me. Augustin's clothes were cheap and worn, but they were clean and they smelled like my mother's sleeping hutch after my Father had lain in it. He was from my clan and he had my Father's wide hands.

But still.

"I can't. I mean, you can't. What I'm saying is, I'm sorry but I'm meeting with my friends after I go to market and I don't know what they might say to having an extra person along."

"Of course, of course. I understand entirely. Well, I'll see you some other time then?"

"Sure," I lied. "Sawa sawa."

But as he left and without my permission, my mind cast off its moorings and drifted off with him, unsteady, unsure of the direction but stubborn. At the market in Parklands, I didn't even notice, until it was too late, the tiny-fisted velvet monkeys creeping through the shadows and the rafters, feeding on corpulent flies and sugar-brown bananas the size of my index finger so adeptly pilfered from my fruit basket. I even neglected to greet my friend Wangebi as he waved to me on my way past the city-center market. Wangebi was one of the spider-legged cripples who begged from a stretching, bleary-eyed dawn until well after sundown outside of the market. I knew him and he knew me because, though I never gave him any money, I always stopped to greet him and share whatever food I had whenever I passed his way.

Lorraine and Idia waited for me on the corner of Taifa Road and City Hall Way, eating chunks of sugarcane from sticky-looking plastic bags and gossiping.

I pushed Augustin out of the way, back behind my ear some-where, and called out "Habari-yako" to my friends.

"Muzuri sana," they answered together. "Sasa?"

"Fit sana, thanks."

"Charlie should be waiting for us down the road a ways. She had errands to run." Lorraine spoke in English for Idia's benefit because Idia was Nigerian and, greetings and curse words aside, she understood not a bit of real Swahili.

Lorraine was a short, sweet girl with a soothing temperament that flowed over other people's minds like a crisp trickle of water over stones. Everybody's favorite. Level-headed. Demure. Industri-ous. A perfect Kikuyu woman. I knew there had to be something wrong with her, only I hadn't found it just yet. Her soft, even skin was the color of a ripe coconut shell, sort of dark for a Kikuyu but beautiful nevertheless. Whenever we all got together, she naturally took the lead.

"Shall we go?" she suggested. "We can meet her coming out of the tailor's place."

"Speaking of tailors, Lorraine, isn't that the new suit you just had made?" I asked. "It's beautiful. I love the color. That shade of blue agrees with you. Just a hint of green, like the ocean."

As she turned to model it, the shirt rose up, exposing four short, perfectly identical slits at the base of her spine.

"Hey, are those your tribal markings?"

"Uh-huh."

"Those are nice, Lorraine. So cute and delicate."

"Yes," Idia agreed. "I like the way you do it over here so much more than the way they do it in some parts of the West and the South. They just slice up your face like they were carving chickens. For the men, it's not so bad. They're men. Who really cares what they look like. But the women. Ei!"

"But of course," Lorraine said softly, "the people who do it would think the scars are beautiful, wouldn't they? So they would most likely see a marked face as much more appealing than an unmarked face. And besides, I hear a lot of guys aren't doing that anymore anyway."

"It's true," Idia said. "A lot of the young people at home are more like me. They don't have them. At least"—she smiled wickedly—"not on their faces anyway."

"You guys!" Charlie called from where she waited in a tangle of passersby at the edge of Mama Ngina Street. Like a gently oiled cocoa bean, broken and smelling sharply of earth, her skin glistened in the light, even from a distance. What I loved about Charlie was that her mind stayed in an almost perpetual state of accelerated motion. She had a bursting spirit that always seemed to be entirely too big for a body that barely came up to even my shoulders. As soon as her eyes caught ours, she peeled off, slicing a path through a crowd of bodies that parted in front of her like storm-blown reeds.

Her name, Charlie, stood in some crazy way for Tshakatumbala. No one ever thought to call her by her Christian name, Marianetta. It just didn't fit.

Over the crinkly gray heads of the bubble-gum-and-match sellers and at least a fabric shop and a bookstore away, she yelled:

"Here I am! Sawa sawa! Now what's going on? Where to?"

We headed back toward Moi Avenue, giggling over the horror of final exams and the marriage proposal that Lorraine had received the week before. She had never met her suitor personally, but the man had heard a stellar report about her through a family friend and had taken it upon himself to visit with her father.

"Are you considering it?" I asked.

"Not really," she sighed. "But my father is. It appears that this man Kangemi is very rich, you see."

We all groaned at the same time.

"He's probably old and fat, with sweaty, stinking balls the size of melons."

"Idia, stop!" Charlie screamed.

"Stop, eh? And which pot's lid are you? You can't tell me to stop. The truth is the truth. Tell the truth and shame the devil. That's what my mother says."

"But you don't know that it's the truth," I said. I had to cover my mouth with my hand so that people passing wouldn't see me laugh. Idia was just plain scandalous.

She rolled her eyes. "It might as well be. But who cares anyway, ya? All Lorraine really has to do is say no. Well, she might have to cry and beg a little, but her parents aren't evil or backward or anything. They won't force her. So let's talk about something else. Something of much greater importance."

"You?" Lorraine wondered.

"Of course. What else is there? Look, you guys. I need your help. I'm doing a project for my Family and Society sociology class, and I have to go out into the field to do some firsthand research. I chose to write about the Samburu so I need to figure out a way to get to the highlands, ya? But I'm not sure how to go about finding someone to stay with. Not a lodge or anything. A real family. What do you think I should do?"

Charlie stopped in the middle of the street and whirled around with her mouth agape.

"But why would you want to go there?" she cried. "Those guys are backward, yaani. They're savages."

I stopped.

What?

"I'm telling you," Charlie pressed, "it's not safe. Those highland tribes can't be trusted. It's like they refuse to come into the twentieth century. All they're good for is herding goats and warring with each other. You don't see any of them at uni do you? There's a reason for that."

"That's a bit harsh, don't you think?" Lorraine asked.

Charlie shook her head and clucked her tongue. "I am sorry, you guy, but that's how I feel. My father used to talk about it all the time, and I agree with what he says. He says that tribes like the Maasai and Samburu get so much attention from outsiders, especially Mzungus, because that is exactly how outsiders want to see Africans. We're supposed to be hunting lions in the bush with spears and pangas and then drinking their blood. We're supposed to still be living in huts with dirt floors and running naked to and fro with bones through our noses. The noble savage. There is nothing noble about it, yaani. Fine, maybe a lot of guys do still live the traditional way, you know, without any modern conveniences. But most of them don't do so because they *want* to. They live that way because they *have* to right now. There aren't so many resources available for the people back in the villages and rural areas. I understand that. But to make romance about a bunch of savages who *choose* to live that way? Ach! It makes no sense to me. Ridiculous. I'm not so much talking about you, Idia, because you're African too, but so many other people don't want to be informed about the other reality, the way the rest of us live.

"I'm telling you, girl." She smiled finally and tried to make light. "They're going to try to marry you off to one of those warriors, and if that doesn't work, they'll try to eat you or some such nonsense. You go study the Luos or the Kalinjin. Now, those are tribes. Kwisha!"

I heard them laughing and knew that they were waiting for me to laugh too. Or to do something, anything at all. But I couldn't. Couldn't move. Couldn't breathe. My thoughts flew high over my head, colliding, diving, rising sluggishly, then not at all, unrecognizable through the thick girders of white sunlight that suddenly separated me from my friends. These tired thoughts of mine lay bruised and scattered on the ground in front of my toes, flitting back and forth like the clouds of fat, black termites that come flying up out of the ground after every heavy rain. I watched my thoughts die slowly in the dirt, like the termites invariably do, crawling about in confused and frustrated circles, their paper-and-vein wings snapped off by vicious updrafts and drifting uselessly on the wind above their heads.

Do they—do I—am I—do they all think like that? Is that how they really see me? What they really feel about me? No. Not me. Because I've never told anyone who I am. And isn't that why I never told? Because I am a coward, because they would think I was

a savage, a

fool. I've been such a fool. What if everything I have ever done, have ever believed in, is as foolish and backward as Charlie makes it sound? What if my parents' lives meant nothing? Then all that they taught me meant nothing. All that my Father fought and suffered and bled for meant nothing. All that my mother clung to meant nothing. All that I was—all that I am—is nothing. Worst of all, it means that Nasieku died for nothing. It means that her life and not her death had been an unfortunate accident. Her death was only an unnecessary one.

"Well, I don't care. I'm going," was what Idia finally said.

And there I was, in the middle of an open road with a bus and a mat hooting at us and Charlie grabbing my hand. I believe she said *What's wrong with you* but her voice blended into the buzz of the traffic and I wasn't sure so I answered the only thing I could get out of my mouth.

"Yes . . . yes . . . I'm coming . . . "

THAT EVENING I sought out Augustin.

I waited until the path leading to the maintenance officers' quarters was empty before I ran up to the door. Afraid of making too much noise and attracting attention, I pushed open the door and peeked my head inside instead of knocking. Augustin sat alone in front of a chessboard drinking a big bottle of Tusker beer.

"Supa," I whispered.

"Supa, siangiki. What a surprise. I was just now thinking of you."

His gingerroot lips parted and his teeth clicked as he opened up his mouth and smiled a smile of eggshells and ivory. The door that opened in his smile shamed me, made me slink away, like Lot's wife, with my back to the setting sun.

"No, no. Don't go. Please come in and have a seat." He patted the wooden chair next to him. "I suppose you don't drink beer, eh? So sorry, but I haven't got anything else."

"No, I'm sorry. I shouldn't disturb you."

"That is nonsense. You shouldn't be talking like that. I thought you were a smart girl. If you were half as clever as you look, you would know that you could never disturb me."

He dropped his head as he spoke, suddenly looking almost as embarrassed as I. "Now, how can I help you?"

I had no idea. I really hadn't thought this thing through any further than knocking at the door. For no reason other than that I had nothing else to say, I blurted, "I was going for a walk. I thought you might join me."

"But of course."

At the back end of the campus we waded through a wall of tall brown grass that hadn't been cut by the maintenance men because the schoolrooms were not yet ready for use. These rooms were like cabins and made out of red wood, with two classrooms in the center, one on the left side and one on the right. They were connected by a walkway into an open-ended square that had two staircases on either side of it. In the center, a plot of upturned earth waited impatiently for someone to remember to plant the seeds that would turn it into a beautiful garden. People would step out of their classrooms, look down, and exclaim, "How lovely!" But for now, the place was barren and forgotten except by the crickets and the tiny, spotted brown frogs that leapt between the wooden planks in the floors and hid inside unused desks. The windowsills and blackboards were peopled with persistent families of red ants that had been disturbed when the earth had been turned upside down. Sausage bugs nested in the rafters, and spindly mosquitoes skimmed the feathered tops of the weeds, searching for the warmth and the heat of fresh blood. Silence clung desperately to the legs of the crickets and ground the reddening sunlight down to dust.

We eased down onto the walkway side by side, with our legs dangling over the edge.

Augustin discreetly turned his face from me before he spoke.

"So, if you don't mind me asking, what seems to be the trouble? And don't shake your head like you've nothing to say. We are family, siangiki. There is no need for false pride. I'll help if I can."

I opened my mouth to say that I was sorry. That I had been mistaken and really, truly hadn't anything further to say. That I needed to be heading back to my flat before it got too dark. But none of those words came out.

Instead, my Father came out. My dead mother came out. All the rest of my dead and dying dreams came tumbling out and I was useless to stop them from falling, from becoming brittle, dusty fodder for a stillborn garden.

And I spoke out all the shame and all the fear, all the doubt and desire, until there were no more tears left on my tongue and my heart had been wrung clean.

By the time every necessary thing had been said, Ngai had blessed the sunless sky and named her Aurora. He'd plucked the cast-off stars from her streaking violet hair and held them close in his cupped hands, preparing for another daybreak.

The last thing Augustin said before I fell asleep on his chest was, "Whether you like it or not, it is your family and your tribe that really shapes you. You can fight against that for the rest of your life if you want, but it's much easier to just accept it. Look around you. You see how crazy guys act around here—here at university, I mean? Well, do you see any of the day students acting that way? No. And I'll tell you why. Because they have to go home every night, where they have parents and uncles and brothers watching them. They wouldn't dare let their families catch them skipping classes or sleeping around with God knows who and all that nonsense. They wouldn't live to see another day, yaani, I promise you. But people like you who are kind of cut off, who have a little bit of breathing space, well, for you guys the sky's the limit! You see, very few are smart enough or strong enough to carry their families and their traditions up here," he said, tapping his forehead, "when they are not right here." And he reached out for my arm.

"Perhaps we are smartest when we leave them and their prejudices and mistakes behind completely," I ventured quietly.

Augustin didn't answer at first. He hummed a snatch of a lingala tune and rocked me to the beat.

Finally he sighed and said, "It's just not possible, yaani. It can't be done."

CHAPTER *Fifteen*

. . . .

CHARLIE'S WORDS HUMMED mosquitolike in my ears until they drowned out every other word in my head that I had worked for over a year to conjure up. And it wasn't simply about her and her prejudices. It was about all the other people around me, laughing loud with their eyes as I walked by but never opening their mouths to offer as much as a simple greeting. On some days I believed it was all in my head. And on other days I knew that the time would come when all of their smart, privileged faces would silently metamorphose into my brother Lolorok's bloated face and I would be shunned and turned out. I had no place, no shield, no shade. My mother's hut had been battered to the ground, and my own, standing by itself in the sun, seemed lost and unbalanced. What would these so-called peers of mine say, the ones who took their holidays in Europe's gold and silver snows, the ones whose parents employed my uncles and cousins to work in their garages and fields, if they found out that both of my parents had been prisoners? That my mother had died a prisoner, and not of any brutal lashing or dramatic attempt at escape, but of her own inability to say no?

I hadn't the energy or the desire to fight even one of them if it came to it. All I wanted was to sit back and breathe deeply. To feel safe, the way I felt with Augustin's throat vibrating against my temple. And as far as I could tell, the only way to do that was to become like them. Like Lorraine. Like Angela. Like Paula, Idia, and all the rest of them. Like Charlie.

To begin with, I took a boyfriend.

He was a soft-voiced, dark-haired German boy named Tobias who had lived in so many different countries growing up that he often forgot which language he was speaking in idle conversation. He would begin a thought in Swahili but end it in Turkish or English or French and be none the wiser until a confused listener dragged his nonsense under his nose and made him sniff it. Tobias's father, the ambassador, had abandoned him at university, racing home to the gentle Teutonic forests of his childhood literally hours after his three-year tour of duty in Africa was officially finished. He never even told his son good-bye face to face. He sent Tobias an e-mail with instructions to call him at the house in Berlin. He could reverse the charges, of course, but give it about three days before ringing up as he and the stepmom needed some time to settle in. That's the reason I liked Tobias. He was just as alone as I was. We had no reason to hide from each other.

But in trying so desperately to fit in, I had made myself obvious and obtrusive. People stared at me when I walked down the street. Tobias said it was because of my beauty. He said it was because I had secrets sitting in the cushion of my lips like flowers to be plucked, and it made me irresistible. I knew it was because I walked arm in arm with an arrogant-looking white man who wore his heel-clicking authority like a tight suit of clothes.

That's when the whispering began. *Nusu-nusu.* I never heard it so much at university, where people appreciated Tobias and his Europeanness. But on the road, in the crowded marketplaces, in bake shops and tilting, sun-burnt kiosks, in those places people pointed me out with a quick stab of their chins aimed in our general direction and spoke in their rustling, nighttime voices about giving away the race. Fifty-fifty, they said and not because of my parentage this time, but because of my choice. Half in, half out.

Nusu-nusu. Young women with babies dangling between their breasts, old women walking curved roads with straight backs and bowed eyes, the dusty, shrunken women at school who washed my clothes, they all said it softly. One morning, about six months into the thing, I stayed the night at his flat. We left for classes the next morning, staggering out into the feel of a cool, pink dawn. I noticed the way the gossamer light filtered through the powdery jacaranda blossoms and then, belatedly, the three barefoot women who slowed down specifically to point and cluck their tongues at me. The noise they made was loud, deliberate. Sounded like Kedua sucking her teeth. Disgusted. Perhaps that's why I almost didn't see them. Instead, my mind roamed steady with my hand over the creases and wrinkles of Tobias's baby finger and the side of his palm. It was Tobias who pointed the women out to me.

We were strolling through the lush suburb where he lived, deep in the twisting Westlands hills just north of Nairobi. All around us, glorious red-tiled houses, mainly of Spanish or Italian design, clung to the cracks and furrows in the hillside, crouching behind rainbow sprays of bougainvilleas and white lilies weeping with dew. Pink roses, licked crimson round the edges, jutted out from behind attended gates made tall with imported wrought iron. Trees on each side of the sloping concrete road formed arches above us, sprinkling and dotting our heads, our laughter, our joined hands with pale sun drops that slipped through pointed, quivering breaks in the leaves. We walked alone on the early-morning road except for the houseboys and maids making their way to work.

I followed the women's eyes back to my own body, my hand specifically, which at that moment swung jauntily enmeshed in the left hand of a white man. A white man whose smiling lips pressed themselves into my ear (in the middle of the road, imagine!) and who languorously, almost drunkenly, breathed in the scent of birch and sunflowers oiled into my hair. A white man who, from the almost feverish way his eyes guarded me as they got close, was obviously not my john. When Tobias pointed them out to me, he chose to laugh at their bare feet and hard eyes, but somehow I couldn't find the humor in being disdained. That triangle of tight jaws and the firm creases in their lips pushed me back into that vulnerable place of my childhood called the Middle. It's a dubious place to be, shadowy and inconsistent, neither here nor anywhere. A space where thoughts and deeds are wide open to ridicule regardless of intent. The place from which he was supposed to be helping me to escape.

More frustrated and uncertain than ever, I begged off from Tobias when we got to campus, skipped my class, and ran straight up the dry-bones path to the maintenance shack. Augustin wasn't in. In his absence, the emptiness that tended the shack's rickety, wind-crippled walls began pushing in on me, squeezing down on my chest. I felt weak enough to cry. But still, I was too embarrassed to ask his whereabouts of the other porters. So instead I asked the one called Peter if he might come and repair the plugged-up toilet in my room at the flats. The little man's barking laugh told me that he wasn't fooled, but he nodded quickly and promised to be up directly after lunch.

Mortified by their smirking silence, I slipped away, wondering how I had gotten so high up and dignified that I couldn't find a way back down to where I needed to be. I stumbled back down the path, tied to my loneliness like a heifer being sat on and stilled by many anxious, blood-wet hands as they truss her for slaughter; bucking in the heat, she is already buried in a death of dusted nettles and loam.

More than seven miles I walked that day, trying to evade all of the confusion and anger and fear that skulked so doggedly behind me. I walked the whole long way into town, in fact, wading in the places where the walkways cracked and faltered or disappeared entirely through feather-headed weeds that crept up under my skirt to tickle my thighs.

I headed down the shoulder of Uhuru Highway, finally stopping to rest in Uhuru Park. With nothing else to do and nowhere left to go, I sat on the hillside in front of the pond and made up stories about the people rushing along like a determined black river below me. The park calmed me. The wide reach of the acacia trees seemed like bright green watercolor brush strokes. Unsteady and intangible. Short, slim-trunked, umbrella-shaped trees with eruptions of sunshine-yellow blossoms on top lined the walkways. In the center of the pond sat a man-made island, crusted around the edges with smoothed-over white, gray, and coral stones. On top of the island's grassy knoll stood a single, droopy palm tree that looked more akin to a willow, its heavy leaves practically touching the ground.

In this place, finally, I felt I could breathe and know that the air filling my lungs wouldn't hurt me. It wouldn't be a chore to exhale and then have to contemplate the rigors of doing it all over again. In this place, I could fantasize about my grandmothers roaming the plains and the forests and not feel inadequate. Watching couples row the small white boats away from the jetty at the foot of the hill, I pictured the happier times of my childhood. The times when I'd trailed behind my mother and her husband, Ngatuny, being alone with them when none of the other children were allowed to follow.

I almost wasn't surprised when Augustin eased down beside me and began speaking. As usual, he skipped cordial greetings.

"So what has been going on, bwana?" he whispered.

To explain his presence is like explaining the bursting, nut-brown banks of the Isiolo River—dry for a lifetime, then suddenly pregnant and throbbing, pushing out the fatted, thundering rains of a healer's prayer.

"Nothing out of the usual," I answered. Then, as my breath began to come back to me, I asked, "Say, bwana, how did you find me, eh?"

"I saw you leave the porters' quarters and I followed you from uni."

"*What?* You joke! You mean to tell me that you walked this entire morning behind me and I never saw you?"

He nodded. "You seemed pretty oblivious to most things, I have to say, not just me. That's why I didn't approach you. Don't laugh, but I remembered some bit about sleepwalkers and how they shouldn't be disturbed for fear that they might hurt themselves. So I left you alone. But I was quite worried, so I figured I'd best stay nearby. Now what were you thinking about?"

"My parents . . ."

". . . and what they would think of you if they could see you sitting here just now?"

I nodded, startled and a bit annoyed at the way he took it upon himself to finish my thoughts. Was I so transparent? So foolish and easy to understand?

"Well, I don't know what they would think," he continued, "but, if you'll forgive me for saying so, I think you're being very selfish and childish."

I laughed and asked, "How so?" in mock bewilderment, as if I was amused by his bluntness. But really, Augustin's candor was like a long, deep gash across the side of my head.

"Because you're sulking like a chastised child when you haven't reason to. I look at it this way: you already live in a sort of dream world, yaani. You drive around with your friends in nice cars, wear designer clothes, and talk about traveling abroad. You listen to all types of hip-hop and reggae music. Maybe some lingala here and there. But do you even remember any of the traditional songs your mum sang to you when you were young? Everything for those guys you hang around with must be newer, faster, and better. What I'm saying is that they're terrifically spoiled. And here you are, crying like the world has stopped spinning because you can't be more like them. But those people only see themselves, yaani, and then only the reflection of themselves that is closest to what they want to believe. It's greed on top of greed. They don't give thanks for what they have, they complain about not having more. And that's what I mean about you. You are stunning to look at, bright and a good person. You have opportunities that most of our women wouldn't even think of. You have a chance to break down walls, but all you can think about is what you don't have. It's disgusting."

"That's not true! I know—"

"Hey, hey, hey, look at who you're talking to. I know you more than you could ever guess. I *watch* you. So denials are no good here. It's futile. But even in trying to deny, and just think about this, what you don't want to admit is that your world stops with you. Even this so-called relationship you have with that Mzungu, it doesn't have anything to do with him, really. It's all about you and what he gives you. With him, you can feel rich and sophisticated and included—even if you're not. Admit it. If he got fat, lost all his teeth, and went bald tomorrow, would you still be so proud of him? The real person? With all of the boasting and the insecurities? Would his whims still control your life? Eh? Speak loudly, now. What was that? Nothing. Just like I figured."

We sat in silence for a long while. There was nothing I could say.

Finally Augustin grabbed my hand and yanked me up off the ground.

"Come on," he said. "We're about to get soaked. Let's go."

Rain clouds that we had thoroughly ignored before now closed in on us quite insistently. We left the park, walking quickly down H. Tubman Road. Then, turning right onto Mbingu Street, we scurried past the Standard Street causeway, and I noticed that it was almost completely empty of the normal crowd of Thursday lunch-hour shoppers. The few like us who were still outside were already running for cover. Bloated, black clouds fell lower and lower, devouring the tall building peaks and dribbling humidity down onto the ground in long, unbearable streams. This late storm might have been the very last of the rainy season, but it also appeared to be rapidly shaping up as one of the worst. When the first heavy beads of rain fell, we began to run, laughing and dodging clinking beer bottles as the wind mischievously rolled them out under our feet. As we passed the steps in front of city hall, the clouds peeled back and the lightning began to drop.

From deep inside the hall, raised voices, thirsty and strong, sang out, "What a Friend We Have in Jesus." The sound mixed with the thunder, bringing its booming a cappella into harmony.

"I wonder what's going on in there," I said.

"It's the Christ Fellowship lunchtime meeting. They meet every afternoon. I know because I used to go at least two or three times a week. But I've been pretty busy lately. Working extra hours so I can send more money home to my parents and such. You know how it is."

In truth, I didn't know how it was to have anybody depending on me, but I said nothing.

The music was transforming. We both slowed down to listen, the calming solace in the song counteracting the sting of slashing spikes of rain. When the voices began to fade away, he took my hand and led me back toward Moi Avenue and (hopefully) a waiting school bus.

The rain shouted and screamed in our ears, drowning out all other sound, almost as if it were a human being in pain. But when we neared the corner of Mama Ngina Street and I saw the first group of the men ahead of us retreating in fear, I realized that the noise that had been sitting on my ears for the last two blocks was, in fact, a human being. I didn't want to see, didn't want to know what was happening, so I tried to turn and run. But Augustin grabbed me and locked me underneath his arm.

"Don't worry," he ordered. "Nothing can happen to you. Just hold on to me."

The chaos on Moi Avenue spread quickly to the surrounding streets and alleys. Police charged at the fleeing men with heavy black batons and whips, flailing wildly, striking anything in their path. The men dodged and shielded their heads as clubs and rifle butts came down again and again. A bearded man in a red shirt lay coiled on the ground, shrieking at an officer to please, please stop.

He wasn't guilty. He hadn't done anything. The officer's whip tore into the man's back and belly, excavating thin slivers of his skin and flesh, into which the rain continued to fall. Another officer leapt over a prone, smoldering body and tackled a fleeing woman, who immediately began crying out to God.

Almost as a second thought, I looked back at the smoking man on the ground. He lay surrounded by car tires, one of which was still wrapped hooplike around his midsection. His skin and his clothes had been burned away in great patches. Writhing on the yellow dividing line in the road, the man twisted and keened and shrieked. The noises came from way down deep in the back of his throat because his lips had also been burned away. I walked toward the man, unaware that I was even moving until I felt Augustin's arm bolted around my waist and lifting me up into the air. He pulled me back just as an officer's baton came slicing down in front of my nose, glancing off my knee. My entire leg exploded into a blaring, paralyzing wall of sound that my numbed and terrified body could not yet identify as pain.

I'm not sure what exactly happened next. I know that the police officer disappeared and then Augustin stood hovering over me with tears and rain and blood dripping off his face and onto mine. Then two pairs of hands lifted me and I floated through the street, my face pressed firmly against the sky with clouds weaving in and out of my hair and thunder rocking between my teeth.

When I woke up we were on the school bus and one of the other porters, a man named Elias, sat next to us.

"Talk to me, bwana," Augustin was saying. "Why did that happen? Why did they necklace that man on the ground back there?"

For a moment it looked as though Elias wouldn't be able to find his voice. He trembled and hiccuped, staring fearfully out of the window until the bus finally pulled off. Only after we'd cleared the roundabout over the Nairobi River and started down Muranga Road did he turn to Augustin and speak.

"They said he stole this rich Mzungu woman's purse all the way out by the Intercontinental Hotel and those sides. She started screaming, 'Thief, thief!' and before you knew it the mob gathered and chased him all the way out here. I saw people running and followed behind asking guys what happened. Then I think the man doubled back or something, so all of a sudden I was right in the middle of the thing. They caught him and wrapped him in tires and tried to set him alight with petrol. But the rain was coming down just too thick, ya? So they stuffed papers and rubbish and such inside the tires and then lit it. It burned somewhat for a minute or two, but not nearly enough to kill the guy. Then the police came and guys just scattered everywhere."

Elias dropped his voice to a whisper. "I saw you fighting with that officer, you know. All I can say is thank God you weren't caught. They surely would have killed you the way you beat that guy."

Augustin didn't answer. He just stroked the top of my head and stared out of the fogged-up window. When Elias spoke again there were tears in his mouth.

"All I wanted was to get to uni on time for my shift, ya? And here it is that I have to see all of that. And for what? For a white woman's purse that nobody even saw the guy with anyway? I just don't understand it, yaani. I just don't."

Augustin carried me to the nurse's station when we got back to campus and stayed with me all through the next week, since my leg was too swollen for me to walk or do very many things at all for myself. I found out later from Elias that he had been docked for all those days' pay, including the day of the necklacing, and was almost fired. Yet each morning when he scratched on my door with my breakfast and the morning papers he never mentioned any of these things.

I found myself writing about him in the evenings after he left my flat and then hiding the papers from Tobias. When the electricity in the flats failed, as it was wont to do every so often, I wrote about him by the light of a dozen candles, flicking like engorged stars. In candlelight, my words ran like tears. Like the earth-river of veins crisscrossing the backs of his hard hands. Like his laughter flowing down the center of my chest and pooling at the bottom of my stomach.

The first night I was well enough to walk, I made my way down the dirt road to the workers' flats east of campus. The cottages were no more than tin-roofed shacks lined up in a row with some goats and a couple of balding cattle milling about the dusty yard. I didn't even know which shack was his. I was about to turn around and hobble home when his voice reached out and caressed my hair.

"So this time you find me, siangiki."

I nodded through the darkness, for once stripped of my shield of words, without thought, without shame.

He walked from the brick well at the far end of the yard right past me. The night sky rocked neither moon nor stars against its breast, so I could not see more than a roaming shadow until he opened the door to his tiny home and lit a lantern.

I followed him inside, full of tears and promises and he loved me, silently, steadily, until it was time for me to go home again.

❧

I LIVED in that shack with Augustin, every night after dark, for the next year and a half.

Tobias followed me there once not too long after I broke things off with him. After spying through the window, he went back and reported to anyone who would listen that I had abandoned him, the ambassador's son, to go off and fuck the Samburu janitor on the dirt floor of his hut. No one dared ask me if these allegations were true, but they flocked to Lorraine, demanding answers.

Lorraine clucked her tongue at each and every face at our door.

"Of course it's not true." She smiled. "Tobias is angry and seeking excuses. Just between us, bwana, he simply wants to ruin her reputation because in spite of all that time alone together and all of his flattery and fancy gifts, she never, ah, well, she never *reciprocated* his feelings, if you follow my meaning. And he could never quite understand why. I suppose he's just making things up to make himself feel better. Who knows. One thing I know that's certain is that no matter how late it might be, she is here each night before I go to bed."

But when we were alone, she was much more direct. One morning, perhaps a month or two before graduation, Lorraine waited up for me as I came sneaking into the room just after dawn. She sat quite still on the edge of her bed, the thick down of her duvet puffing around her body like a petticoat, with her slim ankles folded underneath her and her hands immobile in her lap. The anger never rose in her voice, only in the deepening color of her cheeks.

"You must be more careful, Nasarian. I cannot understand why it is that I continually repeat to you things you must already know. You have no family. No brothers to care for you." (I had never told her about Lolorok.) "If you spoil your name and make it so that you can't find a good husband, what are you going to do then, eh? Where will you live when you leave here? I know first-hand of at least four other guys here at uni who have inquired about you. Sister, I have lied to these men, and I don't like to lie to anyone. Now, I've seen this janitor of yours lurking around the flats looking for you, and I admit that he's quite beautiful. I've even heard the other girls whispering about him. But that's just it. It's only whispering. What could that porter possibly give a girl like you? A girl who is about to get her university degree and probably her master's as well? Someone who can attract the sons of ambassadors and bankers and government ministers? What could you possibly have in common?"

Everything, I wanted to shout at her. But I didn't dare. Instead I nodded, feeling every bit the chastised child that Augustin always accused me of being, and drew my bedcovers up under my chin. The sunlight was already creeping through my window, and I only had about an hour or so to nap before it would be time for me to rise and make my way to my morning class. There was no use in spending that time bickering.

How could I ever explain to a much loved, much petted child like Lorraine what it meant to look into someone else's eyes and see something you have never seen before—a reflection of your honored nakedness, silent and supple, unadorned and still unabashedly complete? What sense could it make that at the feel of the scraping-thin wool of Augustin's blanket my eyes glazed over in tears until my sight was as blinded as my heart? That though the blanket had frayed thin enough so that I could see through it in some places, the fact that it was warmed by his back and his bones sent a brighter, concentric warmth running through it like the sun over my soul? I knew that I had been chosen for a task that meant searching out alien things that had no place in his life. And sometimes when knowing and loving don't coincide, very difficult choices must be made. But as the winter quarter, my final one, whittled its way down to nothing, in frustration, in fear and desperation, I simply chose not to choose.

The month of April came. Classes ended. My graduate school acceptance letters arrived.

I spent the final afternoon of classes talking with the director of the university. My shaking fingers dipped in and out of the dimples sewn into the plush calfskin chair that was too impossibly soft for me to feel comfortable sitting in. Dr. Stevens strode back and forth in front of her marigold-garden window, rambling on about strong women making strong choices. She was an African American woman, but when she had first arrived on campus the previous September her pale skin, green eyes, and deep gold hair had led everyone to believe her to be white. And they'd treated her accordingly. Sitting over a perfect service of raisin biscuits and strong Kenyan tea fragrant with rose hips and cinnamon (her own creation), she spoke candidly of her own loneliness and doubt in those first two or three months.

Besides possibly with my mother, I had never had this type of frank discussion with an elder before. It made me nauseous. She laughed at my sweating ears and dry, puckered lips and said, It's all right to be afraid as long as you don't let your fear stop you from doing the things you know you must. But what, I whispered, if it is not fear that stops you, but love? Her head jerked up as mine immediately shot down. Did I really just say that? I thought. I've truly lost my mind. She bent over me sighing, took my face in her hands, and said, "Then it's still fear, Nasarian, because true and unconditional love never holds you back or ties you down. If it did"—she stroked my cheek with the long, oval nail of her thumb—"I wouldn't be here."

Seeing that I was still unconvinced, she added, "You know, believe it or not, one of my very best friends is an Afrikaans woman named Henrietta Fredrickson. Before I came here, I stopped over in Cape Town to visit her. While I was flying, to kill time I decided to read some literature about the different South African cultures, and I came across the most fascinating thing. There is a word in the Xhosa language, *ubuntu,* which means 'I am because we are.' Now, I want you to think carefully about that word, about the concept behind it. No person, no distance traveled, no amount of time spent apart can ever take the people you love and what they mean to you out of your heart or your mind. Because everything they mean to you, every bit of love you've ever given or received is what has made you the brilliant young woman you are."

Ubuntu. It seemed to describe so perfectly the way I had been feeling about Augustin that I decided right then and there that it would be my own private name for him. Ubuntu. Any time I thought of him or wrote about him I would use that name. Even if I never spoke it out loud, I would think it. Always.

I looked back up at Dr. Stevens. The sureness in her eyes made me wonder who I would be if this woman, and not Nima, had been my mother. Then in my very next thought I wondered why, *why* I was always so quick to want to give away my life, my identity. I abruptly changed the subject.

We went over the various offers I'd received and kept coming back to one choice: the creative writing program at Columbia University. Ivy League on a full scholarship. Most of the other places I'd applied to not only did not give scholarships to foreign students but sometimes charged them up to 50 percent more than American students for tuition and fees. Dr. Stevens insisted that I couldn't get a better education anywhere. She herself had attended undergraduate school there. *Kwisha!* we decided. Columbia. I beamed at Dr. Stevens and then cried so hard and for so long that I vomited all over her cerulean tea service and the soft, soft leather of the chair.

Out to the nurse's station we marched just as, to my horror,

Augustin turned into the corridor, headed toward Dr. Stevens's office with his ever-present mop and pail in hand. In front of the director he dared not speak, but his eyes poked at my back and wrapped tightly around my legs until I tripped over them and went sprawling onto the squeaking clean wood floor. *Oh, Augustin,* I thought, but I refused to cry tears that I couldn't explain. So I jumped up, wiped the red sting off my palms, and ran for the door with a baffled, stuttering director trailing close behind.

The indignities continued on during my physical as the nurse prodded and squeezed and raided my body for various samples. I stood there in my underwear, absolutely humiliated, hopping from bare foot to bare foot on the icy green tiles. The only thing all of this would prove, I was sure, was that I had been overworked and unrested over the past few weeks because I had been so focused on my final exams. Had I vomited before? Well, yes. Once or twice in the past couple of weeks. But it was mainly because I hadn't been eating properly, and so my stomach naturally felt shrunken and irritable.

The nurse said "pregnant" like it was what we both knew, but I wasn't at all sure what was going on, much less what to think about it, so I gathered my things without further comment and crept out the door. Halfway up the road the red-tiled roof and cinder-block facade of the flats came into view directly ahead of me. It was then that I felt the wind lapping with its wide, fast tongue at the brackish sweat between my breasts and I realized that I wore only my frayed black brassiere and skirt. No shoes, no shirt. No pride, no hope. What had filtered through the back corner of my mind as the grating, baby-cry whine of a crowing rooster suddenly became snorts of astounded laughter. In a panic, I stared down at the balled-up silk blouse crushed in my fists and then up towards the flats in front of me. So far. So much hurt and fear to wade through on the way there.

Desperate to cover the hopeless, naked tears sliding down onto my chest, I tied the lavender blouse sleeves under my right arm and over my left shoulder and made a lesso of it. Then I flung myself past the rows and clumps of anxious, flashing teeth that had already sunk themselves deep into my misery. Those gaping people, my classmates, became nothing but swollen, elongated mouths, chewing me over slowly, grinding and swallowing bitter imagination, picking their teeth with the sharp edges of my tears.

If they all thought I was crazy before, well, now they had proof.

Augustin found me upstairs, hiding under my bed and weeping. Strong arms couldn't reach past the fragile dust pockets and the leg clicks of a family of black beetles singing through my hair. Strong words couldn't soothe the secrets stuffed between a slim foam mattress and the white-like-bone-splinters wall. He didn't belong in this sterile place, this place where dreams were hatched, not birthed. No love had ever been had in this room. And it showed.

Unable and unwilling to face him, I grabbed my baby by the feet like a broom, swinging and sweeping, hoping to clear him out.

"Go away! I don't have to tell you anything. No. No, wait. Do you really want to know what the matter is? Good. Sawa sawa. I will tell you. I've fallen pregnant. That's what the matter is. Are you satisfied now? No! Don't you dare speak. Just go. There's no more damage to be done here. In fact, I reckon there is nothing at all that a man like you can do for me. Including care for my child or teach it how to be anything more than an illiterate porter!"

Augustin didn't bother to close the door behind him.

The openness, the stale draft sailing through the corridor,

under the eagle's-claw feet of the wardrobe and around the creaking metal legs of the bed frame, came finally to nest under my armpits and in the fine down on my shoulders. It smelled of tin rooftops and honey. Dust and milk. Dried, cracking eucalyptus leaves and the exasperation of burning hair in a curling iron. It fused with the boy-funk of thrown and forgotten shoes idling on banisters and landings.

People all around and outside of me were doing things, being free and unafraid. Why couldn't I be the same? What was it that kept escaping me? The same thing, I reckoned, that turned around and trapped me time and again. The thing that made me say cruel words that perhaps, at least to a certain degree, I actually meant but that still had no business in my mouth. The thing inside me making sure that, no matter what, I ended up alone.

Nima, whom I called on and begged for and wept over, never answered me. Her spirit of still waters and redemption stayed silent. And no other punishment could possibly have been greater. Instead, my Father, Ngatuny, crept under my bed, lacing himself like wire-thin shoestrings around my thighs and up over my stomach. I couldn't understand why it was his memory that should come to hold my hand in the middle of this deeply personal woman's time. But there he was—his laugh, his clean, rawhide smell, his empty and sullen eyes. He felt so much like Augustin. So much like my future.

Just then, I heard the light tread of his feet and the latch on the door as it clicked softly behind him. After praising God, I wondered why in the world Augustin would come back after the things I'd said.

"Come out, siangiki. We must speak."

I didn't move. I couldn't.

He sighed, bent down, and slid four thick, glittering gold hoops under the bed directly in front of my face.

"Siangiki, I don't pretend to understand these tears and dramatics. I have never met the woman who does not believe that children are the greatest blessing a family can have. Maybe not too many children if, as you pointed out, there are no means to support them. But that is not the case here—no matter what you might think."

"But I am not the woman for you."

"Yes! Yes, you are. I've known that since the moment I saw you." He sat on the floor against the wall at the head of the bed. "Let me tell you a secret I've been holding on to. Two days before we met, I went to my laa manyit to discuss a disturbing dream I had been having. In the dream, I was at home alone in my family's manyatta. All of a sudden I heard the cattle in the boma start screaming—actually shrieking and screaming like they were people. I ran over and found the boma full of vomit and feces. All of the cattle were dead or dying. All but one. The rest looked to have the East Coast fever. Their hides were eaten away and they had open sores everywhere that dripped pus. But whatever the case, they were beyond saving.

"Then I felt something moving around in my mouth. When I opened my mouth, three teeth came rolling out. I put my hand in my mouth to see which teeth they were only to find that I had no more left. I held my last three teeth in my hand. I couldn't believe it, so I opened my mouth even wider to examine further, and that's when the blue ticks, the ones that cause the fever, came crawling out of my throat. A whole swarm of them. This is the point where I always awoke. The laa manyit said the dream indicated change. But nothing like what I was thinking. No one in my family was in any jeopardy. He said that I should watch out because sometime soon I would meet a woman who owned three faces, only two of which I would ever see, whose love I could not conquer because her spirit skimmed both the treetops and the river's rocky bed in the same breath of time. But this, nonetheless, would be the woman for me. I would love this woman beyond all reason and time. She, in turn, would set me free. At this point I was to become her greatest challenge, the mouth of her path to God.

"I don't pretend to understand all of it," he continued, "not by any means. And I know that there was more that he didn't tell me. All I am certain of is that when I saw you creeping through that gate, I knew without a doubt in my soul that you were the woman that he spoke of. I went out that very afternoon and put money down on those earrings lying in front of you. In fact, I've only just finished paying them off. Less than a month ago. We both know I cannot afford the type of bride-price that a girl like you would carry. All I hoped for when I first saw you was that, when the time came, you would love me enough to forgo the bride-price, at least for now, and instead accept these as a token of my devotion.

"Nas, you can't begin to understand how many times I wanted to just run up and grab you and steal you away. But I remembered what the laa manyit said about your love never being conquered. So I waited for you to come to me. And you never did. I am still waiting, siangiki, for you to come to me like a woman comes to a man she loves and respects. In the light of day. Without shame and without doubt. What? Why should you cry again now? Did you think I didn't know? I may be an illiterate porter, as you put it, but I am not a foolish man, Nasarian. Neither am I blind. But the time for waiting and game playing is over. We have a child to look after and care for now. The say-so is no longer yours."

I recoiled when he said that, realizing for the first time that there is a certain freedom to be had in fear and uncertainty. A freedom to change. And here he was telling me that I had just lost something that I'd never even realized that I wanted or needed.

"What are you saying?"

I asked what I already knew just so that the words would be forced to take shape in front of me. So that they could never be called back or denied.

"I'm saying that starting tomorrow morning I'm taking a leave of absence from work and will go home to arrange for your circumcision. Then, when you have healed, we will be allowed to be officially married. My child will have my clan and my name and my home. Nothing else really matters from there. We can make any other decisions when I get back."

"But what if . . . what if I . . . say . . . no?"

"There is no saying no. Not anymore. Listen to me, Nasarian—what do you have in this life if you have no people? No family? No home to return to? You have nothing, that's what. I don't care what lofty ideas have been put into your head about school or writing, you must admit that there is no degree or certificate you could receive that would ever take precedence over your family. Now, I know that my family needs me and I need them. And you need them too, whether you realize it or not. We could sit here and argue this all day, but in the end, I will be with them and so will my child."

He left me with promises of love and a safe, quick return. But did I want him to return? Really? I didn't know. Nothing was certain to me except that someone out there, someone that I had never seen, who lived thousands of miles away from me in a country I had no firsthand knowledge of, had looked at my words on a piece of paper and determined me to be exceptional. Worthy. Ready. But what would that mean to a child who had no father? No home? How selfish did I intend to be with my life?

Augustin was wrong about one thing, however. My writing and my education were much more than just ideas flipping up against my teeth. The need to create had taken on a life of its own inside me. It leeched onto my mind, my body, something like an extra thumb that had grown overnight on a whim and for no more reason than to spite me, to make me drop the things I was sure I had in a perfectly solid grip. The longer I waited and thought about it, the more intensely it twisted and bucked in front of my eyes, a forgotten flag slapped by March wind, bled of all its color and dying. No. I had to go. Anyway, the choice to leave was not particularly mine to make, I felt, because of the way this desire had seeded itself inside me, like a mischievous, petulant child. The words had found me, dogging and haunting me endlessly. Not the other way around. Since Nasieku had died, they had been my reason for walking and sleeping and breathing and crying in a way that Augustin seemed to fear and so had never even tried to understand. My words clung to me, almost as tightly embedded in my womb as my real child, demanding my attention. They kicked hard, feeding off my blood.

Right or wrong, I had to fight for what I needed. Didn't I? Well, what would Nima say? But Nima was dead, so what she thought or would have said hardly mattered I reasoned. (I was such a fool.) And where did that leave me? What was my choice? What would Ngatuny do? It kept coming back to me that my Father would fight. So should I not fight as well? But then again, I was my Father's daughter, not my Father's son. How many things did I want to change at once?

Everything.

While Augustin was gone, I finalized my plans to leave.

I hadn't told Lalasi that I was graduating a full year early, three years instead of four, so as usual, he sent money to me for the next four quarters. I intended to use it for a passport and an airplane ticket. On my way back from the post office, I got to thinking about Lalasi. He must have been broken financially from paying all my fees for so long. He probably had nothing left in the world. *Hiya!* I laughed out loud just thinking about it and did a back-curling, foot-stomping strut in the dust as I skipped, money in hand, down the road toward Dr. Stevens's office at school. It served him right. But he had fulfilled his part of the deal, and I knew I couldn't expect a shilling more. So I planned and plotted down to the last bob how else to spend what I would have left.

With Dr. Stevens to vouch for me, I got a passport within three weeks, even though I didn't have my Father's signature. (Dr. Stevens managed this impossibility, I found out later, by speaking with one of the managers she knew at the passport office in town. The woman's son, coincidentally, had an application for university sitting right on the edge of her desk.) Columbia had a program where I could arrive in early June, so as to get acclimated to my new surroundings and learn to find my way around the campus before being bombarded with work in the fall. I was sure I wouldn't be able to find an affordable airline ticket in time, but even that worked out. I was scheduled to leave Nairobi from Kenyatta Airport on June 5, with a twelve-hour layover in London, and arrive in New York City the next day. I couldn't believe that things had worked out so perfectly for me.

Until Augustin came back.

He sent word with Elias that he wanted me to come to his cottage in the evening. He had a surprise for me. The moment Elias closed my door, I darted into the loo and vomited.

I couldn't go to New York. Not now. Had I ever really wanted to go? Or was I just hiding from the one thing in my life that, up to that trip to the nurse's station, had never caused me pain or grief? No. That wasn't true either. Augustin had caused me pain. Or, more correctly, his presence brought up pains that I would just as soon have ignored.

But I had to go to him. He was waiting.

The yellow light spurting through the holes in his gray burlap curtains seemed brighter that night. Or maybe I stood outside the shack longer. Wondering, weighing my mind, changing my decision thrice and then one last time as my shaking hand hovered above the door handle. How could I tell him I was leaving him in less than three weeks to study abroad when he didn't even know I had applied to graduate school? How could I tell myself that I was staying? Even though, I decided finally, that is what I had to do.

Just as I pressed down on the handle, the door flew open and there he was, smelling of old sunlight. His lips were dry, cracked from road dust and heat, but as he kissed me, I felt the press of silk underneath the gently peeling skin. He lifted me in the air, swaying and spinning. Over his broad shoulder I watched white and brown moths collide, scrambling to get toward the lantern's glowing heat. The odor of good, thick goat stew and ugali wafted up with the moths and then out into the yard. The tender, pungent smell said the meat was ready and waiting to be eaten.

But wait. Augustin couldn't cook.

"Allow me, mother, to carry you in to your surprise," he laughed.

He swooped me in through the doorway and set me down in the middle of the floor.

In front of me on the floor sat an exquisite young woman of about my age. Her ebon skin shone in the lamplight and her scalp had obviously been freshly shaved. Beneath the broad reach of her nose, her lips quivered. Full lips, warm-looking and firm. Sable lips made for smiling demure smiles and saying yes to sharing all that she owned. I couldn't see into her eyes because they were cast down at the dirt floor. Modest. Self-effacing. Good. The woman had obviously washed and changed clothes, because while Augustin was still wrinkled and streaked with sweat stains and grime, she had on a crisp, coral lesso embroidered throughout with crimson roses. In her lap, a small gift lay wrapped in a bottle-green handkerchief.

How much had she spent on this new material? On that gift? All of the money for her provisions for two weeks? Three weeks? How much? How much did she give? And all of this just to meet me.

"Ndama." He addressed her first. "This is your new co-wife, Nasarian. Nasarian, this is your new senior wife, Ndama."

Ndama looked up at me then and smiled prettily. But her eyes lingered on my blue jeans, on the scarlet toenails poking through my sandals, and on my curled hair. She glanced up at her husband quickly before allowing her smile to falter.

The look on my face must have been not just surprised or taken aback but horrified, because Augustin began babbling.

"I hope you're not too startled to sit down and eat with us. Ha ha! You know, I'm thinking that I probably should have explained about Ndama a long while ago. But to be quite honest, I wasn't sure how you would react. However, when all is said and done, this is going to be the best thing that could happen to any of us. Now, I've been considering this situation for the entire trip. Nas, I know that you don't want to settle down in the village just yet. Well, we don't have to. After the marriage and after the baby is born, we can give him over to Ndama to care for at home. She hasn't been able

252 • KUWANA HAULSEY

to conceive yet, even though it's been almost four years now. It's probably all my fault, of course. I don't go home but two or three times a year. But whatever the case, she can mother the baby back at home. That way Ndama has a child to look after, the child will have her and the rest of the family, I can keep my job, and you can get a job here in the city and work as much as you want to. With the money we save over the next couple of years, whenever we do decide to go home, we will be able to afford to live comfortably. What do you think?"

"I'm . . . I'm sorry," I stuttered. "I didn't even really hear you. I'm just standing here thinking about the fact that I have no . . . no gift for Ndama. I feel ashamed. Pardon me, Ndama, but I had no idea . . . about any of this. I have no proper welcome for you. Please, allow me to go back to my room at the flats. I'm sure I can find . . . something. It might not be a proper gift, but at least I will not feel the shame of being empty-handed."

Bowing my head at both of them, I backed out of the door, shutting it softly behind me.

And I ran.

CHAPTER Sixteen

. . . .

I HAVE NO MEMORY of walking the road that night, no memory of the sun dawning over the towering rooftops in town (which is where I wound up, walking the violet streets with the prostitutes, the orphans, and the parking boys—all of us homeless in a sense). All I was remotely aware of were my kaleidoscope thoughts crashing and banging together. Confused and hostile.

He'd betrayed me.

No, actually, he hadn't.

His wives were his business. Back home, sometimes girls didn't know that the negotiations for their own marriages had even started until the groom showed up at the door with the bride-price and the bull for sacrifice to start the ceremony. No, he didn't owe me any of his secrets. And besides, was it not right and just for a man to have many women? After all, my own Father had four wives. I had grown up loving all of them—well, all except Kedua. But people today looked down on that type of thing. Today there was one man for each woman and one woman for each man. *But not back home.* That was the point I'd continued to gloss past. Our families were still different. And what did you have in this life if you didn't have the love and respect of your family? Or the safety, security, and comfort of a home?

If I left, I would have freedom. But the freedom to do what? To try and fail? I couldn't even picture success. What did it look like? How did it taste? And how can you believe in something you can't even see? Not even in your own mind?

Faith. The word stole into my head like a fugitive. Faith: the thing that my mother had in abundance but that still couldn't save her. The thing that my Father, for all of his wisdom, all of his children, all of the influence that his respected position bought him, had lacked almost completely. Did I have faith? Whose child was I? Really? My thoughts fought inside me like little, wounded animals, blinded and desperate, searching for space.

I walked through that morning dazed and cramping badly. This baby was angry, and she refused to hide it. No consideration at all for me. See, it was starting already. One cramp hit, feeling like someone had taken a razor to my intestines, and I doubled over, weeping silently.

Then I heard it again. That same singing I had heard on the day of the storm, the day that I'd found Augustin sitting beside me underneath the spinning yellow blossoms in the park. The song was different, a Swahili song this time, but the soaring, pleading voices hadn't changed at all.

I followed the sound off the sidewalk and up the stairs into the meeting hall, walking in just as the service was about to end.

The arcing wave of the pastor's voice receded to a trickle as the vestiges of the final prayer, the prayer of safe journey, dripped off the eaves of the packed balcony.

"Oh, heavenly Father," he soothed, "guide your children safely back to their homes or their offices or their stores or wherever your spirit will lead them. And no matter where they go, no matter what the devil may throw in their paths to make them stumble or fall, we know that according to your word, they shall be more than conquerors . . ."

No matter where we go. Conquerors.

And the people said, "Amen. Amen."

Hobbled metal chair legs scraped against the concrete floor and, as quietly as I stepped in, I stepped back out, filing out with the brothers and sisters rushing toward the door at the rear of the auditorium. They were anxious, now that prayer was done, to get out of the makeshift meeting room in city hall and back to the kitchens and kiosks and offices where they worked. The churning bodies roused the sleepy shit smell that slid from under the doors of the two first-floor lavatories. The signs above the knobs said OUT OF ORDER, but the doors themselves were wide open. The stench lodged itself into my clothes and into the tears that scraped my eyes as I felt arms and shoulders brushing my body. Too many people. Too close. Too soon. Rushing, pressing, pulling. I began to panic. My throat contracted and suddenly I couldn't breathe. The crowd . . . smelled of simmering urine . . . not them . . . the loo . . . the loo smelled . . . of shit baking in the heat. The odor overpowered me as it poured roughshod through the wide hall, banging through the tall metal doors and roiling out into the street.

The brothers and sisters charged out after it, vanishing down the steps in front of the doors and into a wide mouth of sunlight. Two of the women squeezed so close to me that I could smell the Omo soap in their white blouses. Their wigs, shining with clenched black curls, slipped forward and back on kinky heads, undone by sweat. Sweat beaded its way across my shoulders too, as I stumbled out with everyone else, pushing my way through.

Heading east on Tom Mboya Street, woozy, disoriented, and still struggling with the pastor's final words, I heard Augustin's voice behind me.

He was screaming my name, his voice red and bruised with pain. Violent.

My feet refused to stop. The closer his voice came, the faster I walked.

The road narrowed as I turned off onto Cabral Street. Cobblestones lay broken in the gutters, and gaping holes waited in the middle of the road to pop tires and trip pedestrians. Just outside the door of Aunt Evie's Fishmongery and Hair Saloon and to the left of the Good Times Pub lay an old, overturned fruit cart that was missing two of its wheels. The heat mixed with the awful smell of the rancid bananas and oranges that had fallen off of the cart. The fruit fairly bubbled, hissing out putrid gases from underneath decaying skins as the piles sat in the alley, rotting in the sun. At the sight and the stench I stopped dead, welded to the spot, my head reeling and my stomach heaving. It was there that Augustin caught up with me.

He pushed me hard from behind, but before I could tip over, he grabbed me by the shoulders and spun me around to face him. How could I run that way? he hissed. How could I embarrass him so badly in front of his wife? How would he ever be able to face her again? What more did I want from him? What more could any man give? He had nothing left in his body or his soul that I did not already own. But that was it, wasn't it? It still wasn't enough. He was not now nor could he ever be good enough for me. If my people, my home, were not good enough for me, then how could he expect me to think that he could measure up? How could he compare to my other men (other men?) and their imported cars, their lush homes, their money, their *fucking* university certificates? He had been searching the whole of Nairobi for me since dawn, and all I could give him was a blank stare?

Speak plain, damn it! What did I mean I was going to school? No! That was a lie. Just please stop lying and treating him like a child! He was not stupid. My graduation was set for the coming Saturday morning. School had already finished. I couldn't be . . . What? School abroad?

Abroad?

Smack! I covered my head as his fist raked across my neck. I couldn't breathe. He was choking me. Choking me, spitting and crying. How could I do this? What did I want? What more . . . ? I vomited again, a thin, green stream of bile that dribbled down my chin across the knuckles of his thumbs. The rest stayed caught in my throat, under the pressure of his callused hands. He wrestled me down to the ground, lying on top of me, pummeling my breasts and shoulders (but never my stomach, not even then), weeping.

I reached up and grabbed his face, still soft with tears. I found his eyes with my rummaging fingers, found the crescents of those eyes just next to the bridge of his nose and plunged my nails down hard. Augustin rolled back, howling and clutching his face. I still couldn't breathe, couldn't walk, so I flipped over and tried to crawl away. His hands clutched onto my ankle and dragged me deeper into the alleyway as I shredded my fingernails and then my fingertips trying to anchor myself against the hot cobblestones. Terrified, I glanced over my shoulder.

The face I saw in that moment was not Augustin's face.

It was not the patient, indulgent face of my lover, but my brother's face, glaring and crumpled with rage. I saw Lolorok seething and laughing. Lolorok waiting, hovering, wizened by his hatred of me, dwarfed in the shade of the baobab tree.

I saw him lunge at me. Again. And then he raised a fist. But this time it was not his fist that he raised. The fist I saw was Lalasi's bloody fist.

And I thought hysterically, *My God, he's going to kill me too.*

I couldn't hear myself screaming, "Thief! Thief! Thief!"

But I did.

Suddenly the men who had been standing by benignly and watching roared into action. The man was a thief. Not an angry brother or an agitated lover. He had actually stolen something. That changed the matter entirely. They looked at my expensive jeans, my lace shirt, my gold. They saw Augustin standing over me, fists clenched, mouth slack and panting, matted tufts of hair peeking through his ripped, dirty traveling clothes. The tattered pants, the sockless feet. One sandal lost in the gutter.

Thief.

A bottle crashed through the air and shattered against the curb behind him. The men took up my scream and made it a chant. *Thief thief thief.* They pulled clubs fashioned from wooden chair legs out of their waistbands and switchblade knives from the folds of their socks. The vegetable women who had been selling tomatoes and squash from blankets on the corner ran over to help me up. Their hands were reedy and rough like cornhusks left to dry on curved stones. As they hefted me to my feet, they picked up the chant as well, crying as loudly as they could in Swahili, "mwizi." Thief. A couple of them at the far end of the street threw more Coke bottles at Augustin's now retreating feet to make him stumble.

I still couldn't focus. Couldn't grasp what was going on. I wondered briefly why Augustin was running away and if it was Lalasi who was chasing him. But no, Lalasi was in Maralal, where Nasieku used to be. Where I used to be. And what was I doing here in this street anyway? Who were these women, and why were they fondling me? I didn't want their smell of earth and salt and sea crawling on my skin, their cornhusk hands in my hair plugging up my mind. Why didn't Augustin make them stop? Why did he leave me?

He's busy dying, Nas. Too busy dying to help you right now. Polle sana.

Polle sana. The women's teeth clicked and their hands shot up toward the sky, but I couldn't hear them. I blinked, trying to shake the sweat out of my eyes and the silence out of my head. *Augustin? That's silly. He's never too busy for me.*

I glanced around, set to laugh at my own foolishness, but he still wasn't there. Then I saw him. He was up ahead . . . in the street . . . in the middle of the crowd. The mob had gathered and spread like mist, cutting off his exit.

And that is when I realized what I had done. When I finally understood what was about to happen.

Like a lightning crack, the soundlessness in my head instantly splintered and crumbled and burst. Noise exploded out of the women, out of the screech and whine of retreating cars, out of the drum-thumping sticks and poles and clubs that whacked repeatedly against fragile windowpanes and bones.

No. No, please. Not him. Not him too. Oh God, no!

It was all my fault. I'd done this! But I didn't know. I hadn't meant for it to happen. He'd frightened me and I responded without thinking. That's all. But now look. Look what happened. Look what I'd done.

I broke away from the women and began running through the mob, screaming for them to stop. Screaming that they didn't understand. That he hadn't meant harm. That I was wrong and it was all my fault. I lied! I lied and I now took it all back. He really wasn't a thief. His name was Augustin and he was a good, strong man. Anything, anything to make them stop.

But I got swept away in the current. Pounding feet. Raised fists. Swinging clubs. No thought.

I couldn't stop. They were crushing me.

Ahead of me, Augustin tripped on another overturned fruit cart and the mob fell on him, pummeling and kicking him. The men fought one another for the chance to beat him. His body was whisked up into the air by the momentum of the crowd, his arms splayed and his head thrown back like a grotesque parody of Christ with blood running from his head and from a gash in his side.

"Necklace him! Necklace him!"

As the cry went up, old tires appeared, it seemed, out of the air. They came from alleyways and parked cars. They came from junk carts. All thrown around Augustin's body until he stood, encased up to his neck, in filthy rubber.

"Light the bastard! Light him up!"

Horrified and overwhelmed, unable to control my own body, I vomited again all over myself and onto the neck of the man in front of me.

And then, God forgive me, I turned like a coward to run.

But I couldn't. Couldn't move. Too many packed bodies. Stifling. Crushing. I tried again to reach him . . . I couldn't . . . I . . . I was . . . trapped . . .

I . . . was . . .

I . . .
              I am
lost
              Can't
think

breathe

    Oh God can't breathe

The crowd yanks me, like a dog by its scruff, up off my feet.

I'm trying. I'm trying. I'm trying but I can't resist the forward motion, the stamping feet or the hoarse, chanting voices. The men, they're bigger than me. They steal my air, rob my feet of steady ground. They slam me up against wide backs and sweat-soaked shoulders. Excitement clogs the narrow road as surely as the hundreds upon hundreds of dark bodies that have stopped buses in midturn and sent pedestrians scrambling like ants toward the dark, humid doorways of office buildings.

"Mwizi! Thief!" the men scream.

Their raised voices seem to come from all quarters, seem to come from me. I am screaming, but not to see Augustin burn. I can't get out. I can't reach him. Oh God. I can't reach him.

Another surge and I'm lifted up off the ground again. Lightheaded, giddy almost, I can see over their heads for a second. What's going on up there? I don't understand. Why don't they listen to me? The heat becomes a rough, wet cloth that covers my nose and mouth and I can feel myself, almost as if it is happening to someone else, begin to suffocate. The wheezing starts softly, and before I can talk myself out of it, my chest is hitching and my lungs contract, getting steadily smaller and tighter. A flying elbow jabs me in the neck. The sharp pain focuses my attention and forces me to quit thinking stupid thoughts about what it will be like to die on my feet right here inside the body of the mob.

The crowd starts to pull me back down and, as though I'm treading water, I kick and squirm, trying to stay aloft. But I can't. Arms rise up and I am swallowed bit by bit back into the crush. My head snaps left and then right, still searching for Augustin's face. Maybe. Maybe he got away.

To my left, I see men stalk along the sidewalk where the mob has thinned, racing to get closer, dodging and leaping—with skinny arms and fists raised—over prone bodies. Some carry sticks or jagged wooden chair legs while a couple of others carry battered Goodyear tires gripped tight and held high like a first prize. The crowd pushes forward again, straining with birth pains, waiting to give form to this collective will. Outrage has been mastered by something deeper, something gleeful and contagious. And I'm caught up in the middle of it.

My lungs feel like they're collapsing. Too many bodies pressing on me, dragging me down and up and back down. No, not down. Not under. I snatch hold of the front of a wet brown work shirt. The cheap material gives out under the pressure of my hand almost as easily as ripping tissue. I don't care. I grab another handful and pull myself up, climbing this man's chest as if it were a rope, panting and terrified. Just as I feel myself straighten up and get my bearings, the shoulder of the man behind the first man slams into my chest. This time I push back, shoving him off balance. But the other bodies in the crowd buoy him and keep him on his feet. I glance once at his back (he never even slowed), but when I turn my head around, I'm a second too late and another body crashes into me, knocking me back (forward) again.

I'm staggering drunkenly. I let out a giggle that sounds more like a cry, but I can't cry, not now, so I clamp my mouth shut and try again to bully my way through. But my knees are melting into warm puddles. My lungs haven't enough air left in them and my arms haven't enough strength to keep pushing the bodies away. The heat and the dense funk of labor wafting off these men lodges in my throat, in my eyes. Can't see.

And underneath the smell, pulsing like short, sharp bursts of electrical current, is the more frightening scent of ignited idleness. It's not completely correct to call it a scent, but this presence is too strong, too overpowering and pervasive to simply be called a feeling.

"Mwizi! Mwizi!"

Oh my God, Augustin, where are you?

A hiss sweeps through the crowd and, in spite of myself, I turn to face the same direction in which everyone else is going. What was that sound? The odor of petrol hangs hazily in the air, stronger now that I'm facing into the wind, looking toward the wide circle up ahead.

The circle.

They've encircled him. No one dares cross the threshold of the circle. But everyone wants to see. Again, the wave of bodies picks me up, and for a second, just one second, I see.

A tower of tires encasing him up to his neck holds him straight. It looks to me as though he's wearing a hat of blood, like perhaps the top of his head had been smashed in, but, really, that could just be in my head. I don't know. The fire is sucking the skin off his flesh almost seductively. And, as though partnered in the most sensual of dances, the skin reaches back to be touched by the fire's heart, peeling itself back off my lover's skull, wholly unaware that it is the fire's heart. His eyes are shut now but his mouth is gaping, like the dried salt fish that the old women sell on street corners near the city center.

My heart. My love. He looks as though he died screaming (and in spite of the twitching in his neck, he is most assuredly already dead), but I can't remember hearing him scream. Not that I should have been able to hear him, not in this crowd.

The crowd. The thought breaks the spell and sucks me back down. All of a sudden, I'm choking on the smell of burning rubber and something (say it) else, something sweet (like) and heavy (like burnt pork). Meat. I don't know. I just don't know.

My eyes are so heavy now. So heavy and full. I think I'm going to let them close.

Silence.

Yes, silence, my love. Be silent. Be still.

AFTER

. . . .

THE PASTOR HAD SAID that no matter what happened to me, no matter where I went, I had God's promise that I would be more than a conqueror.

But as I stood on that day facing that moment, I found that I was no conqueror. No warrior of any kind. Especially not for God. Perhaps I was more like a ghost, invisible and fluttering without wings, without benefit of a warning keen.

Most definitely I was a thief. Even bowed and humbled with the weight of God's thumb stroking the back of my neck, I stole. From Augustin, from the crowd who intercepted him and danced, I took life, I took reason. Nothing but a common criminal. A crook of songs, of ideas, a Windigo without shame and out of my season, I had watched my love burn and then stolen away. Stuffing my mouth with silence.

Three days after I got out of Aga Khan Hospital, I came here, to Harlem. I came here only to dream constantly of a place that I'd fought so long and so hard to get out of. To dream now of a home that doesn't exist and of a man who is dead but who I know will never die. In my heart.

I understand now that the past can never, should never be discarded. The feelings/words/images stand always so close at my back, peering over my shoulder and snickering like the tired shades of tribal warriors forgotten by the collective before their war is even over. Old dead with even older, insatiable grudges.

But I am new and I am cold. The fog clings to my cheeks and the baby kicks petulantly inside of my swollen belly. The woman who sparked this thought has disappeared in the fog, coated over completely with cold gray rain, and left far, far behind me by now.

In a couple more months, I think to myself, I will know exactly how far I have come, whether I have truly learned or stood still. My daughter's eyes will tell me.

I turn the corner at the end of the street and duck my head as the icy wind rips open my coat collar and pounds my exposed neck. I stick my arm out and press my numbed fingers against the frozen concrete wall beside me to steady myself. After a moment, I push off, wiping the stinging water from my eyes and trying to walk faster. But the wind has taken a steady hold on my shoulders and grips me tightly as if to say, *No, wait!*

But I won't wait.

All I want to do right now is get off the blustery street and up to my flat. The place where I currently live is a tiny three-room apartment on the third floor of a walk-up on 121st Street. It's not precisely part of the nice area, but it's safe. I applied for family housing through the university immediately after I got here, and they actually gave it to me even though I'm not married. Not anymore.

Sometimes I am amazed at the way God blesses me continuously, although only recently have I begun to see it as such and believe that I could actually be deserving of any blessings at all. Now the largest room in my flat holds a secondhand crib that I painted white to hide the age spots, a tall plastic changing table, and a bureau with pink and green teddy bears drawn on the sides. I work in one of the university's libraries and have recently discovered that I can sell my poetry and my stories for a rather reasonable price. If I've had a good month and there's extra money left over at the end, I send it home to Augustin's wife, Ndama. I like to tell myself that she is starting to understand and forgive me, but I'm not sure if that's really true. Whatever the case, she doesn't send the money back anymore, so at least I feel as though I'm helping the family out in some way.

Things seem to be working out okay. I may even get my green card.

Each day I think of Augustin. I feel him around me, watching, laughing, forgiving. Forgiving both of us for so many things just as I must forgive him and, somehow, eventually, myself. I often wondered at first what kind of life my child could have without a father. But I am realizing now that she does have a father. She will have, through me, Augustin's memory. She will also have my Father. And I will teach her his strengths but I will also teach her to beware of his flaws and his fears (a gift my own mother never gave me). Because another thing that I have realized is that it was his fear—not a fear of death, but of continuing on with life after it has blessed you with changes that perhaps you never asked for or wanted—that kept him trapped in the empty heart that he called his curse. He tried to get out through my mother's love, but not even she had the key to that door.

I tried to get out through Augustin. It took his death to make me see that I had already fashioned my own key. All I needed to do was pick it up and hold on to it. He was the mouth of my path to God. My Ubuntu.

And now I walk, understanding that though I am my mother's heart, I am my Father's daughter. He, like Nima, is with me constantly and will live in my child in a way I never had the courage to let him live in me.

But I am learning how to do that now, day by day.

And I am not afraid, anymore, of the fear, or the pain.

I have learned, and so I say for the one who comes behind me and yet has lit the path in front of me, guiding my feet through sullen twilight although I never knew it: take a chance at challenging pain. Eat with him. Drink from his cup. Trap him in your arms at night and whisper him awake at dawn. He is waiting for it. Call him out, and he will concede.

It has taken me a very long time to begin to understand that freedom needs no validation. Whether I am right or wrong is inconsequential, for even my mistakes are perfect. If they lead me to learn. That has been the most difficult lesson, I suppose, but a lesson that once learned can never be minimized or forgotten. Because try as I might to force, cajole, or beg myself for it, the regret just won't come. Instead, I hear a satin tapestry of music, celestial and bright, pregnant with misunderstanding and thick with promise. And it's all for me. I've found that few are keen, dedicated, and brutal enough to make love to the details and the depths of life. So each day I strive to do that, to be that, to take small, uncalculated risks that will nudge me toward being the woman I believe I am, despite and because of my past. That way I might have a future that transcends place and fear and even me.

For my daughter's sake.

THE RED MOON

A Reader's Guide

KUWANA HAULSEY

A CONVERSATION WITH
KUWANA HAULSEY

Q: *What motivated you to write* The Red Moon? *Where does the title come from?*

A: Sometimes people don't believe this when I say it, but the entire plot for *The Red Moon* came to me while sitting on the floor one afternoon in my apartment in Brooklyn. At that point, I knew nothing about the Samburu tribe and very little about African culture in general. But for some reason, I believed in the reality and the truth of this vision that I had. So I packed up everything, and two and a half months later I was on a plane bound for Nairobi. I didn't know anyone, couldn't speak Swahili, and wasn't really even sure of where I was going to sleep once I got there. All I knew was that I had been given this idea for a reason and I had to see it through to the end. Once I got there and began making friends, I started telling people about what I was doing and asking them if they knew which tribe it was that I had been writing about. The overwhelming response that I got was "Oh, that's easy. That's the Samburu." And when I finally got to Samburu, I found everything almost exactly as I had envisioned it thousands of miles away in my tiny Brooklyn apartment.

On my first trip to Samburu, I stayed in a town called Maralal with the district water chief, a man named Karanga and his sister Christine. Karanga lived at the top of a long, twisting hill overlooking the town. One evening we all decided to go into town to visit the local lodge. Trees lined Karanga's driveway, blocking the view of the mountainside. So when we backed out of the drive and onto the road, I was stunned by the sudden appearance of the full moon hanging down low over the valley. The moon was huge and shaded a deep, radiant crimson. I was awestruck. I had never seen anything like it. After I started to learn more of the Samburu language, Maa, I discovered that the Samburu had a name for that type of moon. In Maa, it is called *Lonyuki Lapa*, which literally means "the red moon." When the red moon appears in the sky four days after the new moon, that is the time for circumcising young girls. That is the only time of the month that the ritual can be performed.

For Nasarian, the red moon at first symbolizes death—the death of her mother, the death of her dreams. But as she begins to evolve, she starts to understand that the essence of death is rejuvenation and rebirth. That understanding parallels the metamorphosis that also begins to take place in her life.

Q: *What do you hope that people reading this novel will take away from it?*

A: Of course, I want people to be entertained and I want them to learn about cultures that they might otherwise never come into contact with. I want the readers to be captivated by the places and people that they meet. And hopefully the experience will open their eyes and minds to beliefs, traditions, and convictions that may not only be different than their own, but perhaps completely opposite to everything that they have ever known or held to be true.

I hope that the character of Nasarian will resonate with people who read this book and that in her they will be able to recognize many aspects of themselves. The situations and circumstances that she finds herself in are extreme, but at the heart of it is a young woman who wants to change her world to reflect her own vision of who she is and what her life will be. I think that is probably the most important theme in the book. Nasarian must discover that life is about making choices. She must realize that even in choosing not to choose, in deciding to give up and be buffeted about by the circumstances that surround her, she is making a very strong, definitive choice. As she begins to comprehend the fact that, moment by moment, she herself is the driving force creating the reality in which she lives, her life starts to take some drastic turns. I believe that this realization of personal power and choice can be a life-altering moment of epiphany, and I want to confront my readers with that idea.

Q: *Tell us about your experiences in Africa.*

A: The time I spent living in Africa was one of the most exciting, fascinating, and awe-inspiring periods of my life. The friends I made in Kenya took me into their lives as if I was family in a way that I could not even have fathomed, being from a place like New York City. In New York, people oftentimes don't care to know their neighbors, much less random strangers who drop in from the other side of the world. In Kenya, I got to do things that I would never have imagined I would do, like hiking through canyons and up mountainsides and volcanoes while herds of giraffes and zebras quietly kept pace a short distance away. I had to sleep with goats inside our hut because we were afraid that the lions that had sneaked inside the *manyatta* before would come back and try to steal more animals. It was the best way to protect the animals, because although the lions might not mind venturing inside our fence, they wouldn't be so bold as to walk right up into our huts (or so I was told).

Q: *Is life really like that today?*

A: The information age has gripped Africa just as it has the rest of the world. Things are changing more rapidly than ever before. Five or six years ago, when I wrote to my friends back in Nairobi, it usually took me at least a month to receive a reply. Now most of the people I know are online, so we can communicate daily if we want to.

But for many people, especially in rural communities and villages, not many things have changed. Moreover, some people and some tribes, like the Samburu for example, have chosen to live in much the same way as their ancestors lived. In those cases, their lives are still very similar to those of the characters in the book. They perform the same rituals, live by the same traditions and beliefs as I described.

Q: *Who are your favorite novelists?*

A: Just like everyone else in the world, I must pay homage to Toni Morrison. Her words tend to melt into your mind. They create pictures and feelings that take time, patience, and careful thought to digest properly. For me, the same can be said of Alice Walker, Zora Neale Hurston, Gabriel García Márquez, and James Baldwin. I also love people like Chinua Achebe, Maxine Hong Kingston, and Maya Angelou. Though their styles are probably as different as they can possibly be, each writes with eloquence, passion, and humor. (Yes, I do find Chinua Achebe humorous—sometimes.) They were pioneers who wrote about experiences and people that might not otherwise have been given a voice in literature. Other writers who are less well known but still incredible craftspeople in my mind are women like Anita Desai, who wrote *Clear Light of Day*, and Ama Ata Aidoo, who wrote *Our Sister Killjoy*. Their stories address the politics of the personal worlds of women in developing nations like India and Ghana.

Q: *Briefly describe your next project.*

A: My next project is a novel called *Angel of Harlem*. It's based on the life of a woman named May Edward Chinn, who was the first black female doctor in Harlem during its famed renaissance in the 1920s. It tells her life from her birth just before the turn of the century up through the 1940s. It also reaches back as far as the Civil War. May was fascinating in that she devoted her life to being of service to others. She broke down barriers that had previously been unassailable, never for personal gain but because she saw people in need and was determined to make a difference. The story has an incredible cast of characters: Paul Robeson, Langston Hughes, Countee Cullen, Zora Neale Hurston, W.E.B. DuBois, and more. The best part of it is, it's all true! Early readers have commented that I must have an incredible imagination to have created the plot of this book. Even though I like to hear that stuff, I have to correct them and let them know that I made up remarkably little. The beauty of this book comes from May's spirit, not my imagination.

Reading Group Questions and Topics for Discussion

1. Nasarian's coming of age resembles her father's in that both grew up outside the Samburu world, but where Ngatuny eventually rejects foreign ways, Nasarian cannot commit fully to either Mzungu or Samburu life. How does she navigate the space between these two worlds? Is she successful?

2. In some ways education is Nasarian's salvation: She escapes the abuses of her brother Lolorok and the repression of her cousin Lalasi by going away to school. Nasarian pays a price for this escape: As she advances in school she becomes more estranged from her culture. Is it impossible for her to remain a traditional Samburu and be educated? What is different about her education and that of her father?

3. Although Nasarian is Samburu, she remains an outsider because of her mother's origins. Does her status as a *nusu-nusu*, a half caste, influence the choices she makes in rejecting certain traditions like circumcision or leaving home? Had Nima and Nasar-

ian been accepted by Ngatuny's other wives and children, would Nasarian have stayed with the tribe?

4. For Augustin, allegiance to family and tribe are the most important values in life; he cannot understand Nasarian's desire to live outside the rules of the tribe. Is he right in saying that without family she will have nothing? Does he love Nasarian because she is different or in spite of it?

5. Lalasi and Ketigile's stormy relationship results in the destruction of the only thing they share: their child, Nasieku. What is the cause of their deep discord? Why does Lalasi send his daughter to be married away even if he does not need the money?

6. In their own way, Ngatuny and Nima live and die out of a strong will—Nima, whose life began among the Samburu as a prisoner and ends when she refuses to marry her dead husband's brother; and Ngatuny, whose life reflected his will to conquer the destruction of his family and retain his tradition. In some ways, Nasarian possesses the same stubborn will. How does it manifest itself? What are the results? What does Nima mean when she tells Nasarian to let go of her will?

7. Try as they might, the Samburu are unable to avoid modernizing influences. How does the process assert itself in *The Red Moon*? Can modernity and tradition coexist?

8. Nasarian pursues two relationships at the university: one with Tobias, the other with Augustin. Although she chooses Augustin over Tobias, there are aspects to both relationships that she likes and dislikes. What are they? Why does she leave Tobias and finally Augustin? Did Augustin's first wife have any effect on her decision?

9. The women in *The Red Moon* are dissatisfied with traditional life at times; we see both the pleasure they gain from strong families but also the pain of polygamy and child marriage. What does the author think about the role of women in Kenya? Compare and contrast the experiences of the two sisters, Taisere and Ketigile.

10. Ngatuny views Jonas Wilheim as his teacher and surrogate father; he is bitterly disappointed when Wilheim severs the relationship after Ngatuny is imprisoned. Was their relationship false? Why can't Wilheim, who spent years studying Kenya, understand Ngatuny?

11. By the time Nasarian reaches the United States, she has left Kenya behind but keeps it in her heart. She seems to have made peace with the legacy of her parents and Augustin. What does she learn from Nima, Ngatuny, and Augustin? What does Nasarian mean by *ubuntu*?

Angel
of Harlem

KUWANA HAULSEY

AN EXCERPT FROM *ANGEL OF HARLEM*

. . . .

IT TOOK SEVENTY-THREE YEARS for my father to die.

He held on, cloaked beneath a broad quilt of memories, peering out his window onto the wide basin of winter below. Memory had creased his face with fresh gullies and markers that ran east, toward the river. When memory escaped him, he searched it out, skating his eyes along the sagging white rooftops outside until he found what he was looking for. Papa refused to wade into the drifts of his understanding, though, to get thick into it like he could have, deep enough to allow for release.

So stubborn, that old man. Just tiring.

And I am nothing but his daughter.

My papa managed to make it all the way to the outskirts of spring in 1936. February and March had been humbling throughout the city, but especially in Harlem. Gutters hardened into icy spillboxes. Streets drained of color and smell, except the heavy, spoiled odor of snow.

Months before, when it still sparkled, I'd plunged into the snow stacks with the neighborhood children, flinging it at little pecan-colored boys with wild hair and hatless heads. They'd scatter and re-form, creeping up like bright-eyed kittens, wiggling and ready to pounce. The children all wore patched sackcloth coats; some had mufflers, some had gloves, but none had both. If I'd taken off their shoes, I'd have found soles tattooed with newspaper ink and tiny, ashy toes wrinkled from adventure.

I adored those children, had birthed two or three, the ones who called me Mama May instead of Dr. May or Ma'am.

On those late afternoons, when the sun deepened and lay like sheaves of wheat or, sometimes, like thick cream over the covered roads, those babies reminded me of truth. They taught me that play created gulfs of unintended joy, then unmasked circumstance—not as an adversary, but a coconspirator in the game. I needed with all my heart to remember the wisdom born inside innocence, to see myself in their eyes and maybe find worth in that unspoiled vision.

So I squealed like a young girl when they yelled, *"Git her!"* and stuffed snowballs down my cotton shirtwaist. I pretended to run so they could foil my escape, sneaking more snow into the pockets of my covert-cloth coat, the first good, new brown coat I'd had in three years. It didn't matter. I giggled anyway, licking snow off my rose-colored palms before the flakes could melt, while they were still glassy and protruding and round.

But by March, things had changed.

The streets were blackened by spitting trucks and feet and mules and human waste in areas where sewer pipes routinely ballooned with cold, then burst. Weals of mud sprouted through the ice and concrete, snaking along the roads all the way out to the river, which itself was hoary and stiff, poised with frost.

By March, the children had long since trudged home. Now the streets stayed empty unless some kind of work refused to wait.

So, things being the way they were, no one came to stand watch at my father's feet. No old-time friend whispered cures or condolences into my mother's ear. No nieces or cousins dropped by, donating heaping pans of simmered greens and crisp fried rabbit as a love offering.

Not even his lost daughters returned to see him off. I'd written Irene the month before and she'd written back, *"Can't quite make it. Much to do here. But I'll pass the word. Tell the old man I said good luck."*

Her response offended Papa in a way that death never could have.

His intention had been to make it back home to Chinn Ridge in Virginia, where all parts of his death would be warm and dusty with road songs, and sweet. He had memories secreted away there, stashed in the swollen, ocher hills like treasure. He had people in those hills, too. Most of them were years dead, but some still lingered, telling stories only he could rightly remember and pass judgment on. True or false was his alone to say. My papa yearned to be with people who allowed him his place. In the end, though, he was too weak to make the trip.

Despite his sincere efforts to wait out the last whispers of winter and escape, my papa died cold. He died shivering like the wind in his bed, while my mother, who was the sun, stood by his pillow playing "Pennies from Heaven" over and over again on the phonograph to warm him. She used burnt rum and music on his fever chills because the Depression was so unyielding that year that we hadn't any extra blankets. Without thinking, I'd given them all away to my patients, every last one. I hadn't been a good enough daughter to save even one warm, gray blanket on which my father could die.

My selfishness and lack of forethought embarrassed me. To

make up for it, I waited on him, trying to get him things he didn't need—an out-of-season apricot, a bit of soft, sky-blue calico, pine-cones to rub against his whiskers and his round, red cheeks, then toss onto the coal in the stove. Then the house would smell of woods, like when he was a boy. He smiled and let me do these things because he loved me more than I'd thought I loved him. All I knew for sure was that I let him down. I'd been distracted by my work, by my own thoughts, hunkered down and birthing other things. I hadn't stayed aware.

Each time my mother passed his bed, Papa mouthed her name . . . *Lulu*. His gaze followed her, sucking up what he could—her black eyes, her butternut skin, her silence.

His spirit lingered around just to be near her, long past his physical endurance. Papa's flesh was bloated by then, fat and ripe with decay. But still he stayed. After a while my mother began to fear, not for the comfort of his body, but for the direction of his soul. Finally, late one evening, she sat on the edge of his bed and took his hand. Leaning in to kiss his eyelids, she whispered, "It's all right, William. Go 'head now. Go on."

She released him.

Just like that, after all that waiting, he went.

No more words passed between them, just a look of simple wonder that crossed my father's face as he let go, a look of grati-tude that said he hadn't known dying could be so easy.

My mother didn't speak again until we'd laid Papa out in the church. Hair parted, tie straightened, she smoothed him over, readied him for all the hardness of the earth. Even then, the only thing she managed to say was, "When shadows fly, they cover the stones below. Remember, May."

Then the Negro seeped out of her face, and she became a Chickahominy again, so silent that I lost track of her breath, so ancient and wide that her presence suddenly felt as inescapable, as untouchable, as the dusky, violet sky. When she was a black woman, my mother railed and sang and cut her eyes. As a Chickahominy, she was free. Lulu became a Chickahominy every time she got mad at my father. So when she stood at the foot of his coffin with her arms akimbo and got free, that's how I knew for sure that she missed him, too.

After a while I asked, "What did you mean by that, Mama?"

It's not so much that I needed to know, but the incredible length of her solitude was too much for me. I wanted to put it away for her, to roll it up like a bolt of cloth over my arms. I wanted to hear its dusty *clap* as it turned and turned, hitting the floor at my feet. But I couldn't. The space that she held was too vast, too dense, much more like the rolling of river water than some dry piece of cloth.

Standing next to my mother felt like wading through the sand at the bottom of a stream. Her solitude rose, filling the ripening red of the carpet, the velvety creases in the drapes, even the gray lapels of Papa's suit. The undercurrent of her grief ruffled the waves in his hair. She sighed so soft and, for once, I knew that her memories of my father had nothing whatsoever to do with me.

"I s'ppose," she replied slowly, "I just meant that you can't untie the past from its present, that's all." She reached behind her, stretched vigorously, and sighed again. "Well, at least his love was good, and it lasted. You can't ask for much more."

I disagreed, but didn't bother to say so. Didn't have to—she already knew what I was thinking. She always knew. She'd spent the past forty years knowing.

Just to prove the point, Mama coughed politely into the back of her hand, raised the long, woolen hem of her mourning dress and limped toward the back door. As she swung the door open, I felt a breeze shift through the funeral parlor. It roused the heavy curtains and antique lace draped over the mahogany tables in the corner, twisting through the worn pews—a breeze with enough April floating through it to catch butterflies. Despite the cold, my father had managed to produce an unseasonably beautiful afternoon for his burial. I had to smile.

"I'ma check on that carriage right quick. Be back shortly, Ladybug."

The carriage was already out back, waiting to take us out of Harlem and up to Woodlawn Cemetery in the Bronx. We both knew that. This was just her way of giving me some privacy to do my grieving.

I stared down at my father William and touched his smooth, firm, pale skin. My heart refused to see the blotted veins congealed in whirlpools around his nose and across his cheeks. In my mind, I stared into his shining hazel eyes, and I took some time to love the way they danced.

It was his eyes. That's what did it. When I finally stopped pretending and looked down at his eyes. The sunken lids, rutted with veins, so fragile-looking, like paper, like if I pressed even slightly, my finger would go straight through. It dawned on me then that my father would never get to see me again. It was over. He was gone.

For a moment, I thought I'd died. Blackness snatched me up—no light, no sound, no breath, no skin. No heartbeat, no pain. Through the absence of everything, one thought rose up, not from within me, but from somewhere off to the side, a child's toy floating by in the ocean: *This is wonderful.*

Grief erupted inside my body. It exploded in a sickening physical blow that crumpled me like I'd been kicked in the chest, harder than Papa had ever had the courage to hit. The pain left me doubled over, my nails digging into the grooves on the side of the coffin, unsteady and shaking with regret. I wanted to cry out for my mother, but I didn't. I couldn't. Instead, I opened myself to the sorrow. I let it come in and shower me, wash me clean.

My father had been a slave, his father a master. Which master, he never knew, but a master nonetheless. The question of it, the uncertainty, had dogged him his entire life. He'd always believed his father to be his Master Benjamin but Grammy Susan refused to tell him one way or the other when he was a child. The question of his lineage had been roundly considered to be grown folks' business and, therefore, none of his concern.

"Shoo, little fly, don't bother me," she'd sing, and sweep him away with her broom or dust him out the door with a crisp cotton rag.

"But, ma'am . . ."

"Boy, I *know* you ain't tryin' to work my nerves with this foolishness. Not today. Now get on outside *and stay out grown-folks' business.*"

That was always the end of it. By the time he grew old enough to know, he'd been alone and on his own for many years, Grammy Susan long since gone. To this day, I believe that my father's confusion over the matter was the real reason he himself never learned to master without controlling, to control without descending into tyranny, or to recognize the wisdom in releasing that which had never belonged to him in the first place.

Proud and brilliant as he was, white people often mistook William Chinn as white. Other Negroes, however, never made that mistake. His carriage and the fierceness of his dignity gave him away as one of them, even though his skin color did not. Still, no matter how he tried, he'd never been able to find any forgiveness for his old life, nor a suitable, painless place in the present. Unmet expectation had chained him to his past because the past was the only thing he had to blame.

As a child, of course, I hadn't understood these things. I didn't know what his feelings were or how to name them. But when I felt the sadness come down on him, thick and clinging to his feet like mud, I'd crawl behind my mother's ancient potbellied stove and cry.

As an adult, I tried my best to ignore his moods, just as he'd sworn to ignore me for the rest of his life after learning I intended to disgrace him by going to college. When Mama told him I'd decided to continue on to medical school, he'd fled the house and hadn't returned for more than three months. When he finally did slink on home, he'd begged my mother to stop my foolishness. If it was all right for a colored woman to become a doctor, he reasoned, then why hadn't they heard of anyone here in the city who'd done it before? Because it wasn't for anyone else to do, she'd explained. The job had been waiting on me.

Papa disavowed me. Again. In spite of the fact that we lived in the same house, he refused to utter a single word to me. He would rage about me to my mother, to the neighbors across the air shaft or off into the sky, ranting that *a cackling rooster and a crowing hen don't never come to no good end!* In fact, he claimed, there were two things he flat out didn't believe in: God and doctors. Somehow, he'd managed to get hooked up with a daughter who thought she was both. Mama would continue to sew velvet or wash the kettle or dust the piano. I'd read my anatomy books in silence. Eventually, he'd skulk out the door with nothing but the price of a bottle in his pocket.

For nearly a decade, I was a ghost to my father. Then one night, about eight years before, he nearly died. In the midst of that first false death, he slipped and said the word, the one word that made everything else in my life begin to make sense.

I STAGGERED HOME during the time of morning so early that you can smell the sunrise long before you see it. The soft, grassy scent of dawn edged up over the river as I crossed the trolley tracks on Lenox Avenue and turned onto 138th Street. As impossible as it seemed, it was only a two-block walk to my flat from Harlem General Hospital, where I interned. My calves clenched and un-clenched in spasms, like a heartbeat, and I stumbled over the curb, nearly falling into the corner lamppost. Under my breath I mur-mured a song, something to distract myself from the fire in my back that came from hefting and heaving a grown man's weight.

"Epiphany! Light of lights that shineth ere the world began. Draw thou near, and lighten the heart of every man."

Railroad ties and twisted nails had shredded my long white skirt, then the skin on my knees beneath. My face was blackened and slick with grease. But I had such a wide, free feeling bubbling through me, something even stronger than the tiredness, so strong that I had to sing it out.

I'd saved someone that night. And though I could barely move, though no one else would ever know, there was joy dancing through my fingers and toes. I knew. That was enough.

Moonlight shivered through the branches of the maple trees. It slid, mirrorlike, across the windows of the fifty-year-old brown-stones and tenements that lined both sides of our street. I was the only person up and about, but I knew that in another twenty or thirty minutes, the street would flex and stretch and come alive for the day. Throngs of people would swarm onto the avenue, crowded together almost shoulder to shoulder, in a teeming brown-and-black wave. I smiled, knowing that I would be warm and lazy in my sleep well before then.

Walking with my eyes half closed, I retraced my steps from memory, stepping high in front of 165 to avoid the oak roots that raised a hump in the sidewalk, to the left around the Wilsons' trash barrel in front of 167. I never even saw the heap sprawled at the bottom of our stoop until I fell over him. In midthought, my feet flew out from underneath me, and I landed hard on the concrete step. The shadow on the ground cringed a little, trying to shield his head with one of his hands. He moaned. When I heard the raspy breath, I knew. I didn't have to turn him over or call his name. I just knew. Shame cut across my body, cool and smooth and bright as the morning moon.

Papa lay on the ground, curled up on his side, smelling old and sharp, funky with cheap liquor. He'd vomited on himself. I could smell that, too. The odor of it wafted onto me, bitterness nestled in my own breath.

Look, Papa,

"Look," I whisper, "look at the horse." The horse bolts from the stable, just past us on the lawn. Its gray muzzle is streaked with long handles of spit and foam. The other men dive for cover while the little blond girl on the saddle struggles not to fly off, screaming, crying, pulling the horse's mane instead of taking the reins.

Papa leaps from our blanket and, as the horse comes round again, he tackles it by the neck and scissors his way onto its back. The horse whinnies and bucks, and the girl begins to tumble. But before she can fall under the hooves, Papa's arm snaps out and catches her. A jubilant cry goes up from the crowd. He holds her by the silk of her little blue dress until he's talked the horse still.

Instantly, a huge crowd appears around him, white men helping them down, clapping his back, white women weeping at the heroism, the daring of it all. He's sweating and shaking, so beautiful that I fall out against my mother and begin to cry, too. I stretch out my arms, but he can't find me. The crowd is too thick, too radiant with his goodness for him to notice me. I'm three years old, so small I can't be seen.

"Come on, fellow, let's us go inside and buy you some drinks. Lord God! Did you see what he did?"

Papa stops. Papa stares. He cannot go inside. The 126th Street Riding Club refuses colored. That is why we picnic, each weekend, on the grass outside. The men don't understand this. They look at his face, at his bright eyes and the strands of hair plastered to his forehead with sweat, and they want to embrace him.

"Oh, what is it, fellow? Your family out here somewhere? Well, bring them, too!"

"Yes, please," says the little blond girl's father. "Please, I must tell your wife what you did. You are a hero, sir. You saved—" He can't go on. He breaks down in tears. The women surround him and applaud softly.

"Where are your people, man? Let's go inside and celebrate!"

Slowly my father turns to face Mother and me, still sitting on our shabby cotton blanket. He does not look at us directly, but over our heads. He's wilted. Papa's sad now, and I don't know why.

Though we are the only two sitting on this part of the lawn, the men still don't understand. There is good-natured, confused silence for a moment. Then one of the men's faces goes blank. Like when I erase anthills in the sandy dirt with my hand. One minute there is life, the next minute everything is smooth. It makes you think maybe nothing was ever there at all.

"He's colored," the man grimaces. "He's a nigger."

"What?" "Yeah. Look." "No." "Yeah. Look, dammit, look." "Lord God. He is, isn't he? Hey, boy, look at me. Hey. I'm talking to you. Yeah, look at him. I bet he is." "Jesus, that nigger had his hands all over your daughter."

The crowd is unraveling, some moving away from Papa, some approaching slowly, with rigid steps. They're deciding something. Before they can conclude, Papa breaks away, strides over to us, and sweeps us up. I hear voices, louder and louder. But I don't understand. I confuse anger with gratitude, joy with splintering rage. Mama's clutching me too tight, squeezing me. Papa's got our blanket, our liverwurst sandwiches dashed into the basket, his fiddle jammed down in the basket, too, getting nasty with meat and jelly. We're flying, flying. We're gone. We'll picnic somewhere else from then on.

Look at you, Papa.

For a moment I watched him struggling to raise his head. Then I stood and turned to continue on up the stairs without him.

But I couldn't move. Tears gathered at the back of my throat and sprouted up in my chest, bursting open like seeds. My father's dignity was a sham. He was nothing but a filthy heap in a doorway.

But if he's nothing, how can I be more?

I looked again and saw that his jacket was open. He'd worn his green wool vest, but no scarf. He never remembered his scarf. Without thinking, I reached for him, ready to cover that soft place at the hollow of his throat with my hands. But then I stopped and glanced around quick. The idea of touching him scared me to where I couldn't think, couldn't see straight. What if I put my hands on him, and he didn't move?

She's so smart she's stupid. Always walkin' crooked to go straight.

Lulu, can't you see?

My father had so many cutting ways about him, so many awkward, tilting truths. He'd used his silence as a blade for so long that my heart became clear water, and my purpose, a whetstone— edgeless, heavy, but unbreaking.

This is what he wanted. So let the old man lie in the bed he made.

Literally.

I turned again to walk away. But I didn't know where to go. Surely not upstairs to my mother, who, at that moment, was probably scowling over her coffee because the two of us were still out of doors, somewhere on the street. It seemed better just to sit down in the dark and disappear. That made much more sense. I'd relax myself, ease, and sink into nothingness. Like him. Struggle accomplished nothing.

All I'd ever wanted was for him to recognize me, for him to stand up as tall as I stood and hold my face and say *yes!* And then nothing else would matter.

I turned back, knelt beside him, and shook him.

"Papa? Papa get up. Come on."

When he didn't respond, I checked his wrist. His pulse gently fluttered under the pressure of my thumb, and his breath came in short, shallow gasps. I pulled down his lower lids. His eyes were bloody with broken vessels, rolled up into his head.

Grabbing one arm, I hauled him to his knees. Then I wrapped his arm around my shoulder and stood slowly, leveraging myself against his dangling weight as it threatened to drag me back down. Step by step, we climbed the stoop, pushed through the heavy door, and started on our way up to the fifth floor. Each time we rounded the corner on a landing, my legs cramped, refusing to go any farther. It didn't matter. We climbed beyond my legs, past the thoughts in my mind and the burning in my chest. If I stopped, I'd just lie where I was until someone found us and called out "Ho!" to my mother, but by then it would be too late.

"Papa? Can you hear me? Come on, stay with me, Papa. Talk to me."

My father's eyes flickered open, and his head bobbed as he tried to turn toward the sound of my voice.

"That's it, Papa! Do you know where you are? Tell me who I am, Papa. Can you do that? Who am I?"

"Fanny?"

My body slumped forward, and we collapsed in a heap on the landing in front of our apartment. Papa's body landed on top of me. He reeked of pot liquor and ashes, and I pushed him off because I couldn't breathe with him so close. My hair hung in my face, dragging on the floor as I crawled to the door, calling for my mother.

Then the door opened and Lulu was there and suddenly we were inside. She carted Papa to his bedroom and plopped me on the sofa in the sitting room. Flying out the door, she yelled over her shoulder something about getting another doctor, someone other than me, because we both knew that's what my father would insist on if he could talk.

It seemed as though the door had just closed when it opened again, and I heard Dr. Jackson's high voice and long stride move past me toward the bedroom. Then he was back, out into the hall, banging on doors, calling the men on the floor to help him carry Papa downstairs. Rolled up in a plaid blanket, they rushed my father across the street to Harlem General. When I moved to follow, Mama said, "No. You stay here," and snapped the door shut behind them.

An hour or so later, she was back. Alone.

"Dr. Crump took him into surgery. Said his appendix ruptured."

She eased herself down at the foot of the sofa.

"You better go see about him. Say what you need to say, even if you don't get to say it to his face."

"It's like that?"

"They wasn't sure. Could be. Dr. Crump said if he makes it through surgery, that'd be a good sign. Come on, Sweetness, sit up. You ok. Let me rub you with some oil and put a little gauze over those cuts on your legs. Then you can go on over. Don't stay too long though. You need to sleep."

"Who's Fanny?"

Mama looked at me so blankly that anyone else would have thought her ignorant.

"You need to wash your face," she said. "Let me help you. You got work again tonight."

I didn't answer, so she said, "You know, when my father used to do things that were bad or that I didn't understand and I asked about it, my grandfather would say: 'Truth tells vivid tales that linger in the mouth of time and can never be unspoken, can never be hushed.' Maybe it loses a little somethin' in translation, but that's the gist. Point is, I knew not to ask again."

"Who is she?"

Mama huffed at me and cut her eyes. "What part of 'mind your business' got you confused?"

"Mama—"

"Those are things for him to talk, not me."

"What if he can't?"

"Look, May, let's let it rest until tonight or maybe morning. We'll talk if you get home early enough in the morning. How's that sound?"

She asked it as a question, so it was mine to answer as though I were rolling around some choices and making a decision. But in reality, the subject was closed. So I said, "Sounds fine," to save face, and let her run out the door.

The sun had risen. She was late.

ABOUT THE AUTHOR

KUWANA HAULSEY, author of the critically celebrated debut novel *The Red Moon*, was born and raised in New York City. She studied theater at Fiorello H. LaGuardia High School of Performing Arts and has been acting on stage and in film for the past fifteen years. She graduated from Rutgers University magna cum laude and Phi Beta Kappa.

Kuwana has led seminars for the Penn Faulkner Institute in Washington, D.C., and at Rutgers University. She's taught writing classes for UCLA and Agape International, both in Los Angeles. She is an actress and currently lives in North Hollywood, California.

Her second novel, *Angel of Harlem*, will be published by One World in 2004.

Visit the author's website at www.kuwanahaulsey.com.